A BACKROOM MURDER

IRENE MATTEI

ISBN: 1540546438
ISBN 13: 9781540546432
Library of Congress Control Number: 2016919578
CreateSpace Independent Publishing Platform
North Charleston, South Carolina

CHARACTERS

<u>West Electronics Corporation:</u>
Martin West- President, West Electronics Corporation
Haru "Harry" Maruri -Controller
Oliver Blakely-Vice President Sales & Marketing (Marilyn, wife)
Ken Ichiwara Western Regional sales manager
Edward "Ed" Walsh-Director of Warehouse Operations
Rick Hanson-Loading Dock Manager
Mark Cranston- Senior Accounting Dept. clerk
Geraldine "Gerry" Fineman-Junior Accounting Dept. Clerk
Sheila Birney-Secretary to Oliver Blakely & backup in front office
Wendy Solomon –Secretary to Ed Walsh & backup in front office
Elinor Sandstrom –Secretary to Martin West (on leave to care for her mother in Minnesota)

Sara Fisher- Temporary secretary from Meacham Temporary Employment Agency
David Marks -Boyfriend of Sara Fisher

Bert Rudner-Boyfriend of Wendy Solomon
Mikey - 15-month-old son of Wendy Solomon

Police:
Michael Roarke-detective
Arnold Spivak-detective

Prologue

Instead of the industrial section of downtown Los Angeles or something closer to the port of Long Beach, Martin West found what he was looking for in Hollywood. It was a bleak-looking, concrete slab of a building, the only one of its kind on a commercially zoned street that had, so far, attracted very little commerce.

An unconventional choice, but perfect for his fledgling electronics company. The rent was cheap, the front offices presentable, the warehouse equipped with a fully functioning loading dock, and the apartment of his mistress was less than a mile away.

He signed the lease in the Spring of 1952. Ten years later, former critics were congratulating him. On that wide, treeless and deserted looking boulevard, West Electronics Corporation was free to thrive, ignored by and ignoring those around them.

Over the intervening years the surrounding buildings, small and one-story high, made of stucco and painted in shades of pink and tan, seemed not to have changed at all. Nor had their tenants: the sign makers, printers, and other small business people whose survival was a testament to how easy it was to get along in those glorious Southern California days, before real estate values would drive them into extinction.

Traffic on the street, human and otherwise, remained practically nonexistent. Shops looked dark behind the doors and windows, as if the owners had gone away, forgetting to put up a sign telling people to come back another time. If they ever had customers, one assumed they parked in the alley behind the buildings, like spies on secret missions.

Across the road was a pale pink wall, forbiddingly high, forming a compound three blocks square. In any other city, it could indicate a prison or a top-secret government facility. In Hollywood, it protected one of the film studios around which the economic life of the community revolved. From the vantage point of West Electronics, it appeared to be solid and invulnerable. To anyone looking closely, the huge posters plastered to the outer surfaces told another story. One of convulsions taking place behind the facade.

The glamourous, larger than life movie stars had been replaced by actors who looked like the boy or girl next door. The once powerful movie studio was now renting space to small and independent producers who were creating programs for a newer medium, one with a more voracious appetite. Very few were making feature films.

Some thought it an ignoble end to what had been a glorious era. Others saw exciting opportunities opening up for the industry. From either point of view, the transformation was enormous. At West Electronics the changes were happening more slowly. They would, for the electronics industry, turn out to be just as consequential.

In 1952, when Martin West persuaded a group of wealthy investors to back him in a plan to import tape recorders from Japan, it was a risky venture. The label "Made in Japan" signaled products that were second-rate; inferior to those manufactured in the United States or Europe. Nobody would buy them.

But West, who had participated in the post-war occupation of Japan, believed those stereotypes were false. He was certain they could be overcome and he had the leadership qualities that allowed him to convince others to finance the gamble. It was paying off.

In the winter of 1962, he was looking for a larger space, ready to leave behind the drab gray building on that quiet Hollywood street. And it was doubtful that anyone on the street, other than the postman and the driver of a canteen truck that stopped in the alley twice a day, would notice when they were gone.

The neighborhood, respectable, if slightly run-down, with the studio at its center, would move on at its own placid pace, seemingly impervious to change until it was forced upon them by the prostitutes and drug dealers who, outgrowing their enclave a few blocks north, would move down and become impossible to ignore. And, perhaps, the blood drenched body to be discovered behind the walls of West Electronics was a harbinger of those things to come.

But nobody can see that far into the future nor, if they could, would they want to. Not on such a bright and sunlit morning when one could still stand on that quiet street in the middle of Hollywood and think how like a small and friendly town it was.

CHAPTER 1

The calendar on Haru Maruri's desk showed the date as February 23, 1962. Next to it, on a notepad, he had scribbled the numbers thirty-five and ten. Fateful numbers. Thirty-five for the years since he'd been born in Japan. Ten for the years since he'd left the land of his ancestors to make his way in the country of the conquerors. On this unseasonably warm and sunny afternoon, he found himself wondering, as was happening more and more frequently, if the move hadn't been a terrible mistake.

His business card announced his title to be "Controller" at West Electronics Corporation, a small company that imported electronic equipment from Japan, but the title was a fiction. At West Electronics he was chief accountant, office manager and the person who got blamed when anything went wrong.

His real job was to make sure everything ran smoothly and, most especially, that Martin West, president of the company, was never inconvenienced. Over the years his salary had steadily increased but his job description hadn't changed and he knew, for as long as he stayed at this company, it never would.

He closed the notebook and gave his attention to problems at hand. They were growing at an alarming rate. The morning had begun with a telex from Japan. Their newest model portable tape recorder, the company's bread and butter, would be delayed. Martin would be furious. Still, Maruri had made a career of handling these kinds of problems. Eventually, the tape recorders would ship and the damage to the company would be controlled.

The problem with Rick Hanson was more complicated. Rick, who worked in the warehouse, hadn't shown up for work that day. Nobody had heard from him and he wasn't answering his phone. Maruri's hand went to the pain in his gut. Rick's loyalty and cooperation were essential.

Ed Walsh, manager of the warehouse, had already gone out on a limb by putting Rick in charge of the loading dock ahead of men with more experience and better qualifications. At first, Rick had been grateful. Now nothing satisfied him. He kept pushing for more. Making unreasonable demands.

It was clear that he shouldn't have been hired in the first place. More crucially, he should never have been taken into their confidence. But it was too late for regrets. Something had to be done and quickly. Rick had to be made to understand the limitations of their position. That there wasn't any more he or Ed Walsh could do for him.

Maruri got up and moved some reports from his desk to the safe in a corner of his office. It was Martin West who concerned him more than anything else. Today Martin was probably with investors. On the company boat or the golf course. Or, he was with his mistress who, like everything else, like Maruri himself, had been imported from Japan.

Maruri didn't much care where he was. He was just relieved that Martin hadn't put in an appearance. Instead of continuing to trust him to handle the nuts and bolts of running the company, the way he'd been doing for years, Martin had begun to ask questions. Difficult questions. If he was becoming suspicious, there would be serious trouble.

Maruri took a fresh roll of antacid tablets from the supply he kept in the top drawer of his desk, opened it carefully, put one in his mouth and the rest into his jacket pocket. He glanced at his desk to make sure it was clear, then turned a key to lock the drawers. He rarely left early, but today it was necessary. After lunch he and Ed Walsh would make the drive to Long Beach.

There was, however, one last item to check on before leaving. A temporary replacement for Elinor Sandstrom was needed. Martin's secretary had received an emergency phone call and flown off to Minnesota to care for a sick mother. An inconvenience for Martin, therefore one more situation, although the least of them, for Maruri to deal with.

"I'm leaving for the day," he told the two people who worked for him in the accounting office and went past them into the reception area. It held an L-shaped arrangement of desks for three secretaries, all of whom doubled as receptionists in the chronically understaffed and rapidly growing company. They grumbled, but they managed.

With Elinor away, only two secretaries were present on this Friday afternoon. He stopped in front of Sheila Birney, peered at her through round black-rimmed eyeglasses and hesitated as he felt the familiar stab of pain shoot through his belly, which the antacid tablet hadn't forestalled.

"Did you call the temporary agency?" he asked.

He spoke clearly, enunciating each word, betraying only the faintest trace of a foreign accent. His English, which he had struggled to perfect, was almost flawless. Still, he rarely allowed himself to speak in haste.

"Of course I called," she snapped.

Anyone looking at the young woman with her curly blond hair and bright blue eyes expected a sunny disposition. More often than not they were disappointed. It was her pronounced and pugnacious jaw that usually ruled the day and, at this moment, that jaw was thrust forward. She stared up at Maruri, refusing to blink or avert her eyes.

"Will they have somebody here on Monday morning?" Maruri prodded, trying not to let her anger bother him and determined not to let her know the degree to which it did. He didn't enjoy provoking her antagonism but he was, by nature, a methodical man who believed that time spent preventing problems was preferable to time wasted in figuring out what had gone wrong after they occurred. By now he was prepared for the hostility that usually greeted his diligence but it would be nice if others would realize that it wasn't easy for him either. He was, after all, only doing his job.

Sheila, who judged him more harshly than anyone else, would not have been swayed by Maruri's need for a more understanding response, even if she'd been aware of it. She didn't care about his problems, she had her own. There was always too much work in the front office and now Elinor had flown off to Minnesota leaving her alone with the office princess, a girl who couldn't even change a typewriter ribbon without help. She glanced over at Wendy Solomon, the young woman sitting at the desk next to hers, and back at Maruri.

"I called the temp agency and everything's arranged," she said.

"And you requested the girl Mr. West especially asked for? The one who's been here before?"

"I told them we preferred to have Sara Fisher and Miss Meacham said they'd do their best to get her. I don't know what else I can do."

"Nothing," he said. "That's all I wanted to know. I'm leaving for the day," he added.

Sheila grunted and watched as he made his exit through the front door. As far as she was concerned, his only authority should be over the two people who worked for him in the accounting department. Her boss was Oliver Blakely, Vice President of Sales & Marketing. The man who, in her opinion, and his, was the most responsible for the success of the company.

She would have quit a long time ago if Mr. Blakely hadn't asked her to be patient. He promised things would get easier after the company moved to larger quarters. And there was her salary to consider. West Electronics paid well and she was saving for a wedding, although the young man she had hopes for had not yet managed a proposal. Still angry, she kept an eye on Wendy Solomon.

While Mr. Maruri was there, the very pretty, child-like woman had kept her back turned, pretending to be working. Once the need to put on a show was over, she went to the plate glass windows that fronted onto the treeless boulevard and placed herself by short, flowered drapes that were pulled back, allowing her to look out while remaining invisible to anyone in the street.

She was slender, with long dark hair that she wore loose, unobtrusive barrettes holding it in place and, while she did not dress provocatively, she managed to project an innocent quality with an overlay of sexual availability. It was a potent mixture to lots of men, although not nearly to as many as she imagined.

"Do you think the agency will send Sara?" she asked.

Sheila was surprised. Wendy wasn't usually interested in anything that didn't concern her directly. "I don't know," she said. "I hope so. It will be nice to have somebody around here who can help. Somebody who knows what she's doing."

Wendy didn't respond to the barb or, perhaps she hadn't recognized it. She was deep in thought. "I hope so too," she said.

"See much out there?" Sheila asked.

There was no response and she hadn't expected one. Sheila knew why Wendy was at the window. She was hoping Rick Hanson might still show up. She was looking for trouble and, with Rick, trouble was exactly what she was going to get.

CHAPTER 2

Haru Maruri was unaware of Wendy Solomon's watchful eye as he walked into the sunshine and descended the short flight of steps that ran along the front of the building.

"Sorry," he said to the stocky, sandy-haired man who waited for him. "Before leaving, I wanted to make sure Martin will have a secretary on Monday morning."

"And everything's taken care of?" Ed Walsh asked, more out of courtesy than interest.

The domain of this retired ex-army supply sergeant was the warehouse where, along with directing the business of shipping, receiving and storing merchandise, he supervised the technical engineers and service people. It was a small crew, eight men in all, but enough to keep him occupied. Problems in the front office neither concerned nor interested him, except when they had to do with the secretary who worked for him. Wendy Solomon.

"All I wanted to know is if she made the phone call," Maruri said. "But, as usual, Sheila had to give me a hard time."

"I would never have her work for me," Walsh declared.

Although the warehouse manager had never married, and his experience with women was mostly limited to transactions for cash, he had supreme confidence in his ability to understand the female temperament.

"Who knows why women react the way they do," he said. "The important thing is, not to let them get to you. If you don't pay attention and you stand firm, sooner or later they forget all about what's bothering them."

He often bragged about how easy it had been for him when Martin West, his commanding officer in post-war Japan, had offered him a job in Los Angeles. There had been nothing to hold him back. No wife to consult with. He'd made the decision on his own, without a moment's hesitation. And it had given him more than he could have hoped for. At fifty-seven years of age, he had a pension from the army, a handsome salary and, in the large warehouse behind the administrative offices of West Electronics, the freedom to construct his world the way he wanted it to be. A man's world, where he could almost believe he had never left the service. Then there was the unexpected icing on his retirement cake, the enterprise he had entered into with Haru Maruri.

"What we need," Walsh continued, as they reached his car, "is a real receptionist out front. It makes for problems when you ask the secretaries to take care of the mail and the phones and all that stuff. We can make room for another desk."

"Don't start on that," Maruri said, digging into his pocket for another antacid tablet. "You know we'll be making the move to larger quarters soon. We can wait until then to add new people, if we need them."

"We need them now. It's too much for Wendy to handle. She has a lot to do and she works very hard."

Maruri knew what Walsh was doing. He wanted to provoke an argument, sidetrack him away from the problems they needed to discuss. It wouldn't work. Not this time.

"They all work hard," he said, "so let's forget about it for now."

He waited for Walsh to open the doors of his new Pontiac Grand Prix, a large blue luxury sedan just off the assembly line in Detroit. He knew Walsh would have preferred a Cadillac but had been wise enough to resist the temptation. Rank did have to be maintained and it wouldn't have done for him to drive the same top of the line car as Martin West. He had settled for the Pontiac instead.

It wasn't until they were both inside the car, with the doors shut, that Maruri allowed himself to raise the subject that was eating at him. "What are we going to do about Rick?" he asked. "You can't let him disappear whenever he feels like it. This morning he never showed up. And he never bothered to call in."

"Don't worry," Walsh said. I'll take care of it."

"When? Nothing will happen until Monday unless you can reach him and set up an earlier meeting."

"I'm not going to call him over the weekend. Do you want to give him the idea that we don't trust him? You worry too much. I can handle him."

"I hope so," Maruri said. "I don't want to think about the consequences if you're wrong."

Walsh shook his head and responded, more calmly than he felt. "You're too hard on him. You have to remember, he's only a boy."

Maruri leaned back and closed his eyes, feeling dwarfed by the big American car, wishing he'd insisted on taking his own Datsun, imported from Japan.

"I don't know," he said. "I'm not sure it's wise to wait--"

The pain in his gut was getting worse and Walsh's words were not reassuring. Rick was twenty-three years old. No longer a boy.

"Trust me," Walsh insisted. "I told you...I know how to handle him."

CHAPTER 3

Wendy Solomon picked at the pleated draperies. She could feel Sheila's eyes on her back but didn't care. Nor was she bothered by the curiosity of the two people in the accounting department. If Mark Cranston and Geraldine Fineman had nothing better to do than spy on her it was their problem. They were all jealous. Elinor too. If Elinor was here today, there'd be yet another pair of eyes watching her. Not that it mattered. The men in the company, the ones who really counted, were on her side. They could see how delicate she was, how special.

"Like a perfect blossom," was how George, her second husband, had described her: "Beautiful, but fragile." He was always so poetic. She'd probably still be with him if he wasn't in jail. He'd be taking care of her. And Mikey, their son. He would take care of Mikey too, was her afterthought.

Her thoughts drifted away from her ex-husband and back to Martin West's secretary. What would happen if Elinor decided to stay in Minnesota and Mr. West had to find someone to take her place? The answer came quickly. She would be his choice. No doubt about it. She had already caught him looking at her. She was much more suited to work for him than Elinor. Elinor was dull. He was probably already wishing Elinor wouldn't come back.

Wendy's imagination made the leap easily. By the time Ed Walsh's Grand Prix pulled out of the driveway she was already Martin West's secretary, picturing how jealous Sheila and the others would be, the ways in which she would lord it over them. And how she would handle Mr. West when, as was inevitable, he would try to make love to her. Maybe she would let him. He was an older man. Much older. Close to fifty, or more. But he wasn't bad looking. It was an interesting possibility, something to be filed away and returned to when she had nothing better to think about.

Her attention went back to the street and anxiety returned. There was still time. Any minute the phone might ring and it would be Rick. Or she would see his Harley. Hear it roar down the street. Why was he torturing her like this? Making her wait?

If Rick didn't call or show up they would miss seeing each other over the weekend and she couldn't bear the thought of not seeing or hearing from him until Monday. There was so much for them to talk about.

It was like a miracle how they had come to love each other even though their time together had been so limited. No more than an hour or two before one or the other would have to be gone. That wasn't enough. They needed a whole night. Time to make love--hold each other--plan for their future together. And an idea about how to make it happen had taken shape in her mind.

Ignoring Sheila, Wendy went into the accounting office, to Geraldine Fineman. "I need to ask you something," she said. "In the ladies' room."

Geraldine, who preferred to be called Gerry, followed. She should have been pleased that Wendy was turning to her. Wanted to talk to her confidentially. But she had no illusions. She knew what Wendy wanted. It wasn't friendship or closeness or anything like that. This would be about Rick Hanson. It happened every time he didn't show up for work. Wendy demanded his home address and Gerry refused to give it to her. Then Wendy would be angry.

But Gerry couldn't do it. Not only was it against the rules, it would be wrong. When, just like she'd expected, Wendy lost her temper and accused her of being selfish, Gerry closed her lips tight together and stopped herself from saying the obvious. If Rick wanted Wendy to have his address, he would have given it to her himself.

Frustrated, Wendy want back to the window in the front office. But she couldn't just stand there, looking out at the empty street, waiting for the phone to ring or for Rick to show up. She had to find a way to be with him.

"Do you have Sara Fisher's phone number?" she asked, turning to Sheila.

"Of course not. Temps aren't allowed to give out their home phone numbers. You know that. We have to go through the agency to reach them. Why do you want to know?"

"No reason. I just like her, that's all and I wanted to ask her a question. She's nice."

Sheila stared with open skepticism. What was Wendy up to? She never had kind words for other women. And why Sara Fisher? What did she have to do with Sara Fisher? But Wendy was once again gazing out the window and Sheila knew that asking questions would be pointless. Whatever it was Wendy was up to, there was no way she was going to tell Sheila about it.

Wendy was formulating a scheme. The idea had occurred to her several weeks earlier but she'd had to set it aside because it involved getting the help of a girlfriend and she didn't have a girlfriend. Then, when Sara Fisher's name was mentioned, it came to her. Sara could be her friend.

Whenever Sara showed up to work at West Electronics, she was easy to talk to, sympathizing and never criticizing or being nasty. Wendy had confided in her more than she ever had to anyone else. Come to think about it, Sara probably thought they were friends already and Wendy almost liked her in return. Especially because she could feel sorry for her.

Sara said she was an actress, but she couldn't be very good at it. If she was she wouldn't be working as a temp. Wendy had never seen her on television or in a movie. She didn't tell stories about acting jobs or meeting famous people or anything interesting. She wasn't married and never mentioned a boyfriend. All this meant that Wendy would be doing Sara a favor. She would be bringing some excitement into poor Sara's life.

"Are you sure Sara will be here on Monday?" she asked, with a little more urgency.

"No," Sheila said. "I can't give you a guarantee, but the agency said they would try."

Wendy left the window, with growing confidence that her plan would work. Once she had Sara's help, her night with Rick would happen. In the meantime, she had to be practical. It was close to noon and the man she lived with would be picking her up so they could have lunch together, like they did every Friday.

She had met Bert Rudner six months earlier when she'd applied for a job at his father's public relations agency. The office manager, obviously jealous, had turned her down but she'd come away with something more valuable. After three dates, Bert had taken her and her child into his home. He had fallen in love. To his father's horror, he was prepared to marry her as soon as the divorce from her current husband, who he did not know was in jail, became final.

Feeling as satisfied as she could under the circumstances, Wendy decided to have the baby-sitter keep Mikey for an extra few hours that evening. Elena could give him dinner while she and Bert ate out. And she didn't have to check with Bert before making the arrangement. He'd go along with anything she wanted.

The phone it rang as she reached for it and she laughed when she heard the voice on the other end. The voice she'd been waiting for. Why had she worried so much about nothing? Why hadn't she trusted him?

CHAPTER 4

"**It might be** my agent," Sara said.

David fell back onto the sofa and wondered why he had bothered to take Friday afternoon off. Sara would take the call, of course, and he hoped an acting job or, at least, the possibility of one, was at the other end of the line. But, even if there'd been no phone call, delay was inevitable. Sara always got scattered before leaving on a trip, even if it was only for a two-day weekend up the coast. He put his feet up on the scarred coffee table and prepared to wait.

David was right, Sara realized, as soon as she recognized the voice of Dolly Meacham. She could have let the answering service get it.

"They need you at West Electronics," Miss Meacham chirped. "'If Sara Fisher is available, that's who we want,' they said."

Dolly Meacham had no difficulty understanding why so many clients had a preference for Sara, although she would never have allowed herself to make such an admission in public. The

Meacham sisters--Miss Dolly and Miss Millie--as they were affec-
tionately referred to by the people who worked for them, always
insisted that every one of 'their' people was equally first-rate.

There were times, however, in the privacy of their two-bedroom
cottage on one of the quieter, tree-lined streets of Hollywood, when
they would admit that some of their people, mostly actors waiting
for their big break, were more first-rate than others. In spite of
their best intentions, they did have favorites and, among these, Sara
ranked high.

"Such a sweet little thing," was how they had described her
when she'd first appeared in their offices looking for work to
supplement her meager income as an actress. And perhaps, back
then, it had been an accurate description although Sara, who had
grown up in one of the tougher neighborhoods of the Bronx,
doubted it had ever applied. Even her doting parents wouldn't
describe her that way. Especially now. Whatever sugar coating
the Meacham sisters had detected was long gone. Worn away
by the intervening years and the realities of her chosen profession. But the sisters hadn't noticed. Their opinion remained
unchanged.

"Are you 'at liberty,' or do you have one of your acting jobs
lined up?" Miss Meacham asked, as she patted the back of her
improbably yellow head of hair. It was swept up into a style made
popular in 1943, the year of her screen test. A year she remembered with great fondness.

"I am free," Sara admitted. She would accept the assignment.
There were worse places to work than West Electronics and she
could use the money. The only acting work she'd had in the last

three months was two days on a TV soap opera and unemployment was running out

"By the way," she told Miss Meacham, "if you and Miss Millie have time to watch, I'll be on 'The Hours of Our Days' the twenty-seventh of this month and the second of next."

"Wonderful. It's going right onto my calendar," Miss Meacham exclaimed.

"Don't go out of your way," Sara advised. "It's just another one of those nameless nurses with only a few lines. If you blink, you'll miss me."

"Nonsense," she said, surprised Sara would make such a suggestion. She and Millie loved watching "their" people on television. No role was too small. No hour too inconvenient. They kept a television set in the office and one at home so they wouldn't risk missing anyone's appearance.

"Alright, but don't say I didn't warn you. And you can tell them at West I'll be there on Monday morning"

"Of course," Miss Meacham said. "They'll be so pleased."

⅄

Sara replaced the receiver, determined to put the state of her career out of her mind. "Let's go," she told David.

He remained seated, watching as Sara gathered up some books.

"Have you seen my sunglasses?"

David pointed to a spot on the coffee table, next to an untidy stack of magazines. "You really ought to marry me," he said. "I could keep you organized and, if I ever manage to find clients who pay, you would never have to work temporary again."

"I can organize myself," Sara told him as she disappeared into the kitchen, her voice sharper than she'd meant it to be.

Marriage was a subject she wished David wouldn't talk about. She did care for him--a lot. She'd been with him for longer than with any other man, but the thought of being tied to one person for the rest of her life provoked the kind of anxiety that had sent her into therapy. She wasn't sure she was temperamentally suited to monogamy. She wasn't even sure she wanted to be.

Returning to the living room, she handed David a glass coffee pot half filled with water. "I can't reach," she said, motioning him towards a somewhat straggly looking Boston fern that hung in a handmade macramé holder over the bookcase.

She took a final look around the bright and cheerful living room with its floral chintz slipcovers and soft green carpeting, the place she wasn't ready to share with anyone, even David. Everything seemed to be in order, at least as much in order as it ever would be.

"I guess that takes care of everything," she said, taking the empty pot back to the kitchen.

"I guess," he agreed, unable to imagine what more there could be for her to do. They were only going away for the weekend. He was going to give legal advice to a grass roots organization working to stop construction of a nuclear power plant in the central valley while Sara would relax in the beautiful country around the foothills of the Sierra. If she'd forgotten anything, it wouldn't be serious.

He carried her canvas tote bag to the door while she grabbed a large and lumpy macramé handbag, crafted by her own hands and dating from the same period as the plant holder. "I'm ready," she announced.

"Right," David said, already out the door. "And, remember, we still have to stop at the supermarket."

"Not only do you not get paid for these weekends, which are really one long consultation," Sara said, as she followed him into the hallway and locked the door, "you also bring the groceries."

"I know. You think I let people take advantage of me. But this group has hardly any funding and they're the ones making the sacrifice. They're out there doing the hard part for the rest of us."

Sara turned and smiled up at him.

"You know what," she said. "Since I'll have some extra money from working at West Electronics next week, the groceries are my treat."

"No way," David protested.

Sara put her hand on the back of David's neck. "Don't argue," she whispered as she raised her lips to his.

He held her tightly and breathed in the subtle fragrance of her scent. She could be difficult and prickly but she was also desirable, smart and funny, with an insatiable curiosity that could be maddening or delightful, but never boring.

"Hold on to the thought until we get back," he said, before letting her go. "We're going to be in sleeping bags on the living room floor this trip, with lord knows how many others."

"One more sacrifice to the cause. And you're going to Seattle when we get back."

"For only a week," he said. "You can handle that."

"I'm not sure," Sara said, teasing. She kissed him once more, lightly this time and started down the terra cotta tile steps. "We'd better hurry. It's getting late."

CHAPTER 5

Rick Hanson allowed his wristwatch--his very expensive wristwatch--to drop onto the crowded bedside table. It was eight o'clock on Monday morning. Time to get out of bed. He rolled onto his back. Slowly, almost insolently, he stretched his arms toward the ceiling. There was no reason to hurry. Nobody would hassle him for being late. He took time to admire the sculptured hardness of his muscles and the evenness of his tan.

Maintaining the golden color was important. He worked hard at it, even during the winter months, lying under the sun whenever time and weather cooperated, turning from one side to the other, taking care to give equal exposure to all parts of his body. Pleased to see it was still looking good, he took a deep breath and, with a surge of energy, shoved aside the dingy sheet.

There was business to take care of this morning. The thought of the possibilities pushed him into action. He moved more quickly now, kicking aside the clothes discarded on the floor, oblivious to the stained, dusty surfaces of the few pieces of furniture provided by his landlord. Since he never brought anybody here, he didn't see why the mess was anything worth worrying about and he didn't

He was happy in this small apartment that had been his home for almost three years. He didn't want to leave. But he had moved up in the world. He had more money now and arrangements for a new apartment had already been made. The lease was signed. Still, he wasn't sure he wanted to go through with it.

In the small bathroom, which was no cleaner than the rest of the apartment, he brushed his teeth then climbed into a chipped and discolored claw-footed tub. The once-transparent shower curtain was clouded with soap scum. Unmindful, Rick turned the faucets and stepped under a heavy spray. He saw no defects. In the small space of this apartment he could be himself. Here, for the first time in his life, he hadn't had to pretend or explain himself to anyone. He didn't bother his neighbors and they didn't bother him. People minded their own business. Not like the town he'd run away from. There, everybody knew everything about everybody else, from the day they were born until they were laid into the ground.

He smiled as he rubbed soap over his body and allowed the water to rinse it away. In Hollywood, everything was different. Exactly the way he'd dreamed it would be. Anything could happen. There was money waiting to be picked up with hardly any effort. And there were girls. Beautiful girls. Especially the actresses. All looking for a break. All eager to get laid by a famous producer's son.

He dried his body carefully, using a corner of the towel to polish a large gold coin he never took from around his neck. It was his lucky charm, an almost-gift from an admirer who Rick was sure would have given it to him had he not pre-empted the generosity by helping himself. So far, it hadn't let him down. Money had come his way and so had women--although he'd never had any problem in that department.

He ran the whirring blades of an electric razor over his face. Coming up with the story about his father being in the movie business had been the stroke of genius. And it had come to him one day when he wasn't even stoned. He used other stories, of course, changing them to suit the situation, weaving in tales about the coin to make them more interesting. But his favorite was the one about his father, the movie producer. How they didn't get along and how important it was for him to prove he could make it on his own.

Rick laughed out loud. His father was a producer all right. He produced gas out of two old and rusty pumps in a rundown service station on the outskirts of a two-bit central valley town. He'd produced three sons, four daughters and a tired wife. Rick could see it all in his mind's eye as clearly as if it was still in front of him. His family. The wooden shack behind the service station they'd lived in. And the flat baked landscape. He hated it all. It was the cruel and arid heartland of California and he had run from it, making his escape before his seventeenth birthday. He had never gone back. His family had no idea where he was and he doubted any of them cared. He certainly had no interest in knowing what had become of them.

He put the razor back on the shelf above the sink. He didn't think he would ever tell anybody the truth about where and what he had come from. The made-up stories were better. He loved telling them and they would work no matter where he lived. The more expensive neighborhood he was moving into would make it even easier.

He frowned. Things wouldn't change just because he'd be paying more rent. Except for having a swimming pool and air conditioning the move would make no major difference in his life. There would still be dope and women. Just more of them and they'd be of higher quality. Anyway, the decision was made.

He took a clean white T-shirt from a drawer that was filled with them. They were his trademark. Everyday a fresh one. They showed off his tan, the blue eyes, the blonde hair bleached even paler by the sun, the breadth of his chest. He pulled it over his head and looked in the mirror that hung over a battered chest of drawers. He focused on himself, oblivious to the reflection of grimy walls behind him and limp curtains on either side of dirty windows. He turned his head this way and that, admiring himself from all the different angles before going to the next step of his morning ritual.

Like he did every morning, he took his key ring from the top of the bureau and, paused to savor the weight of it. There were so many keys on the ring he didn't think another one would fit. It was just like he'd pictured it when he was a child. Even then, when he'd had nothing more than hand-me-down clothing to call his own, he had equated power with the ability to protect himself from the prying eyes and grasping hands of others.

Having a lot of keys had gone together in his mind with being a person of substance. Somebody important who could afford to have secrets and his own private places. Somebody who couldn't be ignored. Now, it was all coming true.

In the kitchen, he used a stepstool to reach into the highest shelf of a cupboard above the sink. From behind some dusty cans of baked beans he took a metal cash box that he brought down to the kitchen table and opened, using one of the smaller keys on the key ring. From its recesses, he pulled a plastic bag filled with tiny, crumpled, brownish leaves and grayish twigs.

Mostly twigs, he noted, but Ken Ichiwara, a salesman who traveled up and down California for West Electronics, wouldn't know the difference. It was cocaine that was missing. Ken had asked for that as well, but Rick had given in to temptation. Over the weekend, he'd done it all himself. His nostrils contracted involuntarily as he remembered how good it had been. More of the white stuff would be available later in the day and, if Ken wanted it, he'd have to come back from Santa Barbara to get it.

Rick returned the box and stepstool to their places. The plastic bag went into the inside zipper pocket of his leather jacket and, ready to face whatever the day held in store, he slung the jacket over his shoulder. He was on his way.

CHAPTER 6

In the passenger seat of a 1962 Thunderbird--bright red--sparkling inside and out--Wendy Solomon held her son on her lap.

"You're driving me crazy," she shouted at the man next to her. "Why can't you leave me alone?"

The child called out, one loud sharp yelp of distress, before going back to making whimpering sounds, his main means of communication. Like a package left behind by mistake, he didn't seem to belong there. His blanket showed traces of dried food and saliva as did the jump suit he was wearing. Once bright blue, both were faded.

Neither his mother nor Bert Rudner, the driver of the car, responded to his cry or allowed it to interfere with their argument and, even at 15 months, Mikey was making it easy for them. While he might not be an attractive child, he was ahead of his age in having learned the secrets of survival. He made few demands on grown-ups and managed to keep the sounds of his despair at a level that wouldn't intrude on their affairs. Rather than being a

27

child that strangers wanted to cuddle, but he had already turned himself into one that was easy to ignore.

"For God's sake. Tell me how these cigarettes got here." Bert Rudner demanded. "That's all. Just tell me how the hell they got here."

He held on to the steering wheel with one hand while, in the other, he clutched the crumpled and almost empty packet he had discovered in the pocket of the car door, next to the driver's seat. He had been groping for his sunglasses when his fingers had come upon the unfamiliar sensation of crumpled cellophane and paper. There were two cigarettes left in the white and gold colored packet. The meaning was clear. Since neither he nor Wendy smoked, a third person had been in the car. And that person had been in the driver's seat. He was bewildered, his feelings alternating between fury and pain.

"You let somebody else drive the car," he accused. "You let somebody else drive my T-Bird."

"I don't know anything about it."

"Then how did these get here? And don't tell me you don't know. You're the only other person I let drive this car."

"How many times do I have to say it? I'll say it again," she shouted. I don't know."

"For God's sake, shut-up," Bert said. His voice had dropped to an angry growl. "She can hear you."

He had pulled up in front of a modest one-family house, painted white with patches of weathered wood showing through. There were a playpen and some toys on the front porch. Elena Sanchez, a large woman with dark eyes and warm brown skin, had already opened the door. Her black hair was streaked with gray. Two of her grandchildren, older than Mikey but still too young for school, crowded into the doorway beside her.

"I don't care who hears me," Wendy said, as she got out of the car, holding on to her child. "You're just jealous, that's all. You're just crazy jealous. You make a big deal out of everything I do."

Bert Rudner couldn't understand what was happening to him. He watched as Wendy carried Mikey up the worn wooden steps. He heard her admonish the child to be a good boy before leaving him without a backward glance. He saw the look on Elena's face, the expression of contempt and a feeling of sadness, deeper than anything he'd ever known came over him. He loved Wendy. He had planned to marry her when she was free. To accept the child. But he was no longer sure that could happen. It was being forced upon him that something in their relationship was going very wrong.

He'd always believed he had a lot going for him. In his thirtieth year, he was, by most people's definition, a "good catch." A nice-looking young man of medium height, with brown curly hair cut short. Well-dressed. A good job, working for his father's public relations firm. Any girl would be happy to have him.

His had been a better than ordinary life and he was grateful for it, never wishing for anything else. There was no secret longing within him for wild adventures. He expected to marry, but until Wendy came along, he'd felt he still had time. One thing he had never considered was living with a woman outside the bounds of matrimony, much less a woman with a child who was still married to another man. Wendy had changed all that.

"You're making a fool out of me," he said, when they were on their way again. His voice had gone quiet. Wendy and his new car, the two things he loved most in the world, had become tainted for him. He was afraid he might break down and cry in front of her, but couldn't stop trying to get at the truth.

"Only two people ever drive this car. You and me. And that was only because you begged me to let you use it when I was out of town or when you wanted to go shopping, like Sunday, when I was watching the game. So, where," he repeated, "did the cigarettes come from? Who were you with? Who are you going out with when my back is turned?"

Wendy stared straight ahead. He couldn't force her to admit anything and West Electronics was only a few blocks away. All she had to do was keep quiet until they got there.

"I want the keys back," he demanded. "Where are the keys to my car?"

"You'll get them back," she said. "Don't worry."

In her lap, her fists clenched. He had no right to be badgering her like this. She hadn't forced him to give her the extra set of keys. He had handed them over of his own free will along with permission to drive his precious Thunderbird. Now he was making conditions on how she used the car. He was lucky she didn't tell him the truth, that she was tired of him and his possessiveness.

Still, she wished she hadn't let Rick talk her into letting him hold onto the keys. And the cigarettes. They should have been more careful about leaving them in the car. It would have saved her a lot of trouble if only they had been more careful. Bert couldn't know the truth until she and Rick worked out a way they could be together. Until then, she needed the shelter and support he provided for her and Mikey. Her only comfort was that once everything was arranged with Rick, Bert and his jealousy would be out of her life.

"The keys. Where are they?" Bert demanded, once again. He had pulled up to the curb in front of West Electronics.

"They're at home," she lied, as she stepped out of the car. "And I have one more thing to say to you," she added, before slamming the door and walking away. "I'm not going to let you ruin my life."

Bert looked after her, stunned. What she was talking about? If anybody's life was being ruined, it was his. He watched her run up the steps and disappear through the front door as if she was hurrying to get away from him. He would have liked to follow her. Find out what she was hiding. He did have his suspicions. Some idea about what was going on. He believed the answer might be inside this building. Right here, at West Electronics.

Chapter 7

Sara barely noticed Bert's Thunderbird as it pulled away from the curb. Already late to work, she turned into the underground garage and concentrated on getting her 1955 Ford sedan within the lines of a guest parking space.

She made it on the first try. An unusual success. True, the car was at a slight angle. But, there was no time to aim for perfection. A quick look at herself in the rear- view mirror showed her short, brown, curly hair going off in all directions. No time to do much about that either. It wasn't until she was out of the car that she became aware of Rick Hanson.

He was looking down at her from the top of a small flight of stairs that led directly from the rear of the garage into the warehouse. She remembered him from previous encounters at West Electronics. She especially recalled having had no desire to know him any better. Beneath his attempts to ingratiate himself she had sensed an arrogance about him that repelled her.

Sara could see it again this morning, in the way he leaned against the heavy door that led into the warehouse, holding it open with the weight of his body; the way he smoked his cigarette, staring at her as if he were stripping her naked in his imagination. What was he doing out here at a quarter past nine? He should be at work.

She looked around, forgetting to hurry. There were few cars in the garage, none in the spaces reserved for executives at the company. Maybe Rick was taking advantage because no one was around to supervise him. She moved forward, prepared to ignore him, relieved that front office workers were discouraged from using the warehouse entrance. But he kept watching her, silent until she reached his motorcycle.

"Feast your eyes," he said. He fingered the keys on the ring he had clipped to a belt loop of his jeans. "We never got around to taking that ride on the Harley the last time you were here. Let's do it tomorrow. After work."

"No thank you,"

Sara's voice was cold, leaving no room for encouragement. Yet she found herself feeling sorry for him. He looked so young standing there, acting like he was God's gift and playing with those ridiculous keys.

Her hand gently massaged the back of her neck, a sure sign that what David called her hyper-active curiosity had been aroused. She wondered why Rick's motorcycle wasn't out back, in the alley, where the other warehouse workers parked their cars. Her eyes held on the key ring, careless of the interpretation Rick would put on her seeming fascination with the part of his anatomy hidden by tight jeans that left little to the imagination.

What could he possibly be doing with so many keys? Was he trying to impress people by decorating himself with keys for which there were no locks? Or did he have that many places to keep hidden away from curious eyes? She remembered the story he'd told her about his father being a movie producer and wondered what kind of a family he really came from.

"Come on," he coaxed. "You might not get another chance. I'm thinking of giving the bike a rest and getting a car. Maybe a Buick. You know, something like the one Ollie drives."

Sara regarded him more thoughtfully. It was strange for someone from the warehouse to be referring to the vice-president of sales and marketing so familiarly. And how could Rick afford the same car Oliver Blakely drove? For that matter, how he could afford the Harley? Those weren't cheap either.

Once again she refused his invitation, this time, more kindly. If she'd thought he'd be able to understand, she would have told him that the kind of motorcycle or car he drove wasn't important. He didn't have to make up stories to be accepted.

Rick would have laughed if Sara had told him what she was thinking. She might act superior but he couldn't be deceived. No matter how hard she tried to hide it, she was attracted to him. And why not? He had more than his looks going for him. He had a technique he was proud of, one he had worked on and used to charm people into giving him what he wanted. Men and women.

Sex itself didn't interest him that much, except as a way to exert power. But he had learned to perform well. Nobody had ever complained. He could even have that dyke in the accounting department if he wanted. Why should this temp be any different?

He smiled as he dropped the butt of his cigarette onto the cement landing and ground it out with the heel of his boot. From a pocket in the back of his jeans, he took a crumpled packet--gold and white. He removed a cigarette, put it between his lips, and patted the pockets of his jeans, looking for matches. He cursed when he realized he didn't have any and put the cigarette behind his ear.

He would have asked Sara for a light but she was gone. When he looked up she was already at the top of the ramp. He could see her silhouetted against the sunshine. She was older than most of the girls he had anything to do with. Probably more than thirty. But she looked good--and there was something about her.

He would try again. She could play hard-to-get all she wanted but he would teach her she wasn't any better than girls who were easy. The ones who threw themselves at him. But he'd have to come up with a different approach. Being the son of a movie producer hadn't been right for Sara. Even though she was an actress, she was also a bleeding heart. He should have used the one about being an orphan. Being an orphan and living with an uncle who beat him. It would work. Sara was just the type who'd go for that one. And then, when she was feeling sorry for him, he would offer her some grass. The good stuff. Something from his own stash. It would have to be the right moment of course. He would have to work it out.

But now, it was time to take care of business. The car he'd been waiting for had arrived.

CHAPTER 8

Sara ran up the steps to West Electronics, ready to apologize for being late and eager to reassure anyone who was interested that she would make up the lost time out of her lunch hour, although she knew, from past experience, that nobody would care unless Mr. West was there, which hardly ever happened, as he rarely arrived before 11 o'clock, if he showed up at all.

Inside the front door Sheila held the phone with one hand while scribbling on a pink message slip with the other. Her jaw protruded and her voice was indignant. "I don't know why he didn't get back to you," she said.

She looked even more disgruntled than usual but her face brightened into prettiness when she saw Sara. She smiled and returned to the caller with less animosity. "I'll give him your message...I'll give Mr. Maruri *all* your messages," she amended, "as soon as he comes in."

At the next desk Wendy Solomon looked like a sullen teenager as she sorted through a mound of Monday morning mail that, even on a good day, was a job she resented. This wasn't a good day. Still smarting from her argument with Bert, she was absorbed in how best to overcome the obstacles he was placing in the way of her happiness. She also worried Sara might not show up. And, if she did show up, what if she refused to cooperate?

"My God, you're here," she exclaimed when Sara's arrival penetrated her consciousness. "I was afraid the agency would send somebody else. That you--"

She stopped abruptly and put a finger to her lips to indicate silence.

Sara's couldn't help wondering why Wendy was so excessively pleased to see her, then caught herself. She didn't want to know and wasn't going to ask. She didn't have to. Wendy was undoubtedly in the midst of some self-induced crisis and looking for a sympathetic ear. Sara had heard enough about these problems during previous assignments at West Electronics to know she wasn't interested in hearing any more.

"Yes, I'll tell him it's urgent," Sheila said as she added the pink message slip to a small stack accumulating on her desk. She hung up the phone and stopped Sara's apology before it could begin.

"Mr. West isn't in yet," she said. "But there's plenty to do." She pointed to Elinor's desk, which was at right angles to her own, facing the entrance to the accounting department office. "I have to go. Mr. Blakely is waiting for me." She instructed Wendy to answer the phones, gathered up a steno pad and pencil, and hurried down the narrow, dimly-lit corridor toward Oliver Blakely's office.

"Is she gone?" Wendy whispered.

Sara nodded and, without pausing, took her place at Elinor's desk. But there was no escape. Wendy moved into Sheila's chair and rolled it over to Sara.

"I'm so happy to see you," she said. "I've never been so happy to see anybody in my whole life." She spoke softly, crowding in on Sara with a disturbing intensity. "We need to talk. In private."

Sara moved her chair back as far as it would go and looked past Wendy at the small room with its flowered drapes, Danish-modern-on-the-cheap furniture and tall potted plants with their improbably shiny, plastic leaves. "We are alone," she pointed out. "What do you want to tell me?"

Wendy shook her head. "Not now. They're watching me. I'll talk to you later...in the ladies' room."

Before Sara could object Wendy had rolled the chair away and was back at her own desk, this time sorting the mail with energy, making herself look busy for a non-existent audience.

Sara's fingers massaged the nape of her neck. Why was Wendy behaving so strangely? Why would anybody be watching her? That she needed professional help, was Sara's diagnosis, although she knew it was something Wendy would never agree to. For her, it was other people who had problems, especially when they got in the way of what she wanted.

Just as aware of her own imperfections, Sara could admit she had brought this intimacy on herself. She had encouraged Wendy to confide in her even after she'd realized Wendy was seriously troubled. But she'd been curious and curiosity was her vice.

Even as a child she would watch the grownups, listen to their conversations and wonder what made them tick. Perhaps it was the trait that drew her to a career in the theatre, where curiosity was an asset. A few night courses in psychology, along with time spent in group therapy, had finished the job. Listening to other people's problems, sharing her own and watching her therapist work had turned her into an incorrigible voyeur into other people's psyches. At least that was the way David would describe it.

He had, more than once, accused her of using curiosity as an excuse for being nosy and she would explain that it had to do with her profession. Actors needed to be aware of the clues people put out, behavior that reveals what they're thinking and feeling, the truth that lies behind the veils we use to protect ourselves. More important, she wasn't harming anybody. It wasn't as if she judged people or tried to interfere in their lives. She just gave what was most needed. A willing ear. Someone to hear them.

But what if, with Wendy, it had been a mistake to listen without trying to help? Maybe she should have been judgmental. Maybe she should have tried to act as a positive influence. But, even if she had made the effort, would it have made a difference? Sara didn't think so.

Wendy didn't want help and Sara knew she wasn't qualified to give it. But she could have stopped listening. She could have walked away. She hadn't and now she was being asked to pay a price she hadn't anticipated. Just when she wanted to put distance between them, Wendy seemed to be assuming a closer relationship than the casual one that had existed in the past, a closer relationship than Sara had meant to encourage.

Sara sighed. Even putting Wendy and her paranoid fantasies aside, the atmosphere didn't seem quite as usual at West Electronics. She tried to get a sense of what was bothering her. Through the open doorway facing her she could see into the large office of the accounting department, the man and woman who worked at desks facing each other, the empty desks set aside for temporary workers and, at the far end, the glass panels of Haru Maruri's office. Nothing out of the ordinary there.

Next to her typewriter were the recorded cylinders Martin West had filled with his evenly paced and easy to follow dictation. She admonished herself to stop imagining problems where there were none and set to work, unaware that curiosity had also been awakened in the accounting office where Mark Cranston and Gerry Fineman were enjoying a rare moment of freedom from observation.

⟡

Haru Maruri had not yet arrived; Elinor, who felt it was her duty to be the eyes and ears for Mr. West, was in Minnesota; and Sheila, who also liked to keep track of her fellow-workers, although they were none of her business, was in Oliver Blakely's office. Mark and Gerry were therefore free to discuss whatever topic was of interest which, at that particular moment, was Wendy, giving lie to Sara's assumption that paranoia was at the heart of Wendy's belief she was being watched.

While Wendy was not, as she tended to assume, the center of everybody's attention, both Gerry and Mark had watched her distraught arrival that morning and had seen the way she'd rolled herself over for a whispered conversation with Sara. Keeping their voices subdued, they pondered the possible reasons for her distress.

"I think he's tired of her," Gerry said, having gone over to perch on a corner of Mark's desk.

"Who's tired of her?" Mark asked, sarcastically. He sat with his chair turned so he could keep an eye out for Haru Maruri's arrival. "You'll have to be more specific. Are you talking about *our* Rick or *her* Bert?"

Gerry giggled. "You mean *your* Rick, don't you? Maybe it's both of them. Maybe they're both tired of her. Not that you care, of course."

Mark sat up in his chair. "Why should I care," he retorted, his face flushed.

He should never have told Gerry about what had happened between him and Rick. He'd feared it was a mistake as soon as his secret spilled out of his mouth. But who else could he talk to? Who else could he confide in? There was nobody. Still, he should have kept his mouth shut.

"It has nothing to do with me!" he said.

"I guess not, since it doesn't look like Rick's going to give you a chance for a repeat performance."

"Maybe not, but that's better than getting nothing at all. And that's all you have to look forward to. Nothing. Wendy wouldn't ever let you get near her."

Ever since Wendy came to West Electronics, he had suspected Gerry had a crush on her but this was the first time he'd given voice to his suspicion and the dark color flooding Gerry's face told him he was on target.

"At least, I would never stoop to paying for it," Gerry responded.

The two friends glared at each other and Gerry, as she turned away, was on the brink of tears. They were each aware they had pushed the other too far. But they had argued before and the anger always faded. It would fade again. When lunch time came, they would join each other once more, unfold brown paper bags, and share confidences while eating the sandwiches they'd brought from home.

In the meantime, calm descended. In the front office, Wendy sorted mail while deciding on how best to approach Sara with her plans. Sara, unaware that Wendy was making plans for her, listened to Martin West's voice and concentrated on transcribing his words as accurately as possible.

CHAPTER 9

"**I almost forget**," Sheila said when she returned from Oliver Blakely's office. She took a folder from her desk and handed it to Sara.

"I typed this report for Mr. West on Friday. But I'm not used to the dictating machine. You should probably review it before turning it over to him."

"I would have typed it up," Wendy said as she dropped a stack of unopened mail in front of Sara and stationed herself there. "But Mr. Walsh likes me to concentrate on his work. And he knows I get a headache when I spend too much time with that dictation thing in my ear." She tossed her hair behind her shoulder with the back of her hand, and called out to Gerry in the accounting department.

"Your mail is ready. It's on my desk."

Gerry came to scoop up the envelopes and lingered, pretending to look through them while hoping for a few minutes of conversation with Wendy and the other girls. It wasn't to be. Within moments, the door from the warehouse, on the back wall next to

Wendy's desk, opened to reveal the arrival of Haru Maruri and Martin West.

On a level that wasn't even conscious, the women stopped what they were doing and returned to their desks with movements almost imperceptible. A reaction so expected--and deemed to be so appropriate--that neither of the men took note.

"Good morning," Martin West said, nodding at Sheila. "Did I have any phone calls?"

Sheila shook her head and pointed to the obvious: Sara sitting at his secretary's desk.

"The man from the insurance company called again," she said to Haru Maruri. "He wants to set up an appointment to come in. I promised you'd call him back this morning. He said it was urgent."

Maruri took the slips of pink paper she held out to him and stuffed them into his jacket pocket, his face stiff with disapproval.

"He wasn't very nice about it," Sheila added. "He said the insurance company wasn't going to send a check until they got more answers to their questions."

Martin West, who had paused to greet Sara and ask her to bring him a cup of coffee, turned an inquiring gaze on his controller. "Are those the losses from September? I thought they'd been paid off on."

Maruri shrugged. "You know how insurance companies are. Always trying to delay the inevitable."

"It should have been settled by now," he said. "Take care of it."

West was tall, with the air of a man who had no doubt his instructions would be obeyed, yet he looked troubled as he turned away and walked toward his office at the end of the corridor.

His breakfast meeting with Maruri and Ed Walsh had not gone well. He trusted both men. They had been with him from the beginning. But he felt their answers to questions about possible problems at the company had been evasive. Now there was this business with the insurance company. Claims he had been allowed to assume were settled were being challenged. What other problems were being kept from him?

Maruri's watched him go, his hand moving to the pain in his belly. Mail and phone call messages were confidential, to be handed over without comment, unless there was an emergency. All the girls had those instructions and he knew Sheila was aware of what she had done. But he was too angry to deal with her now. And, he certainly didn't want to risk calling even more attention to the phone calls from the insurance company. He turned towards his office, only to be interrupted by the newly arrived Ken Ichiwara.

"Good morning, Harry. What are you looking so miserable about?" Ichiwara asked.

"I'm fine," Maruri said. He didn't mind when Martin or Ed Anglicized his name but it infuriated him when Ken used the American diminutive. Especially this morning. Anxiety had kept him from getting any rest over the weekend and breakfast with Martin had been a strain. He was exhausted.

"You don't look fine," Ichiwara said, slapping Maruri on the back, a gesture he knew would cause further annoyance.

The Western Regional Sales Manager for West Electronics, a short, muscular man who sported a well-tended moustache and exuded energy, was gifted with the *bonhomie* of a natural salesman and the thick skin necessary for success in his profession. Hardened to rejection, it rolled off his back. Maruri's obvious disapproval didn't bother him at all.

Maruri forced himself to smile before he once again moved toward the sanctuary of his office. For a time, he had tried to act as a positive influence on Ichiwara who was Nisei, born in the United States and a perfect example of what happened when people drifted from their roots. But the salesman had rejected his attempts and Maruri had come to accept that it was too late for Kenzo Ichiwara, who now called himself Ken. The only things about him that were still Japanese were his surname and his appearance. He might as well be Caucasian.

Ichiwara grinned and turned his attention to Sheila. "Hey, you look great this morning. Any messages?"

She shook her head. "Aren't you supposed to be in Santa Barbara today?"

"I'm leaving now. As soon as I pick up some stuff I forgot to take with me on Friday."

"What are you doing here?" Oliver Blakely asked. "You're supposed to be on the road."

The National Sales Manager had come down the corridor from his office which was next to Martin West's. He was a big man, solidly built, who filled the entrance to the narrow hallway that began where Sara's desk left off.

"I'm on my way. Just need to pick up the demo tapes I forgot when I left for the weekend."

Ichiwara paused, trying to maintain his carefree attitude. If he hadn't been seen talking with Rick in the garage he could have left without coming into the building, the way he'd planned. Now, he was stuck, making lame excuses. For nothing--or practically nothing. There had only been a handful of grass. And Rick wanted him to drive back from Santa Barbara that evening, like an errand boy. Maybe he should have refused. But what Rick had promised for tonight was too good to pass up on.

"I haven't got your sales report for last week yet," Blakely reminded him.

"Right! As soon as I get back. On Thursday. I'll work on it at night, in my hotel room. What else is there to do when you're on the road?" He smiled, angled his head toward the women and winked, inviting them to conjecture about how he really spent his nights. He never tried to hide his extra-marital exploits, except from his wife. And even there he wasn't overly scrupulous.

Blakely grunted. He didn't care where or how Ken spent his nights. Meeting or exceeding sales quotas was the important thing and Ken was one of the best. But, he liked his men to be honest with him and didn't believe Ken's excuse for being here this morning. He would have to keep a closer eye on his number one salesman. If Ken was burning out, he wanted to set him straight or get rid of him before the problems showed up in the sales figures. He rattled the change in his pocket as he walked past Sara's desk.

"Has Mr. Walsh come in yet?" he asked Wendy.

"I haven't seen him, but I'll check for you."

"Not necessary. I'll see for myself," he said and turned to Sheila. "I'm going to take the car in. Someone from the service department at the dealership can drive me back."

"I don't know where everybody else was this morning, but I was here at nine," he said to Ed Walsh. "Waiting for you to show up."

"Sorry. There was a breakfast meeting with Martin and Harry that went on forever."

"It must have been rough," Blakely said. "You look like hell."

Walsh forced a laugh. "It wasn't that bad," he said. "Nothing serious."

"I have to get my car back to the dealer," Blakely said. "But I didn't want to leave without checking on that delayed shipment. I've got customers waiting for the product and I'll have to make some soothing phone calls as soon as I get back. I don't want cancelled orders."

"I don't want that either," Walsh said. "Believe me, I need the information as much as you do. It's Japan, you know. The factory."

"And what about the merchandise that went missing, doesn't that have something to do with it?"

Blakely hadn't been able to resist throwing that in, but he didn't wait for a response. He'd already heard Walsh's excuses and had no interest in hearing them again. "At least," he continued, "the factory should be able to give us an approximate delivery date. Something I can tell my dealers."

"I'll do my best to have that for you," Walsh assured him. "Maybe by the time you get back."

Blakely didn't have time for an argument. He nodded although he knew there would be no information from Japan until the next day at the earliest. Not with the time difference between

Osaka and Los Angeles. Ed should stop pulling that crap and just be honest with him.

He walked out of the small, glass paneled enclosure that was Walsh's office, once again jingling the coins in his pocket. A few feet away, on the landing outside the garage door exit, Rick Hanson was waiting for him.

"Hey, I need to talk to you for a minute," Rick said.

"I don't have time right now," Blakely said, moving past him, towards his car.

Rick followed and blocked his way. "I'm only trying to do you a favor. I'm going to call that friend of ours this afternoon and I thought you might want me to put a little something down for you."

Blakely drew away. "Not interested," he said.

He felt disgust for Rick and anger towards himself for having gotten involved with him on any level. He'd been taken in. Now, he wanted nothing further to do with him and thought he should be fired. Why Walsh put up with him? Not only put up with him, why had Rick Hanson been promoted when he was already puffed up beyond endurance?

He moved again to get to his car. "If there's nothing else, get out of my way," he said.

"As it happens, there is one other thing," Rick said. "I'm a little short of cash and I was wondering if you could advance me a few bucks.

Blakely stared at him, incredulous. "Just how many bucks are we talking about," he asked.

"Not much. Fifty should cover it."

"Fifty," Blakely echoed the casual tone Rick has used with him. "As it happens, I'm a little short myself, right now."

"If that's the way you want it," Rick said, stepping aside. "You know I don't want to cause trouble for anybody, but I do need the money."

Blakely didn't bother to respond. If anybody was looking for trouble it was Rick and he was a fool if he thought anyone would allow themselves to be blackmailed over placing some penny-ante bets with a bookmaker. But Rick might be involved in other, less savory, enterprises. There might be others Rick was trying to extort money from. If so, then he'd better be careful. Blackmail was a dangerous game.

Chapter 10

"**Is Rick out** here," Ed Walsh asked of the two men who were preparing cartons for shipment near the loading dock at the back of the warehouse.

"He was over there about an hour ago," the older of the men said, pointing towards the other end of the warehouse, "by the garage door."

"Yeah," the other man confirmed. "He was talking to Mr. Blakely."

Walsh nodded. That was more than an hour earlier. Where had Rick gone off to? He turned away, moving slowly in the direction from which he'd come. He felt unsure of himself and didn't like it. How was it that Rick seemed to disappear and reappear like a magician? He peered down the shadowy aisles created by huge pallets of tape recorders, as if the answer might be found there.

This was ridiculous. He straightened his back and walked more briskly, ashamed for having let his imagination run away with him.   When he reached the service department work benches, he could see Rick shutting the door to one of the lockers used by warehouse workers. He called out, greeting him with the mixture of jocularity and authority that he believed, however mistakenly, worked with young men like Rick.

"I thought we might have lunch together," he said, when he got closer. "There are some things we need to talk about."

"Yeah," Rick said. "I need to talk to you, too. But, it can't be lunch. I need to take care of something for a sick friend. In fact, I'll probably be gone for a couple of hours."

It hadn't occurred to Walsh that his offer to a subordinate would be refused. What was going on? Rick had always been eager to accept these gestures of camaraderie. Why the change?

More disturbing to the former Staff Sergeant was the way Rick had declared he was taking a long lunch hour. Instead of asking permission he had just announced his intention. This wasn't the way Ed Walsh ran his department but he wasn't sure how to respond. He wasn't sure how his relationship with Rick had become so complicated. He swallowed and struggled to cover his confusion. A sick friend, he rationalized, had to be attended to.

"That will be alright," he said. "We can talk this evening, around five, after the building has cleared out."

Rick smiled. "Sure, that'll be just great. By the way, I'm running a little bit short right now, and I need to pick up some medicine and groceries and things for my friend. I need to borrow a few bucks."

Ed Walsh swallowed again. He could feel perspiration breaking out on his forehead. It wasn't possible that Rick was blackmailing him. He was just a kid and didn't realize how the request sounded. And, of course, Rick wouldn't cause trouble on purpose. But what if he got angry?

"How much do you need?" Walsh asked, reaching into his back pocket for his wallet.

"A hundred bucks ought to do it."

Another swallow. A hundred dollars was a lot of money. More than the weekly wage of most of the men in the warehouse. "I don't carry that much cash on me," he said.

"Don't worry about it," Rick responded, cheerfully. "I'll take what you've got and you can give me the rest later."

Chapter 11

The pink message slip had been folded in half, then folded again. To spy size. Small enough to be passed from one palm to another without detection. Thankfully, Wendy hadn't tried that maneuver. She had contented herself with placing the slip of paper on Sara's desk, accompanied with no more than a meaningful look.

"I think this is for you," she said, before turning away and using the accounting office as her passageway to the ladies' room. A gesture of defiance, since she knew Mr. Maruri didn't like people using that office as a passageway.

Sara watched until Wendy made a right turn into the corridor next to Haru Maruri's office and was no longer visible before she unfolded the message.

Wait a minute or two before coming to meet me in the ladies' room and <u>*DON'T*</u> *follow me through the accounting department. Go the other way.* <u>*HURRY.*</u> *We won't have much time. Tear this up after you read it.*

Sara couldn't help smiling as she tore the paper into small pieces. With Wendy's talent for melodrama, it was a wonder she hadn't instructed Sara to swallow the note. More to the point, why the warning against going through the accounting department? What difference could it make how she got there?

Sara looked over to see if Sheila had observed the note passing transaction. Apparently not. She was still concentrating on transcribing her shorthand notes. Quietly, Sara got up from her desk and, taking the longer way around to this top-secret rendezvous in the ladies' room, her fingers massaged the nape of her neck. What was all this about?

Still, despite that inescapable twinge of curiosity, Sara was determined not to be drawn in--no matter what the crisis turned out to be. She'd had enough of Wendy and wanted nothing more to do with her.

"She's like a little doll," was often people's first impression of the younger woman, but Sara knew better. Wendy more closely resembled a barracuda, especially when it came to getting her own way. Wendy had confided in her, had told her things nobody else at West Electronics knew about. Only to Sara had she revealed stories about her past which contained enough material for a full-length biography with enough shock value to create an instant best-seller.

Although she was only twenty-four years old, Wendy had already abandoned two children and divorced their father, leaving them all in New Jersey. Her third child was fathered by a second husband who was in jail for forgery in Nevada. They were still married but wouldn't be for much longer. She was seeking a divorce. A friendly one, it seemed, because it was on his amiable advice that she had gone looking for greener pastures in California. That was where he had connections who might be of use to her. And they had been, providing false references to go along with her job applications.

As it turned out, it hadn't taken long for a third man to enter the picture, one who was willing to take care of her and the child. They were planning to be married as soon as her divorce from husband number two was final. The plots of the soap operas on which Sara occasionally appeared, paled by comparison.

Sara turned left and continued along the U-shaped configuration of corridors, passing the empty offices of Oliver Blakely and Ken Ichiwara. Turning left again, she went by a supply room and a small kitchen until she reached the ladies room.

"What took you so long?" Wendy whispered. She stood by the sink, pretending to dry her hands. "You go in there," she commanded, pointing to one of two stalls. "If anybody else comes in, lock the door and make believe you just got here."

Sara declined to follow instructions. Since Sheila Birney and Gerry Fineman were the only other women working for the company, she couldn't see what Wendy's precautions were meant to accomplish, unless she was about to find out that West Electronics Corporation was a nest of spies.

"I don't intend to be here that long," Sara said. "So why don't you stop playing KGB and tell me what this is about?"

"Don't make fun of me, Sara. I'm desperate. If you don't help me I don't know what will happen. I'm frightened."

"Okay, I'm sorry. But whatever it is, I don't see how I can help you."

"Don't say that!" Wendy's voice grew more desperate. "You have to help me. Bert has been driving me crazy and I need to get away. He's drinking and he's jealous and I'm afraid of what he might do. There are things about him I can't tell you about. Not here. I need time to think...to work things out.

"What do you want from me?"

"All I want is to tell him that you asked me to spend the night at your house."

Sara had not expected anything like this. Her relationships at temporary jobs had never extended beyond the office and she wasn't about to change that now.

"No," she exclaimed. "Tonight is not a good time. It's impossible. Maybe some other time...if you give me more notice."

"I wanted to reach you," Wendy said. "I tried. But you aren't listed in the phone book and Sheila wouldn't give it to me. She said she didn't have it."

"That's right," Sara said. "She's not supposed to have my phone number. The only way to reach me is through the Meacham Temporary agency and that's the way I want it." Sara started for the door.

"Don't talk that way," Wendy said, grabbing her arm. "I'm desperate. I don't know what will happen if you don't help me. Can't you understand? He's capable of anything."

Sara looked at her and saw the terrified face of a drowning person reaching for a life preserver and she was it. She felt desperate herself as she tried to think of an excuse to put Wendy off but couldn't find one.

"I told you. It's impossible," she said, as she struggled against Wendy's grip.

"You've got to help me. If something terrible happens it will be your fault." Her grip tightened.

"Let go," Sara said. And then, before she could check the words, she heard herself acquiescing. "Okay," her voice said, as if it were coming from somebody else. "I guess it will be alright."

Wendy let go of her and leaned against the sink. She looked as if she was about to faint. "You don't know what this means to me."

Sara nodded. There was, she supposed, no more to be said. She wished she had been able put Wendy off, but what if, this time, she really was in serious trouble or in danger? She certainly looked frightened. Sara frowned.

"What about your baby?" she asked, remembering that Wendy had a very young child. A boy, she thought.

Wendy ignored the question. "I knew I could count on you," she said. "The minute I saw you this morning, I knew you wouldn't let me down. Just remember," she continued, "if anybody asks, you broke up with your boyfriend and you're feeling depressed. You need somebody to stay with you."

Sara couldn't believe what she was hearing. The frightened woman had disappeared, replaced by the one who always got her own way. "What are you talking about? What's going on?" she demanded.

"Don't worry. The question probably won't even come up. But just in case. We have to get our stories straight."

"Just in case of what?" It was Sara's turn to lean against the sink. She had been suckered. This was going to be more complicated than having an overnight house guest.

"In case Bert should get hold of your number and try to check up on me.

"It's not possible for him to get my phone number."

"You don't know him. When he gets an idea in his head he's like a wild animal. The most important thing is that you don't answer the phone."

"Don't answer the phone?" Sara exploded. "What has answering the phone got to do with this?"

"Keep your voice down." Wendy's eyes widened. "If Bert calls and you answer the phone, he'll find out I'm not there. He's trying to destroy my happiness. But I won't let him."

"Wait a minute. If you're not at my place, where will you be?"

"I'll explain everything later. I have to go now."

"No. I won't do it. Wait," Sara called out to the closing door.

She turned and took a long, serious look at herself in the mirror. This simple request of Wendy's had turned into a sordid scheme. She was being used to deceive a man who had taken Wendy and her child into his home, being asked to believe Bert's character had turned violent when all Wendy had ever said about him in the past was how kind and generous he was

Sara wasn't pleased with what she saw in the mirror. She had tried to resist but not hard enough. Why hadn't she continued to refuse to help Wendy? What kind of signals was she sending out that told Wendy she could be manipulated like this? They were almost strangers to each other, yet Wendy had taken it for granted she could get Sara to help her and not betray her confidence. And she was right. No matter how much Sara disapproved, now that she had agreed to help she would go through with it and she would keep the secret.

This was, Sara told herself, exactly what she deserved. Retribution for all the times she had listened to Wendy's stories and enjoyed them with smug detachment, believing she could remain an outsider. At least she could be relieved David was out of town. He wouldn't have to know about this. At least not right away. Maybe never.

CHAPTER 12

Gerry Fineman didn't think of herself as the sort of person who pried into other people's business. On the contrary, she kept mostly to herself and hardly every asked questions of anybody. She did, however, like most people, take an interest in what was going on around her and, fortunately, given her natural reticence, could see enough of the reception room from her desk to keep up with the comings and goings out there.

She had, for instance, just by leaning forward at her desk, been able to see Wendy stop by Sara to drop off a note. Then, Wendy had walked through the accounting department, without so much as a smile or a word greeting, and headed towards the ladies' room. A few moments later, after reading the note, Sara tore it up and left her desk. It was very odd.

"I wish I knew what it was all about," she said, after she'd described to Mark what she'd seen.

He nodded. His mouth too full of ham and cheese to give an immediate response. It was their lunch hour and they were sitting at his desk eating sandwiches brought from home and drinking soda from cans purchased from the catering truck that stopped in the alley behind the building several times a day.

"Sara went toward Mr. West's office," Gerry added. "But I'm sure she was going to meet Wendy in the ladies' room. They must have something to talk about. In private. And it's strange because they hardly know each other."

Mark agreed. It didn't take a great leap of imagination to figure out that Wendy and Sara were having a private talk. It was more difficult to guess what they could have to say to each other that would demand a secret meeting.

"Something's definitely going on," he said, "and I think you should have gone in after them. That's what I would have done."

"It wouldn't have made any difference. You know they would have stopped talking as soon as I got there."

"Maybe. But you would have made it a little bit harder for Wendy to get away with whatever it is she's up to."

"What's that supposed to mean?" Gerry exclaimed.

"You know what I mean. She thinks she's better than everybody else and she's always trying to get away with something."

"You always make it sound like she's doing something wrong. Just because she's pretty and Rick likes her."

"He doesn't like her," Mark vehemently replied. "It's that she's always throwing herself at him. He could have anyone he wants. He doesn't need her."

It took an effort, but Gerry kept her mouth closed. She didn't want to argue with Mark again and she certainly didn't want to hurt his feelings. Not after the mean things she'd said to him earlier in the day. She still felt bad about that, and even though it was obvious he didn't like Wendy because he was jealous, she determined to keep silent now. This wasn't the time to point out that Rick was the one at fault. That the way he teased Mark was cruel, leading him on and then pulling back.

The mean words only slipped out when she was too angry to control herself. She wasn't angry right now. She was just sad because she wished Wendy would let her be a friend. She wanted Wendy to confide in her the way she seemed ready to confide in Sara who was only a temporary worker and hardly ever there. That was all she wanted, wasn't it? Just to be friends.

Chapter 13

Rick was in his kitchen at a small table, part of the furnishings provided by his landlord. It had stainless steel legs and a gray-flecked Formica top. Around it were four chairs with matching gray plastic on the padded seats and backrests. He rarely used the table for its intended purpose. He rarely ate there, unless he called out for a pizza. This was where he worked.

On this afternoon, while others were having lunch, he was setting up the paraphernalia necessary for the job at hand. Of all the money-making activities he'd been involved with since coming to Los Angeles this was his favorite. He was slow and careful as he laid out the tools of this particular trade. Handling them was part of the pleasure. Some were expensive, like the finely made set of brass scales he was working with now. Others, like the green plastic grinder, had cost no more than a few dollars. He appreciated them all.

From a stack of tiny weights, he took the one marked '1 gram', and upset the balance of the scales by gently setting it onto the right-side tray. From one of two clear plastic bags, he carefully spooned a fine white powder into the bowl of the tray on the left of the scale and kept adding the powder until the tray was about two-thirds of the way back down again. He knew the trays should be even. He should continue until the full measure of one gram had been reached. But the temptation was too great. He wanted to keep some for himself, before it was further adulterated.

Rick had no illusions about where he stood in the hierarchy of drug dealers. He was close to the bottom of the food chain and, although his source swore the cocaine had only been through the process once, he knew that, by the time he made his Mickey Mouse buys, it had probably been stepped on several times already. He shouldn't be diluting it again, but he couldn't resist. He put the original plastic bag aside and used the contents of a second bag, a cheap powder filler, to bring the scales into balance. In color and texture, the two powders were almost indistinguishable from each other. He was sure none of his customers would notice the difference. They never had before.

He took the mixture from the scale, put it through the green plastic grinder, then transferred the fine powder onto a small square of white paper. He might have been taken for an origami master in the careful way he folded the paper around the drug. The resulting small, neat packet went into an inner pocket of his leather jacket. Now it was time for his reward.

Before cleaning up and putting everything away, he would do a couple of lines for himself. He took the original plastic bag and spread some of the contents onto the surface of a small round mirror with beveled edges. The powder was already so fine, it hardly needed to be worked with the razor blade, but he enjoyed that part. He chopped at it, drawing the powder in with the side of the blade and spreading it with sharp movements of the fine edge. Finally, he shaped the drug into two thin lines and, using a short straw, lowered his head to the mirror and inhaled it, one line into each nostril.

Rick Hanson was suffused with good feeling. Life had never been better.

Chapter 14

Haru Maruri didn't want to sound petty but the words came out that way, despite his efforts to control them. When he was worried or frightened, this was how he reacted and both of those feelings were fighting it out in his gut, warring to see which would take precedence.

"Can't you ever close the door?" he said.

"Can't you ever relax?" Ed Walsh snapped back.

He was as apprehensive as Maruri, but he'd be damned if he'd let it show and he certainly wasn't getting up to close the door. Instead he sat in the chair next to Maruri's desk, his back to the offending portal, and waited.

Maruri kept silent as he went to the doorway. The day was drawing to a close and he didn't want to end it with an argument. He willed himself to be calm. Told himself everything was under control. In less than an hour he would go home. Maybe get some rest. Nothing helped. He still felt as if he was at the end of a rope and the rope was about to strangle him.

At the open door, a blur of voices reached him from the front office. He noted Sara Fisher, her face set in concentration as she transcribed Martin West's words from the receiver in her ear. The area around his office was deserted. Mark and Gerry were nowhere to be seen and there was no one in the corridor next to his office.

Still, his anxiety was not appeased. It was still there along with a slow, simmering resentment. Someone could have been out there. Someone could have overheard what they were saying. He went back into his office and closed the door as firmly as his temperament would allow. He was no longer sure why he'd asked Walsh to meet with him or what he thought they could accomplish.

"Well? Is anybody hanging around out there?"

"No. But it doesn't hurt to make sure," Maruri responded.

"Satisfied?" Walsh asked.

Maruri shook his head. They'd had this disagreement before. He believed they had to be scrupulous about the precautions they took to protect themselves. No exceptions. Ed Walsh believed his standards were unreasonably high. But Maruri expected as much from himself as he did from others and was convinced that only by adhering to those strict standards could they avoid catastrophe.

"We can't afford to take chances," he insisted. "Why can't you understand the seriousness of our position? Isn't it bad enough the insurance company is acting up and Rick is causing problems? We don't need to add to our troubles by getting careless. The last thing we want is to have people around here getting curious and starting to ask questions."

"Of course I understand," Walsh said. "But right now no-body is asking questions or getting suspicious. It's in your imagi-nation. All you need to worry about is the insurance company. I'll take care of Rick."

Walsh spoke with conviction, having given the assurance so often, it had become routine. But this afternoon, even as the words were coming out of his mouth, he knew they were no lon-ger true. All day he'd been asking himself if it was possible he'd been wrong about Rick. What if they had made a mistake? What if it turned out Rick couldn't be trusted?

Walsh swallowed and played with the open collar of his shirt. He didn't want to give Harry a reason to get more worked up than he was already. He wouldn't tell him about the strange snatches of conversations he'd overheard, or the way Rick had announced he was taking a long lunch hour without bothering to go through the motions of asking for permission. Nor would he mention the money Rick had requested. There was no point in talking about it until he could check out what Rick had meant.

"This is the last time we can get away with making a claim," Maruri said. "You have to make Rick understand. I can get the insurance company to pay out this time. They won't do it again."

"We've been through all this before," Walsh said.

"But you don't seem to understand how serious this is. When we took Rick on, we made it clear that we weren't going to inter-fere with merchandise from the company. We set up rules and he broke them."

Walsh nodded. He too had been disturbed by what Rick had done, all on his own, without checking with either of them.

But he had believed Rick's excuses, even the second time it happened. He'd accepted it was all a misunderstanding rising out of Rick's youth and inexperience. Hadn't Rick always been respectful and obedient in the past? Grateful for the opportunity they were giving him? There'd been no reason to doubt Rick's promise that it wouldn't happen again. And, more troubling, what was the alternative?

He took a handkerchief from his pocket and dabbed at the mist of perspiration on his forehead and upper lip. Walsh knew very well the mess they would be in if company merchandise disappeared again. He wasn't stupid. He just didn't want to sit around talking about it. Knowing was bad enough. He wished Maruri would understand that putting it into words only made it worse.

"He's just a kid and he didn't understand," Walsh said. "It won't happen again." He pointed to the dial of his wristwatch with a stubby finger. "It's almost five. When the office empties out, I'll have a chat with. I already told him I want to talk to him and I'll make sure he understands how things have to be. You don't have to worry. I know how to handle him. He trusts me and he'll listen."

"I'm sick of it. That's all you ever do. Tell me not to worry--"
Maruri broke off as his office door opened.

"Come in," he exclaimed, with as much warmth as he could manage. He stood up to greet Martin West and struggled to look pleased to see him.

Startled by the interruption, Walsh also stood, grateful for the unexpected reprieve. "We were finishing up," he said, as he turned to face the head of the company. "I was just leaving."

"No, you stay," West told him, motioning both men back into their chairs. "I'll only be a minute and this concerns both of you. Before leaving today, I want to check on where we're at with the insurance company. I want to be sure you've got the situation in hand. What's going on there?"

"Nothing serious," Maruri assured him. "There was a mix-up with the shipping documents for the missing merchandise, some forms filled out incorrectly, but it's all straightened out now. I spoke to their representative about half an hour ago. He wants to come in tomorrow and look around the warehouse. Ed and I were just going over the problem and we're working out procedures so this sort of thing doesn't happen again."

West nodded. "Okay," he said. "I want to be sure this takes care of it."

West didn't want to overreact, but he was troubled by the recent losses of merchandise. He could understand why the insurance company was asking questions. He had some of his own. However, Haru Maruri and Ed Walsh had always been reliable, and he wasn't ready to start looking over their shoulders. He had other things on his mind, matters only he could deal with. New model tape recorders and negotiations with Japanese suppliers demanded his full concentration. Still, he wanted everyone to know he was paying attention.

"I'm going to stay on top of this one," he told the two men. "If the insurance company gives us any more problems, I want to hear about it. Right away."

⋏

Confident that he had made his point, West left them. He walked across the accounting office and stopped in front of Sara.

"I'm leaving for the day," he said.

Wendy and Sheila, he saw, were at their desks with several other employees standing close by. He strode past, pausing only for a moment to glance over at Wendy and to nod an acknowledgement to the respectful "Goodnight Mr. Wests" that followed him until he was out the door and into the warehouse.

They had stopped whatever they were talking about as soon as he'd appeared and he knew they wouldn't go back to it until he was out of sight. He had also noticed that Wendy was an exception. His presence had not stopped her from going on with what was obviously a personal and contentious phone call. She had been aware of him. He saw her glance up as he passed, but she had continued with the conversation as if he wasn't there.

If she hadn't felt constrained by his presence to end the phone call, she could at least have lowered her voice. The office was no place for loud and emotional scenes. He made a mental note to talk with Ed Walsh about the possibility of letting her go.

Hiring Wendy had been a mistake, he thought, as he walked down the steps into the garage. But Ed had been pleased when she'd come to work for him. She'd had such glowing references.

Sweet looking and innocent was how he'd described her. And West, although he'd thought she looked sly, didn't like to interfere with those kinds of decisions. There was, however, behavior he couldn't overlook. Also, he felt she was too pretty. He preferred the women who worked for him to be plain, like Elinor, his secretary. She was perfect for him and further acquaintance with Wendy had done nothing to change his opinion on that account.

CHAPTER 15

"**Y**ou can yell all you want," Wendy said. "But you can't stop me. I don't need your permission to spend the night with Sara and I don't want you to drive me there. I'm not going to say it again. Don't come here to pick me up."

It was strange. Wendy, usually so secretive, was arguing with Bert and making it easy for Sheila to listen. But if people wouldn't stop pestering her she would miss the best parts. She glared at Mark Cranston and Gerry Fineman, both of whom seemed rooted to the space in front of her desk.

"Mr. Blakely might still show up," Mark said. He handed her a sheaf of papers he'd been using as his excuse for being there. "I do need to speak to him about these orders."

Sheila handed them back. "They can wait until tomorrow.

With that gesture of dismissal, she turned away. Neither Mark nor Gerry took the hint. They wanted to hear Wendy's conversation as much as she did except that Gerry was starting to feel uncomfortable. She'd been pretending to wait for

Sheila to answer Mark's questions before asking one of her own. But she didn't want anyone, especially Wendy, to think she was listening on purpose. She decided to make a move. Reaching past Mark, she placed a bunch of envelopes on Sheila's desk.

"It's the accounting department mail. Would you take it with you when you leave? Mark and I are going to work late."

Wendy's voice rang out, even louder. "I told you. Sara is depressed. She didn't want me to tell anybody, but her boyfriend walked out on her and she doesn't want to be alone. She needs me and I promised I'd stay with her."

Sara tried not to react. She focused on the sheet of paper in her typewriter and pretended to be unaware of the eyes that had turned towards her. It was her face that gave her away. It had turned bright red.

"You never think of anybody except yourself," Wendy said. "But you don't have to worry. I know Mikey is my responsibility and he's taken care of. I already spoke to Elena. She's going to keep him overnight and I'll pay for whatever extra it costs to keep him there until tomorrow."

Sheila had strong ideas about the obligations of motherhood and Wendy fulfilled none of them. She treated her son like a piece of baggage that she could park here or there, according to whim. More shocking, she had brought him into the home of Bert Rudner, a man who wasn't his father or her husband. If that wasn't bad enough, Sheila now suspected Wendy was cheating on Bert and that the temp, who she had previously believed was respectable, was assisting in the deception.

Sara, who supposedly needed Wendy to comfort her, didn't look depressed. And even if she was, why would she have turned to Wendy for help? They barely knew each other. Sheila rolled her chair over to the temp's desk.

"It's disgusting the way she treats that child," she said. "I'm surprised you're going along with it."

Sara stifled a desire to shove Sheila's chair back to where it belonged. Instead she shrugged her shoulders. Short of standing up and announcing to the world that Wendy was a liar, how could she explain? And Wendy was still on the phone, raising embarrassment to a new level.

"I tell you Sara is desperate," Wendy said. "How do you think I would feel if she harmed herself? That's the question you should be asking yourself. Think about it and get it into your head that I won't abandon her. So...for the last time...I won't be going home with you tonight. And that's final."

Wendy dropped the receiver back onto its cradle. The show was over. Mark and Gerry returned to their office and Sheila rolled back to her desk. Sara envied them. For her, escape was not yet possible.

"Better start getting it together to go home," Wendy called out.

"It's only four-thirty," Sara said.

"Four thirty-five and don't worry about it. I told Mr. Walsh I had to leave a little early tonight and Mr. West is gone, so he won't care. Come on, let's get out of here."

"You'd better hurry," Sheila said. "The princess doesn't like to be kept waiting."

Sara put a cover on the typewriter and grabbed her handbag. "I'll make up the time tomorrow," she said.

Sheila didn't respond.

Chapter 16

Wendy examined Sara's car with a look of disapproval that bordered on disgust. "I didn't realize your car was so old," she said. "What year is it?"

The condescending attitude did nothing to make Sara more kindly disposed to her uninvited guest. She almost expected Wendy to declare the aging, sun-bleached Ford too disreputable for her to be seen in.

"Forget about my car and tell me where I can let you off," she said as she unlocked the doors. "The sooner this is over with the better."

Wendy was surprised. "I don't know what you're so angry about. All I did was say your car looks old."

"My car has nothing to do with it. This is about you on the telephone and the lies you told. You made me look like a pathetic wretch in front of the whole office," Sara said, as she turned the key in the ignition.

"You knew what I was going to tell Bert."

"I knew you were going to *lie* to Bert, but why did you do at the top of your lungs and in front of everybody? Why did you have to make up that ridiculous story about my needing you to comfort me because I'd been dumped by my boyfriend? About how you were worried I might harm myself?"

Wendy's large eyes opened wide, filled with a pretense of remorse, ready to bring forth a tear or two if necessary. "I'm sorry," she said. "I never thought about anybody listening to me or that you would mind. I mean, you being a temp, I didn't think it would matter."

"It does matter, but there's nothing we can do about it now. Just tell me what happens next. Where do you want me to drop you off?"

"We can go to your place," Wendy said. "Unless you want to stop somewhere first...you know...have a drink. My treat."

"I don't want to go out for a drink and why would we go to my place? You're not staying with me tonight. Wasn't that the point? You aren't going to be there and that's why I'm not supposed to answer the phone."

"Right. I'm not going to stay with you."

"I don't understand."

It was an understatement. Sara felt like Alice, tumbling down the rabbit hole with no idea of where she was going to land. Nothing Wendy said made sense and part of her wished she could allow herself to stop asking questions. But she did want to know how long before she would be rid of Wendy and, in spite of her resolutions, she couldn't quell her curiosity. After having been drawn into the situation against her will, it was only fair that she find out what was behind the lies. Wendy owed her that.

"Why don't you explain?" she said, as she drove out of the garage. "Where do you want to go and why do you need an alibi for where you're going to be?"

Wendy laughed. "You're making it sound like something criminal and it's not like that at all," she said. "I want to go to your place but I'm not going to stay there and I have to do it this way because of Bert. He's always watching me. He's so much in love with me that he's obsessed and sometimes I have to get away from him. You don't know what that's like."

"I wouldn't want to know." Sara said. She didn't think any of her lovers had ever cared for her to the point of obsession and she hoped no one ever would.

Wendy sighed at the heaviness of her burden. "My life is a misery."

"Really? So, what you're telling me is that all the stories you made up are just to get away from Bert for an evening...to be on your own? That's what all this is about?"

"Exactly," Wendy exclaimed. "I knew that once you gave me a chance to explain, you'd see my side of it. I've tried to make Bert understand that I'm not like other girls, but every little thing makes him jealous. I mean...I can't help it if men are attracted to me. And just because Mikey and I are living with him doesn't mean he can control my life. I did offer to pay some of the rent."

"Alright," Sara said, although she didn't believe a word of it. "He loves you and he's obsessed with you. Now tell me why he frightens you. You told me that you're afraid of him. Has he ever hit you?"

"Oh, no." Wendy laughed again. "Bert would never do anything like that. But you wouldn't have helped me unless you thought I was in danger."

"I see," Sara said. At last, something believable had come out of Wendy's mouth. Bert's violent temper was one more lie on top of all the others.

"And where," Sara continued, "are you going to spend the night? If you don't mind my asking."

"Oh, didn't I tell you? I thought you knew."

Another lie. Sara let it pass. "Go on," she said.

"I'm going to be with Rick. We're going to spend the whole night together...for the first time. We never could before because of Bert and that's why tonight is so important. That's why when I told him how much I needed to be with him he even cancelled his bowling game with the guys from the warehouse."

"Bowling with the guys from the warehouse?" Sara was surprised that Rick, who she saw as wanting to move higher on the social and economic ladder, would stoop to socializing with people who he would see as being of no use to him.

"He bowls with the guys from the warehouse? Do they have a team?"

"Yes...and Rick hardly ever misses a Monday night because that's where he makes his connections."

An interesting word to use. "What kind of connections?"

Wendy looked unsure. "You do ask the silliest questions," she said. What difference does it make? Why are we talking about bowling?"

"You brought it up. What should we be talking about?"

"About Rick and me. That's what's important. Bert keeps causing problems and Rick is very depressed about it. He thinks we might have to break up because we won't be able to work things out. Tonight I'll be able to tell him my plans and explain how we can be together forever. That's why I need your help. Rick is the most wonderful thing that ever happened to me and I'm not going to let Bert spoil it."

Sara drove carefully, keeping her voice neutral and her eyes on the road. "You are going to break up with Bert so that you and Rick can be together? Is that what you're saying?"

"We love each other."

Sara nodded. This was what the lies were about. Poor, foolish Wendy believed that she and Rick were going to go off into the sunset to live happily ever after. Was her child going with them? Had Wendy thought that far ahead? It didn't matter since none of it was going to happen, although they deserved each other. Two dishonest, selfish, self-involved narcissists coming together, each one the center of their own universe. What could possibly go wrong?

Sara had no more questions. Silently, she turned onto her street and found a parking place directly in front of the small, stucco apartment building she lived in, one that Wendy would undoubtedly find was as far beneath her dignity as Sara's car. "This is it," she announced.

"Wonderful!" Wendy said, radiating sincerity although she couldn't imagine how anybody could live in such an old building where there was no sign of a swimming pool or air conditioning.

"This is perfect. I can relax until nine o'clock. Then I'll take a taxi back to the office to meet Rick. That's when he's expecting me." She paused, waiting for Sara's offer to take her on the short drive back to West Electronics.

"Those taxis are so unreliable but if you wait long enough they come," she added.

"That's true," Sara said, as she led the way through a small terra cotta archway and up the flight of stairs. "Eventually, they do show up."

There was something in the stiffness of Sara's back that told Wendy this was not the moment to push for a ride. Later on, if she looked sad enough, Sara would change her mind. If not, she'd take a cab although she didn't understand why Sara was being so unreasonable. This was an exciting adventure. She should be grateful to be part of it.

"I 'm so excited because we're going to Rick's apartment, Wendy said, as she inspected Sara's living room, "I've never been there before and I told him he couldn't keep it hidden from me forever.

Sara nodded. She tried to imagine what Rick's place would look like and found she couldn't.

"And the only thing you need to remember," Wendy said, "is not to answer the phone after I've left."

"Right," Sara said, although she had no intention of following the instruction. Whether Wendy accepted it or not, there was no way for Bert to get her phone number. And she wasn't about to miss a phone call from David.

"I'm not going to cook," she said. "We'll call out for pizza."

Wendy didn't argue although she didn't like pizza. She smiled. Food was the last thing on her mind. Something Sara wouldn't understand.

CHAPTER 17

Sheila was preparing to leave the office, clearing papers from her desk and checking Mr. Blakely's calendar. She had to admit that today had been interesting. And tomorrow promised more. It was possible Wendy had gone too far this time. That whatever she was up to could get her into trouble. Maybe get her fired. She would keep her eyes and ears open.

In the accounting department, Gerry was also absorbed in speculation, but for more generous reasons. If she knew what was troubling Wendy, maybe she could help.

"That was so weird," she whispered, leaning over Mark's desk. "All that business with Sara and Wendy. What do you suppose it's about?"

He gave her a warning glance and mouthed the word "later."

Gerry nodded. Ed Walsh was leaving Haru Maruri's office and, although he ignored them both as he went by, it would be better to put off any discussion until everybody else had gone home.

Gerry could wait until then. She and Mark often worked late together, alone in the building, and this was going to be one of those nights. It was an easy way to earn extra money, time and a half for overtime. Best of all, they would be free to talk and be themselves, without worrying about anybody guessing the truth, a dangerous truth that would make them even more outsiders than they were now or, more probably, get them fired.

In the meantime, she would go back into the reception room to see if there was anything more to find out before Sheila went home. It was no secret that Sheila and Wendy didn't like each other, but they did work together. Sheila must know something more about what was going on.

"What do you think?" Gerry asked. "I was so surprised. I had no idea Sara was depressed. Did you? I mean, it must be really bad if she asked Wendy to spend the night with her."

"Don't be silly," Sheila declared. "If Sara's depressed then I'm Joan of Arc."

Gerry giggled. "Then why do you suppose they left together?"

"I don't know," Sheila said. "But I can make a very good guess and I think it's disgusting for a woman who has a child to be carrying on like that."

"Carrying on like what? It's not fair. I mean, you're jumping to the conclusion that Wendy is doing something wrong and we don't know that."

"Well, what do you think it's all about?" Sheila demanded.

"I don't know," Gerry said. "But I think you're being too hard on her. She's really very nice."

"You wouldn't say that if you had to work with her. She's useless. But Mr. Walsh lets her get away with anything she wants and Mr. Maruri looks the other way."

Gerry shook her head. "Maybe they're being kind and understanding. You have to take into consideration that she's probably had some very rough times in her life."

Sheila snorted derisively. "Rough times? What does that mean?" she asked. "When it comes down to it, what do you really know about Wendy?"

"She's told me a few things," Gerry said. "Not much. But it can't be easy to raise a child on her own."

Sheila shook her head vigorously. "There's only one thing you can know for sure about Wendy. She's a liar. You can't believe one word she tells you."

Gerry turned away. Like with Mark, she suspected it was jealousy that caused Sheila to make such bitter accusations. "I'd better go back to my desk," she said.

The sound of the front door stopped her. It had been pushed open, violently, as if the person coming in was determined to fight resistance on the other side.

"Where's Wendy?" Bert Rudner asked, his voice loud and angry.

Sheila and Gerry looked at each other then back at the man who stood in the doorway. The suddenness of the intrusion had startled them and his attitude was threatening. They recognized him, of course. He had been there before to pick up Wendy and they'd gotten to know him a little at the office Christmas party. But they had never seen him like this.

"Wendy. Where is she?" he repeated, coming further into the office and letting the door shut behind him.

"She left," Sheila said.

"That's right," Gerry confirmed. "She's gone."

He stared at them suspiciously. "When did she go? How long ago?"

"It was about a quarter of an hour," Sheila said and Gerry nodded. "She left early."

"Was she alone?"

The women glanced at each other. Gerry was beginning to panic. Bert looked dangerous to her. Sheila, less easily intimidated, saw no reason why she shouldn't tell him the truth.

"She went home with Sara Fisher.

He looked from one face to the other, as if he hadn't heard her.

"The temp who works here sometimes," Sheila clarified, although she knew he'd already heard all this from Wendy.

He continued to stare at them, trying to figure out if they were lying. They could be in a conspiracy with Wendy to make a fool out of him. Probably they were. Probably they all knew she was cheating on him and he was, like the pitiful character in all the jokes people told, the last to know. Now, he was making it easier for them. Bursting in here, completely out of control, giving them more to laugh about.

He knew he was behaving badly, but he had to find out the truth. He needed to see the deception with his own eyes or Wendy would twist him around and make him doubt himself all over again. Her desk, he saw, was cleared and the typewriter was covered. The temp was nowhere to be seen. Still, he didn't believe that Wendy had gone home with Sara Fisher.

"Where's Rick?" he asked. "I know he's around here, somewhere."

The question frightened Gerry even more and she was relieved that the commotion had finally brought Mark out from the accounting department.

"What's happening?" he asked.

"Where's Rick?" Bert repeated. "His motorcycle is still here. I saw it. So he can't be too far away."

"If he hasn't gone home yet, he's in back," Sheila said, pointing to the door behind Wendy's desk. "Go on and look for him, if you want to."

Bert hesitated. If Wendy wasn't back there, what would he do? What would he say to Rick?

"I don't think that's such a good idea," Mark said, glaring at Sheila. "We can't have people just wandering around the building."

That did it. Opposition must mean they were hiding something from him. He was gone before anybody could stop him.

"I'd better go after him," Mark said.

Gerry put a restraining hand on his arm. "Stay out of it. Rick can take care of himself."

"She's right," Sheila said. "And, Mr. Walsh is still back there. He can handle it. Maybe it'll do some good. Maybe it'll open his eyes to some of the things his little princess has been up to.

"Okay," Mark said. "But if Bert's not out of there in a few minutes, I'll check it out."

"Do you think we should tell Mr. Maruri what's happening?" Gerry asked.

Mark walked toward Maruri's office. Through the glass panel, he could see the man's head bent forward in concentration. Whatever he was working on, it had his total attention.

He went back to the women. "I don't see what good it would do to get him involved. Not yet, anyway."

Gerry nodded. She saw Sheila take the stack of outgoing mail from her desk and put it down again. It was after five o'clock but she knew Sheila wouldn't leave without knowing the outcome. It didn't take long. In just a few more seconds, Rick came into the room and Bert followed. He still looked flushed but seemed to be in control of himself.

Mr. Walsh must have calmed things down. He was in here as well, having come in behind them. Probably to make sure Bert left without any further trouble. But he looked pale, not at all like himself. He had stopped on the far side of Wendy's desk and was watching what was happening as if it nothing to do with him. It was strange.

"Hey, Mark. Just the guy I was looking for," Rick said. "What do you say we go up the street for a beer. I'm ready to get out of here."

Mark tried to look casual. "Sure," he said. "Sounds great."

Of course he wanted to go with Rick. He glanced at Gerry. She was the only one who could possibly guess how excited he was. And he was sure she wouldn't mind about tonight. They could work late anytime.

To everyone's surprise, Rick then turned to Bert Rudner. "Why don't you come too," he said. "It'll be us guys. Sometimes you have to get away from the women. I mean...sometimes...they can really be a pain."

He looked around for affirmation, but wasn't bothered when it didn't come. He smiled at them all and continued. "Sometimes they just don't know when it's over...when it's time to let go."

Bert looked like he might burst into tears. His face was swollen with the effort to keep them back. "I want to know where Sara Fisher lives," he said gruffly, struggling to maintain his composure. "What's her address?" he asked, looking from face to face for an answer.

Gerry turned away. The man was continuing to humiliate himself. She wished she knew how to make him stop. Why was Mr. Walsh was just standing there, next to Wendy's desk, letting it all go on?

"What's her address?" Bert insisted.

Once again, it was Sheila who responded. "Sara doesn't work for the company. She's a temp. We don't have an address for her."

"That's right," Mark said. "She comes from a temporary personnel agency. And," he added, with belated rectitude, "even if we had her address we couldn't give it to you. It's against company policy."

Gerry nodded, hoping that Bert would understand the need for such a policy and not be too angry like Wendy was when she'd asked for Rick's address and Gerry couldn't give it to her. Bert, she saw, was accepting the refusal with some grace and her sympathy for him increased.

"You win," he said, before walking out the door. No one there was going to help him. He had provided entertainment. Something to gossip about. He had made them a party to his shame and he wasn't sure who he despised more, them or himself.

"Hey, I tried to be friendly," Rick said, looking pleased with himself. "It's not my fault if the guy's a jerk."

"If he's a jerk, he's not the only one," Sheila said. Her final words on her way out.

Rick grinned at the insult and turned to Mark. "Let's get going," he said. "I'm thirsty."

"Just give me a minute to clear my desk." Mark moved quickly and Rick followed him into the accounting department.

Gerry, lonely and deserted, went to the front door and locked it. She didn't want any more surprises. When she turned back, she saw Mr. Walsh, still standing by Wendy's desk. He hadn't moved or said a word since he'd come into the room. He looked odd, not at all like his normal self. She would have liked to ask Mark what he thought the problem might be, but she couldn't. Mark had Rick with him.

"I'm sorry about tonight," Mark said, coming back into the room. He had his jacket on, ready to leave. "We'll make it up later this week. Okay?"

She nodded and smiled to show that she understood, as if she didn't mind being left behind. "I'll be leaving too," she said.

At West Electronics, women weren't allowed to work overtime unless at least one of the men was with them and Gerry had no problem with the policy. After all that had happened, she had no desire to be in the building by herself.

"You could come with us," Rick said, unexpectedly. "She can come, can't she?" he said to Mark. "We can make an exception for Gerry."

Mark smiled gamely. "Sure," he said. "She can come."

Gerry shook her head. "I don't want to."

"Well then, what are we waiting for?" Rick walked around Ed Walsh as if he wasn't there then turned back and spoke softly, close to the older man's ear. "Don't forget that loan for my sick friend," he said before opening the warehouse door and calling out: "Let's go."

"Right," Mark agreed quickly. He couldn't imagine anybody turning down an invitation from Rick and didn't want to give Gerry time to change her mind. "See you tomorrow," he said.

"Yeah," Rick's voice floated back to them. "See ya tomorrow."

CHAPTER 18

The casual "see ya tomorrow," that Rick had called out continued to echo in Ed Walsh's ears. He remained motionless by Wendy's desk. If anybody had asked, he couldn't have told them how much time had gone by. He didn't know and he couldn't make himself care. Time had ceased to have any meaning.

For the first time since he had enlisted in the army, so many years ago, he felt confused. Or--he groped in his mind for another word--maybe it wasn't confusion. Maybe the unfamiliar feeling had another name. Maybe it was fear.

Harry had been right about Rick. All the terrible things Harry had been afraid of were about to happen. Rick had turned into a person he no longer recognized, blackmailing them and threatening to expose them if they didn't go along with his demands. But the demands Rick was making were impossible.

Ed Walsh pulled a handkerchief from his back pocket and wiped the sweat from his forehead. It was necessary to make Rick understand there were limitations on how much he could expect to squeeze out of them and he wasn't sure he could find a way to do it.

"Mr. Walsh...Mr. Walsh...are you alright? Is anything wrong?"

It was, he realized, Geraldine Fineman. "Wrong? Of course not," he replied. He looked around, as if rousing himself from a deep sleep. Gerry almost expected him to say, "Where am I?" Instead, he wanted to know what time it was.

"It's a quarter after five," she told him, wondering why he hadn't consulted the large watch on his wrist.

He was surprised. It seemed to him, as he tried to fight the lethargic state he had fallen into, that hours had passed since Bert Rudner had burst into his office and accused Rick of having an affair with Wendy. He looked at Gerry and had an urge to ask her if she thought such a story could be true. Wendy was such an innocent little thing. Was it possible that Rick had corrupted her? He couldn't believe it and his eyes pleaded with Gerry to answer the question he couldn't ask.

He wiped his forehead again and tried to concentrate. "Are we the only ones left in the office?" he asked.

"Mr. Maruri is still here."

He nodded. How could he have forgotten that Harry would be waiting, needing reassurance, wanting to hear that Rick was under control. That Rick would cooperate.

"Are you alright?" Gerry asked again. "You don't look well." It was an understatement. Mr. Walsh looked like a man who was only partly conscious.

He summoned what energy he could and focused on her. She was questioning him with so much concern, as if she really cared. But, he couldn't be sure of that, could he? His faith in his own judgment was shattered. He didn't think he would ever be sure of anything again. "I'm fine," he said, finally. He didn't seem to realize that his reply had taken too long to come. She was still concerned.

"Are you sure?" she insisted, torn between her desire to leave and unwillingness to walk away from someone who appeared to be ill.

"You just go ahead home and don't worry about anything," he said. Then he remembered the way Bert had burst into his office, like a crazy man. "I'd better see you to your car," he told her, "just in case that boyfriend of Wendy's is still hanging around."

Gerry accepted the offer with gratitude.

He walked with her through the door next to Wendy's desk and watched from the top of the garage steps until she drove off in her small brown Chevrolet. Rick's motorcycle was still there. He could, he supposed, wait for Rick to come back. He shook his head. He wasn't ready to see Rick again. Not yet. First, he needed some time. He needed to think through what his next step should be.

He went to his office, moving slowly, like an old man in a dream, looking around him as if he were searching for a clue to explain what he was doing there. It came to him that he should be going in the other direction, to see Harry, who was waiting for him. There was no way to avoid the meeting and it would be better if he got it over with before Harry came out here, looking for him. He would have more control that way.

His mind was working again. He would close down the warehouse before going to see Harry. That way he'd be able to get away quickly before Harry had a chance to ask questions. He still wasn't sure what he would say. He could tell Harry the truth and face the recriminations he deserved. Or he could stall for time, giving himself the space he needed to talk to Rick again. Maybe get him to see reason. He would decide when he got there.

Walsh moved more quickly now. He turned off the light in his office, went past the workbenches in the service department and crossed the length of the warehouse. Increasingly anxious, he hurried to make sure the loading dock gate and the door next to it were locked then almost ran the length of the warehouse back to a panel of switches on the wall next to the garage door. One by one, he moved them down, until only two dim red lights remained: one at the far end of the warehouse by the loading dock door; the other over the door to the garage. The darkness was almost complete. Everything was ready when he walked back into the light of the front office.

Maruri was still bent over the papers on his desk, lost in numbers. Like a fish in a bowl, Walsh thought, as he stood outside looking through the glass panel, summoning the courage to go in. He had decided what he was going to say.

"I told you there was nothing to worry about," Walsh said, as he stuck his head inside the door. "I spoke to Rick and everything's okay."

"Wait a minute. What did he say? Did you explain our position to him?"

"I went over all the things we talked about. I'll fill you in on the specifics in the morning. I just didn't want to leave before I let you know that there isn't anything to worry about."

"And he agreed to everything? It was that easy?"

Walsh swallowed and forced himself to laugh. There were beads of perspiration on his forehead. He hoped Harry wouldn't notice. "Didn't I tell you I could handle it? But, listen, I've got to get out of here. Janice is cooking dinner for me tonight and I forgot all about it. I'm late already." He didn't know where Janice's name had come from. He hadn't seen her in months. He stepped out of the doorway and started to close the door.

"Leave it open," Maruri called out. "And don't forget. The insurance adjustor will be here first thing tomorrow morning."

"I'll be in early," Walsh assured him. He waved and tried to sound cheerful. "See you then."

He didn't relax or let down his guard until he was in his car. Once there, he rested his arms on the steering wheel, dropped his head, and did something he couldn't remember having done since he was a little boy. He burst into tears.

CHAPTER 19

Anger didn't come easily to Haru Maruri, but it had taken hold of him now, surprising him with its ferocity. He had been patient as he waited for Ed; waited to find out exactly what Rick was demanding; waited to find out if Rick was prepared to be reasonable. And Ed had repaid him by rushing off without telling him anything of substance, forcing him to keep on waiting until tomorrow to get answers, as if a dinner with some girlfriend was more important than their business together.

It wasn't right. Their problems were too urgent to be treated so lightly and the same old assurances Ed had offered weren't enough. He took off his glasses, misted them with his breath and wiped them carefully with a clean white handkerchief, one that he kept in his desk drawer for that purpose. He was tired, his head ached and the pain in his belly was getting worse. He wanted to go home.

Haru Maruri usually took his family for granted but tonight he look forward to being with them. He didn't show it very often, but he was aware that he'd chosen well when he had married Michiko. She made a good home for him, where he was respected and nobody questioned his authority. And she never complained, like he knew other wives did, when he came home late or forgot to call or forgot her birthday or their anniversary. She was everything a wife should be, quietly attending to his needs, doing whatever she could to make his life comfortable and she was a good mother to his children. The two boys were as quiet and obedient as any father could wish.

He reached for the phone to tell her he was on his way. It was an unusual courtesy on his part and he was soothed by her expression of gratitude, which he didn't doubt was sincere, and her assurance that she would be pleased to see him whenever he chose to make an appearance.

He gathered up the oversize worksheets on which he'd been adjusting cash flow projections for the rest of the year. Would he still be in this office to accept praise for his accuracy? Would he be there to receive Martin West's appreciation which was always accompanied by a generous bonus? Or had this phase of his life already unraveled?

Maruri frowned and put the projections into a black leather briefcase which, from force of habit, he locked. Slowly and methodically, he cleared his desk and locked that as well.

The resentments still simmered. It didn't seem possible that Rick had given up on his demands and suddenly become manageable. On the other hand, he couldn't believe that Ed would lie to him. But it had been wrong of Ed to rush away, leaving him alone with his anxieties. He should have stayed long enough to properly discuss the situation and dispel any lingering doubts.

When Maruri stood to put on his jacket, he found he'd been subject to yet another desertion. Through the glass panel he'd expected to see Mark and Geraldine at their desks. He put on his glasses and looked again. They had told him they would be working late, but the accounting office was empty. When he went out he found their desks were tidy and the file drawers were locked. He thought he might find a clue as to why they weren't there, a note perhaps. But there was nothing to indicate why they had gone.

Maruri frowned. Discipline in the office seemed to have broken down completely. There was no excuse for Mark and Geraldine to have changed their plans without saying anything to him. He would speak to them in the morning. One more thing to take care of.

He put two antacid tablets into his mouth before moving forward with his normal routine. He circled the corridors, checked the offices and left lights on for workers from the janitorial service who would be arriving at six o'clock. It was just ten minutes short of that time when he came back around to the front office. Everything was in order until he got to the connecting door next to Wendy's desk, the one that led from the reception area to the warehouse. It should have been locked.

After five o'clock nobody was supposed to pass from one side of the building to the other unless they had a key to that door. It was part of the system he and Ed Walsh had worked out to avoid theft.

On the administrative side, where security wasn't as important, all the men, along with Martin's secretary and the supervisor of the cleaning crew, had a key to the front door. But access to the warehouse was restricted. Only three people, Martin, Ed and himself, had a full set of keys. Nobody else could get in or out of the warehouse after it was locked-down.

Maruri recalled when Rick had wanted all the keys and how firmly he had vetoed the request. How he had insisted on maintaining the integrity of the system even though Ed hadn't seen any harm in getting them for him.

"What," Maruri had asked, "would we say if Martin or Oliver Blakely were to find out Rick had those keys? How would we explain why such a junior employee had that privilege?"

Ed had backed down. How much better it might have been if he had said no to Rick's requests more often. Perhaps those requests wouldn't have turned into demands.

But while Ed was not always as careful as Maruri would have liked, especially where Rick was concerned, he had always been scrupulous about locking up. Until tonight, there had never been a problem. Maruri fumbled for his own keys and went into the darkened warehouse.

The door to the garage was only a few steps away and he moved towards it quickly. Although he was not naturally given to morbid imaginings, on this evening he found the darkness disquieting and was eager to be out of there. It was a shock to find that this door, one through which any outsider could walk into the warehouse unseen, had also been left unlocked.

He stopped and set down his briefcase not knowing whether to be angry or concerned. Something must have happened to upset his partner and Rick was the only thing Maruri could think of. He looked toward the red light at the other end of the warehouse, knowing he had to force himself to see if the back door had also been left open. Like a child afraid of shadows, he switched on more lights and made his way across the length of the building.

It was a relief to find that the loading dock and the door next to it had been secured. At least Ed had taken care of this end of the warehouse. He paused to look around, still uneasy, then hurried back to retrieve his briefcase, turn out lights and lock the door behind him. In the garage, however, his departure was delayed again

As he had expected, his was the only car in the underground parking. But Rick's motorcycle was there as well. And he couldn't think why. Could Rick still be in the building? If so, he must be hiding and he would be locked in. But that made no sense. There could be no reason for Rick or anybody else to hide themselves away in the warehouse overnight.

He told himself there must be some simple explanation and started towards his car. He stopped again when he reached the motorcycle. No matter how many assurances Ed gave him, he didn't believe they could trust Rick. He cursed the day when he'd allowed Ed to talk him into allowing Rick to join them in their enterprise. But he also wished they had never embarked on their misbegotten scheme in the first place. He cursed the ambition that had driven him to it and the foolishness that had allowed him to believe they could get away with it. Most of all he cursed the day when he'd allowed himself to be persuaded by Martin West to leave his homeland to make his way in this land where he'd always be a stranger.

But it was too late for regrets. He had to look ahead and he did have contingency plans should he ever need a quick way out. His wife and children could be on a plane for Japan in a moment's notice and there was the house in the outskirts of Tokyo for them to go to. In the meantime, he wasn't going to give up without a fight.

Where Rick was concerned, he could no longer rely on Ed's judgment. He would have to handle the matter himself. For a moment he was tempted to wait for Rick to come back. He would have to return if only to reclaim his motorcycle, but there was no way of knowing when that would be. Rick could be spending the night somewhere else and might not show up until morning. A note was the way to do it.

He pulled a small spiral-bound note book from his inside breast pocket. "It's time to put an end to your nonsense," he wrote. "Be in my office first thing tomorrow morning." He added his signature, ripped out the page and left it, clearly visible, in the space between the seat and the handlebar.

Chapter 20

A cool night breeze moved through the open windows of Mark Cranston's car, doing nothing to calm the feverish anticipation he felt as he drove towards West Electronics. With Rick Hanson by his side his fantasies had come to life.

They had gone to a bar on Hollywood Boulevard, one he wouldn't have dared to suggest himself but Rick had chosen it. It was noisy and crowded and that was okay because it seemed to draw them closer together and after a while they'd managed to find a quiet corner table where they had a few more drinks and then, because Rick was getting hungry, they had ordered hamburgers and French fries and talked as if they'd never run out of things to say to each other.

With Rick being so friendly--asking questions--personal questions--and listening like he was really interested in the answers, the time had flown by. Then Rick had gone on to talk about himself, telling Mark details about his family, things Mark was sure Rick had never told anyone else. It was better than anything he could have imagined and there would be more to come.

Rick, by no means feverish, was also satisfied with how the evening had progressed. Mark had fulfilled his purpose, providing entertainment while Rick waited for Ken to get back from Santa Barbara. He had paid for the food and drinks, as expected, plus a bonus of twenty dollars for the sick friend, all Rick felt he could ask for after glimpsing the meagre amount of cash in Mark's wallet. Not a bad return for listening to Mark's pathetic little confessions, which he hadn't minded as it was this kind of information which could prove profitable in the future. And he'd enjoyed coming up with more "true" stories about his own life.

He had returned to the one about his father being a high-ranking officer in the military who used to beat him because he was different and rebellious and then beat his mother when she tried to protect him, the same story he used with Ed Walsh. Tonight he tried out a new ending about how she had died after a fall that Rick did not believe was an accident. Mark lapped it up like a hungry.

"Perfect timing," Rick said, when they turned into the underground garage. The van belonging to the cleaning people was pulling away from the front of the building. Everything was going according to plan. Now, he needed to get rid of Mark, in case Ken turned up early. That would be easy. He would enjoy it.

"Don't bother to park," he said, and opened the door while the car was still slowing down. "Just stop," he commanded.

He was out of the car the instant it came to a halt, smiling as he walked away while listening for the inevitable reaction.

"Where are you going? Mark called. "I thought...wait a min-ute...please...I thought..." He struggled to find the words but was unable to get past his confusion. He got out of his car.

Rick had been so nice while they were at the bar. He hadn't said anything explicit but the understanding that their evening together would continue was unmistakable. After all, it was Rick who brought up the secret place they had shared only once before and Rick who talked about it with pleasure. The prom-ise was unspoken but it was clear. They'd go back to that place tonight.

"You thought what?" Rick asked. He turned back, his voice no longer quite as friendly. He looked puzzled, as if he had no idea what Mark was talking about.

"When we were at the bar...I thought you said that...maybe we would go inside and talk for a while. You know...in private."

He was pleading with Rick and that wasn't fair. Rick had not only held out a promise with his words, indirect as they were, he'd also asked to borrow twenty dollars, with the suggestion that this gesture cemented their friendship and would lead to further intimacy.

"Hey, you got it wrong. I've got things to do," Rick said. "And I'm not in the mood for company."

"You can't do this," Mark said. "What about the twenty dol-lars? I gave you twenty dollars."

Rick stopped by his motorcycle. "That's right," he said. "And you practically begged me to take it. If you thought you were buying something for your lousy twenty bucks, you were wrong. Now get out of here. I don't want you hanging around."

Mark got back into his car, still unable to accept what was happening. He saw Rick pick up the note that had been left on his motorcycle. Maybe he should wait. Maybe Rick had another date and the note cancelled it. Rick, he saw, had crumpled the note and tossed it away.

If the situation had changed, maybe Rick would want to have some company after all. Maybe he hadn't meant to be cruel. Maybe he just had other things on his mind. It couldn't hurt to try one more time, to give Rick another chance. He stuck his head out the window and called out, "Are you sure you want me to go?"

"God damn it! I'm sick of you. Get out," Rick shouted.

Stripped of his illusions, Mark drove out of the garage, sick with himself for having been willfully blind to Rick's true character and furious with Rick for making a fool of him. "I'll get even," he told himself and spoke the vow out loud. "I'll find some way," he said. "I don't know how, but I'll find a way to get back at him."

Rick couldn't hear Mark's words and, even if he had, the threat wouldn't have troubled him. He reached for his key ring and selected one that he wasn't supposed to have, one of the keys Ed Walsh had warned him to keep secret. "Mr. Maruri doesn't think you need them," Ed Walsh had told him. Well, that was something he wouldn't put up with anymore, Haru Maruri's superior attitude. He could open any of the doors in the building and he didn't care who knew it.

Inside the warehouse he turned on some lights before opening the connecting door to the front office. The key to Bert's precious T-bird was another one he wasn't supposed to have. This one he removed from his key ring and placed it in the top drawer of Wendy's desk. Tonight would bring an end to Wendy and, with her out of the picture, he wouldn't be driving that car again. But he did like the feel of the T-Bird and maybe, instead of a Buick, he'd get a T-Bird for himself. Not red, like Bert's. Another color. It was definitely something to think about.

In the meantime, after Ken picked up his gram of cocaine, there would be Wendy to get rid of. She had become more trouble than she was worth, coming up with plans for them to live together. Her and the kid. What a joke. She would, of course, cry and carry on when he told her it was over. But that would come later, after he had screwed her one last time. He would get off on that, knowing it was the last time. Then--like with Mark--he would have the pleasure of telling her to get lost.

He looked at his watch. Time to get moving. Ken Ichiwara would be arriving soon and this time he would have to pay extra from the wad of cash he kept in his wallet to impress the tramps he hooked up with on the road. After all, Ken couldn't possibly refuse a loan for a sick friend.

Yes. It had been a very good day and tonight was promising to be even better.

CHAPTER 21

Wendy shivered in the back seat of the taxi. She had considered asking to borrow a sweater from Sara, but given the mood Sara was in, she probably would have refused. Jealousy, of course. What other reason could there be for why Sara was being so difficult? Forcing her to wait more than half an hour for a taxi. Making her late to meet Rick who didn't like to be kept waiting.

Wendy had expected more cooperation but she held no hard feelings. In fact, she felt relieved as she realized that Sara no longer mattered. Girlfriends could never be relied on and she didn't think she'd ever need her again. Sara had served her purpose and Wendy was glad to be rid of her.

She leaned forward, close to the driver. "It's right ahead,' she told him. "You can let me off in front, by the driveway."

The taxi driver looked uncertain as Wendy put three dollar bills into his hand and told him to keep the change. "Are you sure this is the place?" he asked. The building and the street around it were deserted. He didn't think it was any place for a woman alone, especially a pretty little thing like this one.

Wendy smiled at him. He was a nice man and it was sweet of him to worry about her. "This is it," she assured him.

"Maybe I should wait."

"That's so kind of you. But I'll be fine."

She got out of the cab still shivering and anxious to get inside. There was nothing to feel nervous or frightened about. This wasn't the first time she'd come to the deserted building to meet with Rick and she knew she'd be safe. He would take care of her. Soon she would be in his arms and they would have all the time needed in which to plan their future.

She turned to wave the driver on his way and laughed as she started down the ramp. This was the first time she would be going to Rick's apartment and the first time they would spend all night together. And this was the first time she had arrived by taxi. What an adventure tonight was turning out to be.

Anticipating the hours of pleasure to come, she hurried through the empty, echoing vault of the garage, ran up the few cement steps and pressed down on the buzzer next to the door. It was large and red, meant to be used after hours. There was a similar buzzer by the loading dock and a smaller, less conspicuous one next to the front door.

Wendy twirled from one side to the other, enjoying the way her gauzy full skirt swirled around her legs. She stopped and pushed the buzzer again, more impatiently this time and with greater force. In her excitement she moved around the landing, unable to stand still. Still, there was no response. She rang again, pressing her ear against the door. She could hear the ring and then there was silence. She turned the knob then banged on the door with clenched fists. He had to be in there. His motorcycle was here.

Could he be punishing her for being late? She went down the steps and touched the bike, reassuring herself it was real. She wasn't dreaming. She went back to the door and banged again. "Rick," she called. "Open up. Please. I'm scared." She started to cry. Being alone in the underground chamber without the certitude of Rick on the other side of the door was frightening her. It was terrifying to be alone here, surrounded by shadows. She rang the bell again and called out to him. Where was he? Why wasn't he answering?

She sank onto one of the steps and buried her head in her hands, still calling Rick's name and sobbing.

CHAPTER 22

"**We won't be** getting there before ten o'clock," Sara said. "We're running late." She hung up quickly, imagining Sheila's frustration at being unable to interject even one sarcastic remark.

Satisfaction faded as she remembered her own frustration, the intractable, self-pitying, sodden mass of misery that had taken over her living room. She had been trying to get Wendy to move for more than an hour, each time finding herself back where she'd started. The phone call to the office taken care of, she braced for another, this time more forceful, attempt.

"I called the office," she said, as she swept back into the living room, like a leading lady making an entrance on stage. "I told them we'd be there soon so you've got to get moving."

The performance was lost on her audience. If Wendy heard the words she gave no sign. Still wearing a flimsy white cotton nightgown, borrowed from Sara on the night before, she looked like an abandoned child sitting in the center of rumpled bed-clothes on the flowered chintz covered sofa. She hugged herself, holding tightly to bare upper arms and stared blankly at an arrangement of dried flowers that sat in the recess of the no longer functioning fireplace on the other side of the room.

Her clothes lay on the floor close to the sofa where she'd dropped them the night before. On the coffee table a jumble of contents from her oversize handbag was spread carelessly over almost the entire surface, covering scars left there by years of use and probably adding a few new ones.

"The coffee is fresh," Sara said. "I'll get you a cup." She carried a brightly colored ceramic mug from the kitchen, filled with fragrant steaming liquid. "Would you move some of that stuff out of the way?" she asked, looking down at the mess on the table.

Wendy continued to ignore her. Sara shoved some of the objects aside and dug out a magazine on which to set the coffee cup. She liked having a table she could use without worrying about scuffs and scratches but that was her prerogative not Wendy's.

"Drink it while it's hot," Sara ordered. "I'll make some toast while you get ready."

Sara had hoped the prospect of food would get Wendy to move. Instead, it brought on a fresh outpouring of grief.

"I can't eat anything now, Wendy sobbed. "I just want to be left alone."

Sara ignored this latest of too many outpourings of emotion and drew open the green drapes that covered the windows, one on either side of the sofa, allowing sunshine to flood the room.

"That's better," she declared.

Despite the grieving sounds coming from the sofa, bright morning sunlight did lift some of the gloomy atmosphere that had built up ever since Wendy's unexpected and mysterious return to the apartment the night before.

Wendy was oblivious. In a further paroxysm of despair, her body fell sideways onto the sofa and the intensity of the tears increased. "Just leave me alone," she wailed.

"No way," Sara said. "You stop crying and then I'll leave you alone."

Her irritation had reached the tipping point. Wendy wouldn't allow herself to be comforted, and she wouldn't tell Sara what happened the night before. Was it that Rick had grown impatient and left without waiting for her? Or had it been something more serious? There hadn't been so much as a hint as to what these outbursts of sorrow were about.

⚓

The phone call from Wendy had come a little after ten o'clock, from a service station on Fountain Avenue, and Sara had been unable to refuse her plea to be picked up. In other cities there might be the hope of a taxi or a bus but not in Hollywood where getting around without a car was always difficult. After dark, it was close to impossible and dangerous. Especially for a woman alone.

Sara had gone to get her and they were back to her apartment in little more than an hour from when Wendy had left. There had been no explanations as to what had happened or why she was back so soon. Questions were answered with tears. Offers of solace were rejected with more tears.

It was after midnight when Sara gave up on trying to stem the flow. She arranged a bed for Wendy on the living room sofa and retired to her bedroom, exhausted and positive that sleep would come as soon as her head touched the pillow. It didn't. The walls of the old, Spanish-style building, thick as they were, hadn't been enough to muffle the sounds of weeping that continued all night long. By morning all Sara longed for was to be rid of Wendy. To deposit her back at West Electronics and out of her life.

"We've got to get going," she called from the kitchen. "So, why don't you shower and get dressed?"

She poured a cup of coffee for herself and returned to the living room where there was progress. Wendy was sitting upright and had lifted her cup from the table.

"I've put towels out for you in bathroom," Sara said. You've got about half an hour to get ready."

Wendy stared soulfully at her hostess then looked down at the litter she had dumped onto the coffee table as if her disappointed hopes were laying there.

Sara looked at the mess as well. There was a key ring with the figure of a unicorn suspended from it and two keys, which Sara assumed were to the house or apartment Wendy lived in with Bert. There were several lipsticks, a comb, compact, a few coins, loose tissues, not unlike the jumble of objects in her own handbag. There were also the things a girl would need for a night away from home: make-up, toothbrush, hairspray, an extra pair of hose, and a small zippered bag which Sara recognized as the sort gynecologists provided to hold a diaphragm.

It was well thought out, an example of how organized Wendy could be when she was motivated. Underneath all that helplessness, Wendy knew exactly what she was doing.

"You'd better start getting it together," Sara said. She didn't raise her voice but there was steel in it. "I'm leaving here in thirty minutes and you're coming with me whether you're ready or not. I'll get you out into the hallway and leave you there, if I have to."

Wendy sniffled and wiped the tears from her face with one of the many crumpled, linty tissues scattered on the table. "First, you have to promise that you won't tell anybody what happened," she said.

"I don't know what happened," Sara replied. "So how can I tell anybody?"

"I mean about me and Rick and that I went to meet him last night. You have to promise."

"I promise. I won't say a word."

"Do you swear?"

"I swear. I promise. I'll agree to anything you want as long as you get dressed so we can get out of here."

Wendy nodded. "I'll get ready," she said, and carried those items she needed into Sara's bathroom.

The end was in sight. Sara opened the front door and went down half a flight of steps to pick up two copies of the Los Angeles Times. One of them she dropped on the straw mat in front of Marissa's doorway, her neighbor who lived across the hall. The other, she took back to the table in the small dining area next to the kitchen. She drank from her now tepid cup of coffee and scanned the front page. Nothing new, she saw, and turned to the small theater section to see if the play some friends of hers were involved with had been reviewed yet.

Chapter 23

Sheila Birney had begun the day with high expectations and her mood brightened even more when Martin West arrived. She fairly bristled with good cheer when she saw him. Her smile radiated sunshine. Her blue eyes sparkled. Her voice trilled.

"Good morning," she said. "I have a message here for you."

Being by herself in the front office, with no one to help field phone calls or open the mail, would normally have put her into a very bad mood, but this morning, she could hand Mr. West the pink message slip with enthusiasm. He was here early, way ahead of his usual time. What a stroke of luck.

Martin West looked around the office, then at his wristwatch. "Where are the other girls?"

Sheila made an effort to sound neutral. This was the question she'd been hoping for but she didn't want to appear eager. She didn't want Mr. West to think she was trying to get anybody into trouble.

"They're not here yet," she said, with apparent reluctance. "But Sara did call a little while ago to say that she and Wendy would be late and they'd both be here soon."

"Both? They're coming in together?"

Sheila confirmed that he had understood her correctly then, before he could get away, went on to make an explanation he hadn't called for. She told him that Sara was having problems and Wendy, to provide comfort, had offered to spend the night with her.

"They should be here by ten o'clock," she added.

"I see," Martin West said.

He didn't care where Wendy had spent the night, or with whom. Neither did he wish to concern himself with exactly what time she or any other employee came in or went home, as long as the privilege wasn't abused. People, he believed, worked better when they were allowed a certain amount of latitude and, for as long as the business ran smoothly and he wasn't inconvenienced, he didn't interfere with that sort of thing. When anyone overstepped the boundaries, it was Haru Maruri's job to correct the situation.

Recently, however, he had begun to pay more attention. Was he imagining it, or had there had been a subtle shift? It seemed as if his company was no longer running as smoothly as it had been. Were there problems Maruri should be telling him about? Problems he should be made aware of?

"Tell Mr. Maruri I want to see him in my office, right away," he directed.

It was a measure of his displeasure that he wanted Sheila to give the instruction and she was aware of it.

"Mr. Maruri is in the warehouse," she told him. "He and Mr. Walsh are with the man from the insurance company and they'll probably be tied up for most of the morning."

"Well tell him when he's free," West said with mounting irritation. "And tell the temporary...Sara...that I want to see her as soon as she gets here."

"Yes, Mr. West, I certainly will."

Sheila almost purred with satisfaction. It would have been better if she'd had the opportunity to work Bert Rudner into the conversation. Been able to explain how Bert had burst into the office and frightened them all the night before. Mr. West did have a right to know what was going in his own company. But, all in all, she was content. For the moment, Mr. West had heard enough and the day was just beginning. Maybe she'd get a chance to tell him more later on. Or even better, maybe somebody else would tell him.

CHAPTER 24

Sara pulled the rear-view mirror back to where it belonged. "Leave it alone," she said.

"I only wanted to make sure I look alright." Wendy fidgeted with a strand of her hair, curled it around a finger and let it go, all the while looking at Sara expectantly.

"Well? Do I look alright?"

In the few minutes since they'd left Sara's apartment, it was the third time the question had been asked and responded to.

"How many times do you have to hear it? You look fine."

Wendy took her handbag from the floor of the car and rummaged through the contents until she came up a small round mirror. She held it up and examined her face carefully.

"I look awful," she declared.

Sara glanced over. Actually, she looked remarkably well. She was calm now. So calm, you would think the histrionics of the previous night hadn't happened. Her face showed hardly a trace of sleeplessness or tears and what there was only added to her attractiveness. It wasn't fair. Wendy looked even prettier than usual.

"I'm the one who looks worse for wear," Sara said. "You, at least, look like you got a good night's sleep." One of Sara's hands left the steering and gently massaged the nape of her neck.

She still wanted to find out what had happened to bring Wendy back to her apartment and this might be her last chance to get an answer. Was it that Rick didn't show up? Was that what caused the hysterical tears? Or had there been an argument? Or, was it something more serious, like an accident?

Sara wanted to know. On the other hand, asking questions would give the impression that she wanted to stay involved. Not a good idea. It would be wiser to keep quiet and, although it wasn't easy, she decided to stifle her curiosity. A few minutes later, when she pulled into the garage at West Electronics, the opportunity was over. Even if she'd wanted to give into temptation, Wendy was out of the car before Sara could turn off the engine.

"I'm going in through the warehouse," she called out and was gone.

"You're welcome," Sara muttered. She walked around to close the door Wendy had left open and was disappointed to see that none of the parking places for regular employees was still vacant. Almost everyone had gotten to work ahead of them, including Mr. West. He almost never arrived at the office before eleven, but this morning, there it was. His Cadillac. Parked in the first stall.

And Rick's Harley was exactly where she'd seen it the day before, next to the small flight of steps leading to the warehouse.

Wendy's rush into the building was obviously to look for him, and Sara was grateful for the small favor. At least they wouldn't be walking into the office together. Even so, there was no escaping the awareness of how inextricably her arrival was bound to Wendy's and how conspicuous their lateness was going to be.

In the hollow loneliness of the garage, a long forgotten incident came back to her. She remembered being eight years old. Late to school. And dreading, as she'd walked the silent empty corridors, doors to the classrooms already closed, what her teacher would say. It had been was worse than she'd imagined it would be.

Miss O'Malley had scolded her in front of the class. She'd been angry--or pretended to be--refusing to hear an explanation and adding to Sara's humiliation by writing a note for her to take to her parents. Sara had cried all the way home, picturing the disappointment of her mother, who always expected perfection from her darling girl.

What a serious child she'd been. Well, she was grown up now and didn't have to be perfect anymore. She wasn't going to hurry. There was no need to feel guilty because she was getting to work an hour late, an hour for which she wouldn't bill the client. The nice little girl from the Bronx who never wanted to disappoint anybody was gone, although Sara had to acknowledge that traces of her still lurked--ready to show up when least expected.

She shook off the shadow of the warehouse as she walked up the ramp, savoring the relief of having the weight of Wendy lifted from her shoulders. She was out of it, and best of all, there was no reason for David ever to know about last night. She wasn't proud of the way in which she'd allowed herself to become en-snared in an ugly deception. And she'd rather he didn't find out about it.

As for the people at West Electronics, she couldn't imagine anything more irrelevant than what any of them believed or thought about her.

CHAPTER 25

"**A**re you feeling better," Sheila asked.

It was almost comical, the way she leaned across the desk and looked at Sara with exaggerated concern.

"I'm fine," Sara said, in no mood to find humor in the situation.

"You do look tired," Sheila conceded. "Where's your new roommate? Did she get lost or did her boyfriend find her?"

"She's coming in through the warehouse," Sara replied.

She went to her desk, trying to avoid Sheila's inquisitive gaze. She'd been so preoccupied with Wendy that she'd forgotten the broken heart she was supposed to be suffering from. Wendy might be out of her apartment, but the story she'd told was going to linger on. Suddenly, she stopped and turned back.

"What do you mean, 'did her boyfriend find her?'"

Sheila smiled. "I guess you didn't realize what you were getting into," she said. "He showed up here, last night. Looking for her. And he was very angry."

"You mean, Bert?" Sara asked.

"Of course. Who did you think I meant? He wanted your address."

"My address!"

"Don't worry. We don't have it and even if we did we wouldn't give it out."

"That's right," Gerry said, coming out of the accounting office. "We never give out home addresses. I am glad to see you. We were beginning to worry."

"I'm fine," Sara said.

It was nice of Gerry, even if she had doubts about Wendy's story, not to let them show. Sheila, on the other hand, made it obvious that she hadn't believed a word of it. And who could blame her? The dishonesty was so transparent.

"Wendy's boyfriend made a terrible scene. It was scary," Gerry said. "He just busted in here--"

"I hate to interrupt," Sheila said. "But Mr. West does want to see Sara. He's been waiting for almost an hour."

Sara grabbed a pad and pencil from the desk and made her escape. With Mr. West there would be no need for pretense. She would apologize for being late and, even if he had overheard anything about the broken-heart Wendy invented for her, he would be too considerate, too disinterested, or both, to mention it.

She was mistaken. While Martin West was usually an easy--and sometimes charming--person to work for, he could be the opposite when a problem became so glaring he was forced to deal with it himself. Sara was about to see that side of him for the first time.

"You're late," he said and held up a hand to halt her apology.

"I appreciate how reliable you've been in the past, and if you can perform the job you've been hired for, I'd like you to stay on until Elinor gets back. If not, we'll get somebody else. By that, I simply mean that personal problems should not be allowed to interfere with your work and it certainly will not be allowed to influence the work of other people in the office. If those terms are alright with you, no more need be said. If not, let Mr. Maruri know. I'm sure that the temporary agency can come up with an adequate replacement by tomorrow."

Sara gaped. He was sending her away without giving her a chance to explain or defend herself. He had reached for his phone and was dialing a number as if she had already left his office.

She could barely contain her outrage. She didn't mind being ignored, but no matter how humble her position with a company, she expected to be treated with respect. Mr. West had crossed that line. She couldn't blame him for wanting her to be on time. And, although she'd expected him to ignore whatever it was that he'd heard about her personal problems, he had a right to ask her to leave them at home. But he had treated her dismissively and denied her the right to explain herself.

It was the third grade all over again, only this time she had some options. He had offered her a way out and she would take it. The Meacham sisters could find somebody else to meet Mr. West's exacting standards. Watching interesting situations from the outside was one thing, getting into the middle of them, was something else. She would get out of this one as soon as possible. Instead of going back to her desk, she turned towards Haru Maruri's office.

Chapter 26

"**S**ara, over here. I'm over here."

The voice was low, almost a whisper and Sara froze when she heard it.

"I have to talk to you."

Sara walked past Oliver Blakely's office and stopped where Wendy waited, just inside the doorway to Ken Ichiwara's office.

"We can talk in here," Wendy said.

Sara refused to cross the threshold. "There's nothing to talk about," she said. "I'm sorry you're having problems and I hope everything works out for you. But, from now on, you're on your own. I don't want to hear about it."

"I have no one else to turn to," Wendy said.

"We've done that one before," Sara replied. She moved to get away but Wendy grabbed hold of her arm.

"It's Rick," Wendy whispered. "He's not here. I asked everywhere in the warehouse and nobody's seen him."

"What do you want me to do? Form a search party?"

"But his Harley is in the garage."

"Listen carefully," Sara said. "I'm not interested in anything you have to say or in anything to do with Rick. I'm sure he can take very good care of himself, so if you want to waste your time worrying about him go right ahead. But leave me out of it." She shook loose from Wendy's grasp. "If you want to worry about somebody, I suggest you turn your attention to your child. Or you might think about Bert. Remember him? He's the guy you and your son are living with. He showed up here last night. Looking for you."

"News sure travels fast around this place," Wendy said, a picture of injured innocence. "Sheila told me how he barged in here and made a scene in front of everybody. He even went back to see Rick. Can you believe it? I told you he was trying to ruin my life." She sighed. "Even Mr. Walsh is angry with me now."

Sara looked at her in disbelief. "Don't you ever think about anybody but yourself?" she asked. "You are the most selfish person I've ever come across."

"I'm not selfish!" Wendy's face flushed with self-righteous indignation. It wasn't the first time the accusation had been leveled against her, but her interpretation never changed. Sara was jealous, just like everybody else.

"Then, think about Bert for a minute," Sara continued. "Try to imagine what he's going through. The guy loves you and you treat him like dirt. Why don't you give him a break? Pick up the phone and call him before he treats you like you deserve."

Sara turned away. Haru Maruri's office was still her destination but a stop in the ladies' room would give her a few moments to calm down. She needed that after the encounters with Wendy and Mr. West. No point in going to see Mr. Maruri while she was still so angry. She looked around to make sure Wendy hadn't followed her before opening the ladies' room door and, once again, was greeted with the unexpected. It looked like somebody had tried to take a shower in there and used a sink to do it in.

Traces of water and what looked like blood were everywhere, splashed on the walls and mirror, with trails and streaks where somebody had tried to clean them. There were murky pools collected in the crevices and corners of the gray tile floor. Soiled and crumpled paper towels had been tossed into the tall metal trash can and others had missed their target.

Neither Sheila nor Gerry would have left the room in this condition. Wendy, even if she was so inclined, wouldn't have had time to do so much damage. And none of them showed signs of having hurt themselves. It must have been one of the cleaning people. And whoever it was must have cut herself.

A nasty cut, Sara surmised as, using a clean paper towel, she picked up the soiled ones and pushed them into the already overflowing basket. But that was no excuse for leaving the room in such disorder. Moving quickly, she did her best to dry the floor, pulling fresh towels from the container and using her foot to push them around until the bloody puddles disappeared. She wiped the mirror and, finally, sloshed water around the basin and used more paper towels to wipe it dry. The room was as presentable as she could make it and she was a mess.

Nothing was going right. She'd stopped in here was to collect her thoughts. Instead she was perspiring from the clean-up and water had splashed the front of her skirt and sweater. She made a few ineffectual attempts at improving her appearance before giving up. What difference did it make? She knew what she wanted to say and how she looked didn't matter. She wasn't coming back to West Electronics and Mr. Maruri would have to call the agency to find somebody else to take care of Mr. West.

But when she got to his office, the only sign of Mr. Maruri was his briefcase lying flat on the desk, as if he'd been about to open it when he was called away. Otherwise, every surface was bare except for a black pad to protect the desk and a photo in a silver frame, the subject of which Sara couldn't see until she went around to stand by his comfortably padded black leather chair, not quite as impressive as Mr. West's, but very nice.

It must be a picture of Mrs. Maruri and their children, two boys, all looking curiously old-fashioned in their solemnity. Something else caught her eye. There was a crumpled piece of paper on the gray industrial-style carpeting. He must have meant it to go into the black plastic wastepaper basket and it had hit the floor instead.

Strange. He was obsessively tidy and unlikely to have overlooked the stray piece of paper. She stooped to pick it up and, after a quick glance through the glass panel to see if anybody was paying attention to her, pulled open the creases of a page apparently torn from a pocket-size notepad. On it were several handwritten lines from Mr. Maruri to an unnamed person, saying he wanted to see that person first thing in the morning.

To Sara, it was obvious that the peremptory tone of the message limited the number of intended recipients and, after considering the possibilities, she came up with Rick Hanson as the most likely candidate. If that case, had Rick ever seen it? If so, could a desire to avoid Mr. Maruri be the reason for his absence? Most curious, whoever the intended recipient, how had the note come to be discarded on the carpet of Mr. Maruri's office?

She also asked herself why she was so interested in something that was probably insignificant and was certainly none of her business. Feeling foolish, she closed her fist around the note and dropped it into the wastepaper basket.

"Will Mr. Maruri be back soon?" she asked, standing in front of Gerry's desk.

"I don't think so," Gerry said. "He's showing a representative from the insurance company around the warehouse and he'll probably be with him for the rest of the morning. Can I help you with anything?"

Sara thanked her and shook her head. She had done her best to see Mr. Maruri and tried to give him enough time to replace her by the next morning. She would continue to make the effort. But it wasn't her fault he wasn't unavailable. And she wouldn't allow it to become her problem. When she did catch up with him, she would make it understood that working for Mr. West for even one more day was out of the question.

CHAPTER 27

C louds moved across the morning sky, softening the sunlight as it shone into the front office, hiding defects and making everything look better wherever it reached. Even the unnatural brightness of the orange Naugahyde furniture seemed more inviting, the glossy fake leaves of the potted plants looked almost alive, and there was a warm glow around Sheila Birney and Wendy Solomon.

The two women, sitting side by side, both pretending to concentrate on their work, were too wrapped up in their own expectations to be aware of the pretty picture they made. One fair haired, the other dark. One cheerful and looking forward to what the next few hours would bring, the other filled with gloomy imaginings.

Sheila was waiting to give Haru Maruri the message from Martin West that she believed would mean trouble for the controller and maybe for Wendy as well. Wendy, anxious about the whereabouts of her lover, waited for noon, when the office would empty out and she could try again to find out what had happened to him.

For her, this level of anxiety was a new experience. She had never before felt herself to be thwarted wherever she turned, with no man to turn to for help or sympathy. There were pale green copies of shipping orders spread over her desk and she shuffled them aimlessly while she vacillated between worrying about Rick and being angry with him for treating her so badly. Toward Sara, whom she had trusted, she was unequivocally furious. Sara had let her down. She had been mean and insulting when all Wendy asked for was a little help and advice.

Disapproval, especially when it came from other women, was usually easy to ignore. But Sara had deceived her. Until last night she'd been taken in by the way Sara seemed to understand and accept her. Now, she knew it was all phony. Sara was like every other woman she had ever known. Even her own mother. They were all jealous.

Wendy bit her lip to keep the tears from flowing again. This was all Sara's fault. If Sara had given her a ride back to the office to meet Rick, she would have been there on time and Rick would have been waiting for her and none of this awfulness would be happening. And this morning, all Sara had worried about was being late to work. When she'd needed time to pull herself together, instead of understanding, Sara had been rushing her. What was the big deal? She was only a temp, what did it matter if she was late? What did she have to be so angry about?

Wendy was vaguely aware that her code of conduct was different from that of most people, but that was because she was special and anyone who recognized that should accept her way of doing things, especially someone like poor, dull Sara, who pretended to be nicer and kinder and better than most people, but turned out to be worse.

Wendy gathered the papers into a pile then spread them out again. She didn't see how she could possibly forgive Sara, but maybe she should try. It was possible she might need Sara's help again and Sara did say some things that made sense.

Most of Sara's harsh words were already erased from Wendy's memory. But what she'd said about Bert still echoed. Even though he'd been making life difficult for her, she knew he loved her. And, as Sara had pointed out, he was willing to take care of her--and Mikey. She did have to think of Mikey.

She continued to shuffle the papers, feeling dejected all over again. If only Rick would turn up. Last night she'd assumed he was purposely making her suffer for being late. She had thought that maybe he was with somebody else to try to make her jealous, or he hadn't realized how important it was for them to be together all night in his apartment. Maybe he didn't understand how urgent it was for them to firm up their plans for being together. But he'd never before stood her up and she was worried about him.

On the other hand, she did have to be practical. "You have to think of yourself," was the unspoken caution that came into her mind, and this was one she could easily embrace.

As Sara came back from her failed attempt to see Mr. Maruri, Wendy was dialing the number for Rudner & Rudner, the public relations firm owned by Bert's father.

"Honey," Wendy said, when she heard Bert's voice on the other end. "I didn't sleep a wink last night. I was so upset because you were angry with me."

⚓

"Mark and I are driving up to the Tick-Tock for lunch," Gerry announced. Anybody want to come with us?"

"No sandwiches today?" Sheila's blue eyes opened wide in feigned amazement. "What happened?"

"I just feel like eating out," Gerry replied, sounding defensive in spite of herself. "Do you want to come?"

"Sure," Sheila said. "I haven't been up there in ages."

"How about you?" Gerry asked, turning to Wendy. She was surprised Sheila had accepted the invitation and glad, but Wendy was the one she most wanted to come along.

Wendy looked around vacantly. "No," she said. "I have to cover the phones for Sheila."

"Sara can do that," Sheila said.

"I said I would do it," Wendy snapped.

Sheila shrugged. "Okay." She patted her blond curls and smiled. "Then Sara can come with us. We can cheer her up."

Sara saw two options, neither of which was appealing. Be alone with Wendy for the next hour or go out with the others and deal with Sheila's sarcasm about her non-existent broken romance. She chose the office where, at least, there would be no need for pretense.

"No thanks," she said. "I'll get a sandwich from the truck and eat here...to make up for being late."

Gerry had trouble hiding her disappointment. Having Sara join them would have been some consolation for Wendy's refusal. And maybe, over lunch, they could have found out what was going on. Like the real reason Wendy had spent the night with Sara. Painful as it was, she had to admit to herself what she wouldn't admit to anyone else, she didn't believe a word of the story Wendy had told.

"Why don't you get Mark?" Sheila suggested. "It's still early. If we leave now, it'll be easier to park."

She would forego the pleasure of giving Mr. Maruri his message from Martin West in person. He was taking a long time with the insurance adjustor and she was hungry. Instead, she took the pink message form to his office, placed it in the center of his desk and moved the family photo to anchor it in place.

"Let's go," she said and led the way out the front door.

Wendy could barely able to contain herself as she waited for the rest of the office to empty out. It didn't take long. Martin West came into the front office at noon, with Oliver Blakely following closely behind. He stopped at her desk, ignoring Sara, to announce that he and Blakely were going to lunch and asked for the whereabouts of Mr. Maruri.

Wendy, too preoccupied to enjoy this special attention, told him she wasn't sure, but thought he was still in back with the insurance man. West nodded and, with Blakely in tow, walked out to the garage via the warehouse where he'd be able to check on Haru Maruri's presence for himself.

Shortly afterwards, Haru Maruri and Ed Walsh emerged from the back of the building, as if, it seemed to Sara, they'd been waiting for the front office to clear out before making an appearance.

"Mr. Maruri and I will be back within the hour," Walsh told Wendy.

"Mr. Maruri, I need to speak with you," Sara called out, nearly knocking over her chair in her rush to get his attention.

Maruri didn't pause. "When I get back from lunch," he said, and was out the door before she could stop him.

"Damn it!" Sara exclaimed. "If they can't get someone to take my place, it's their problem. I'm not coming back here tomorrow."

Wendy paid no attention. She was on her feet, looking out the window. When she saw Maruri's Datsun pull out of the driveway she turned to Sara.

"Answer the phone," she commanded.

She was going back to the warehouse. By now, the men who worked there would be eating their sandwiches and probably passing around a joint in the sunshine behind the building. Nobody would pay any attention to her. It was a trip she had already made several times that morning but this time she would be able to have a more thorough look around.

CHAPTER 28

While Wendy was searching for a clue to Rick Hanson's whereabouts, Haru Maruri and Ed Walsh were on their way to a luncheonette less than a quarter of a mile from the office, a tense silence between them.

Overnight the positions of the two men seemed to have reversed. The large, self-confident, authoritative man, the one who had created his own fiefdom at West Electronics, who was always ready to offer reassurance to his more anxious partner, that man had shrunk into a timid, frightened shadow of himself. And Haru Maruri realized that the burden was on his shoulders. Ed Walsh was looking to him for a way out of the morass in which they found themselves.

Maruri waited until they were seated and had given their order to the waitress--a hamburger for each with cups of coffee to be served at once--before he broke the silence.

"I still don't understand," he said. He took a paper napkin from the stainless steel dispenser on the table and wiped the bottom of his cup. "Explain it to me. You said that Rick has conditions. Are you sure he didn't say anything else? He must have given you some idea of what he wanted."

"I told you. We were interrupted. Wendy's boyfriend showed up out of nowhere and started yelling at us. Wanting to know what was going on between Rick and Wendy. Acting like there was a conspiracy to keep Wendy hidden from him. It was crazy talk and Rick made it worse. He started to laugh like it was all some kind of joke and the boyfriend got even more agitated. By the time I got the guy to calm down, it was too late. Rick announced he was leaving."

"And you let him go?"

"What was I supposed to do? I told him to wait. That we needed to talk. But he walked out anyway. Into the front office. Said he wanted to go out for a drink. He got Mark to go with him. Then Wendy's boyfriend left and it was all over."

"You should have stopped him," Maruri said.

"Do you think I should have risked making a scene in front of everybody in the front office? What would that have looked like?"

The two men fell silent as they sat in their booth by the window, facing each other across a Formica topped table upon which a disinterested waitress had just placed two heavy plates which were more gray than white, each one bearing a skimpy patty of ground meat between a stale hamburger bun, a slice of unripe tomato, two slices of watery pickle, and a wilted leaf of lettuce.

Maruri looked down at the unappealing plate in front of him and back at the man who was his partner. "Still, it wasn't right...the way you walked out last night without telling me what happened."

"I didn't want to worry you. I kept thinking that if I had another chance to talk to Rick I'd find a way to handle it. If he been there this morning maybe I could have--"

Maruri waved away the excuses. "Are you telling me the truth?" he asked. He was calm. Perhaps, because the initial shock had worn off, the shock of finding out that the man he had trusted, had been less than candid with him. Had in fact lied to him. Perhaps it was because anger was a luxury he couldn't afford. Getting at the truth was more important. He needed that in order to protect himself. In order to protect both of them.

"Are you telling me all of it this time?"

Walsh couldn't resent the question. He hadn't been honest with Harry the night before. He had run away. Even now--. He averted his eyes and swallowed hard. "That's it," he said. "There's nothing more."

Maruri nodded. "I hope so," he said. "Now...for when Rick turns up. The first thing is to find out what he wants. What he expects from us and what he is threatening if we refuse."

Walsh wouldn't hazard a response. He wiped the perspiration from his forehead and upper lip. There was no point in telling Harry about Rick's whispered reminder about the money he'd asked for, the money to help his sick friend. He couldn't see why Harry had to know about that.

Maruri pushed away the untouched plate. "How could Rick disappear without leaving a trace?" he asked as the waitress approached with a fresh pot of coffee.

"Except for his motorcycle," Walsh said.

Maruri nodded. The motorcycle was exactly where it had been when he'd left his note at six o'clock the night before. "And you're sure that Mark has no idea what happened after he dropped Rick off?"

"That's what he told me. He left Rick in the garage around seven-thirty, figuring he wanted to pick up his motorcycle and go home."

"And Rick couldn't have gone back into the building because he doesn't have a key?"

Ed Walsh heard the question mark at the end of the sentence but kept silent. He couldn't bring himself to admit that, against Harry's fierce objections, he had provided Rick with a key to every door in the building. That he had given in when Rick had pleaded, saying it would seem like they didn't trust him if he didn't have the keys. This was yet another secret he had kept from his partner, another mistake for which he owed an apology. But not yet, no more recriminations, not right now.

"You say you tried to call him at home this morning and there was no answer?" Maruri asked, a trace of weariness in his voice. The coffee wasn't helping the almost constant pain in his stomach and he reached into his pocket for the ever-present antacid tablets. "And nobody has seen Rick at work this morning?"

Walsh nodded.

"Then, why is his motorcycle in the garage?"

"I don't know! Why are you asking me all these questions when we've been through them all before?"

"Because you're the one who said you could handle him," Maruri said. "He can't have disappeared into thin air."

"Maybe he's playing some kind of cat and mouse game...trying to up the ante?" Walsh said despairingly. "I don't know any more than you do. But I would have bet my life we could trust him."

"You did bet your life," Maruri said. "And mine too. Now we have to figure out what we're going to do next."

CHAPTER 29

The luncheon exodus had emptied the offices and left a soothing silence behind. It was a welcome respite for Sara, to be left alone with the voice of Martin West in her ear accompanied by the soft rapid clicking of electronic typewriter keys as she transcribed his words to paper.

She had come to dislike the man, but had to admit his dictation was, as always, clear, steady and easy to understand even though the memo she worked on was more complicated than usual, full of technical details, demanding her total concentration. She didn't hear Wendy return from the warehouse. Nor was she aware of anyone coming up behind her until she felt a hand clutch her shoulder. It startled her out of her chair.

"You nearly scared me to death!" she exclaimed. "What's wrong with you?"

Wendy was pale and gasping for breath. She tried to speak, but the only sounds emerging from her struggle were childlike whimpers.

"What's happened? What on earth is the matter?" Sara looked at the other woman more closely. Wendy was terrified. The color was drained from her face and her entire body was trembling.

"I don't know what to do," Wendy said. Her voice quavered.

"About what?"

Wendy shook her head helplessly.

Sara forced herself to speak gently. "I can't help if you won't tell me what's wrong," she said. "Is this to do with Rick?"

Wendy nodded.

"Where is he?'

"I found him."

"Yes," Sara said. "Go on. Why are you so upset? What did he say?"

Once more, Wendy was unable to reply. She was looking at Sara with those mournful frightened eyes.

"Where has he been?" Sara asked. "Did he threaten you? Did he hurt you? Answer me."

Wendy shuddered convulsively. "I think he's dead."

"Dead!" Sara shook her head. "Don't be ridiculous."

"It's true. It's true," Wendy repeated, like a child trying to convince a grown up. Tears were now spilling out of her eyes leaving traces of mascara as they ran down her cheeks. "You've got to believe me."

Sara stared at her, unwilling to accept what she'd heard and unable to come up with a reason for why Wendy would make up such a story. "Okay," she said. "Where is he?"

"In the warehouse," Wendy whispered, the words coming more quickly now. "There's a space back there that he made just for us, behind some boxes. Nobody else knows about it, that's why I had to wait till everybody was out of the way before I could go look for him. He's lying there, covered with blood."

"Take me there," Sara demanded.

"I can't," Wendy protested hysterically. "I can't go back there."

"Then tell me how to find it."

Wendy, still sobbing, went to the door next to her desk. She opened it, stepped a few feet in and pointed toward the end of the large warehouse.

There had never been any reason for Sara to be back there and she'd never thought much about what went on in the warehouse until now. She looked around, curious. Just inside, to the right of the exit to the garage, she saw what she took to be Ed Walsh's office. On the left there were several workbenches for the technicians who handled quality control and repairs. Beyond the benches there was a bank of lockers for the use of the men who worked back there and the rest of the vast space was filled with large cartons of tape recorders, piled high on wooden pallets arranged in orderly rows.

"Stay on this side," Wendy said. She was barely able to speak, as she indicated an aisle closest to the left wall of the warehouse.

"Go on," Sara urged.

"You have to go to space just before last set of boxes then turn left and walk until you reach the wall. She grabbed hold of Sara's arm. "It was too horrible," she cried.

"Is that it?" Sara asked. "Is that where you think you saw Rick."

Wendy shook her head. "On your left-hand side, you'll see a space between the wall and the cartons." She struggled to control her tears before she could go on. "You have to squeeze through that space. Between the wall and cartons. And go a few more steps. Then you'll see. It's like a little room. And that's where he is." Once again sobbing hysterically, Wendy turned away and left Sara on her own in the warehouse.

Sara moved forward slowly. It couldn't be true that there was a body back here. Whatever Wendy thought she'd seen it must have been the product of shadows and her overwrought imagination. It would be easy to be carried away by morbid thoughts in this dim, cavernous space. Even she felt a bit frightened and vulnerable, dwarfed by the giant islands of cartons.

There was no comfort from the voices of the men who were just outside the building. In the bright sunshine they seemed unreal, framed by the loading dock like characters on a movie screen, laughing and talking, chewing on sandwiches, drinking from bottles of soda, smoking cigarettes and totally unaware of her existence. Could they also be unaware that a body was hidden away back here? Of course not. The idea was ridiculous.

Except, where was Rick? And why had he left his motorcycle behind? Sara fought the feeling of foreboding that seized her as she approached the final pallet of master cartons. In a few moments it would be over. She would discover the reality of what Wendy thought she had seen and be out of here. She would be able to assure Wendy that, wherever Rick was, he wasn't dead or lying wounded behind a pile of cardboard boxes.

She turned left into an aisle formed by two sets of pallets and went toward the wall that looked like it would turn out to be a dead end. When she got there, she found a passageway, just as Wendy had foretold. She went forward for several feet until coming to an opening between the cartons, entrance to a an enclosure that was no more than five feet wide and seven feet long. How very clever of Rick. There were cushions and straw mats. There was an ashtray and two burnt out candles on top of a small carton that had been covered with a tie-dye cloth. She moved forward and paused. It felt like she was stepping on small stones or pebbles. She looked down, straining to see in the semi-darkness. They were keys, quite a few of them, different sizes and shapes, like the ones Rick Hanson had been so proud of.

They were scattered, leading to the body of a man about whose identity there could be no doubt. His head was turned away from her, but Sara could recognize what remained of the blonde, crisp, curly hair. She stood, paralyzed for a few moments, then moved forward.

It had to be done. It seemed impossible, but he might still be alive and she couldn't leave him lying there without being sure. Using all the willpower she could muster, she crouched to touch a corner of his back: broad, muscular and scarred with bloody gashes where the skin was ripped from his body. She recoiled from the sight. Gasping, she backed away and leaned against a stack of cartons for support. There could be no doubt. Rick was dead. Where her fingers had touched him, the flesh was ice cold. There were wounds all over and blood. A lot of blood. A sickening smell. No wonder Wendy had been horrified. Sara groped her way out of there. She would be sick to her stomach if she didn't get away.

⚓

Wendy, she discovered, had made a remarkable recovery. She was standing by the door connecting to the front office, holding it open like a hostess ready to greet a guest. The sobbing had stopped. The trails of tears and mascara were almost invisible, just faint smudges where she had wiped them away.

It was Sara who trembled now, she who was close to tears as she stopped to lean against Wendy's desk and struggled to regain her composure.

"You didn't believe me but it was just like I told you," Wendy said. "You saw for yourself, didn't you? He's back there and he's dead, isn't he?" There was no grief in her voice as the questions poured out, just a detectable note of triumph at having been proved correct.

Sara ignored the questions. She barely heard them. "We've got to call the police right away," she said. "Do you want to do it or shall I?"

Wendy's newly regained control disappeared in an instant. "Are you crazy? Why should we call the police?"

"Because Rick is lying back there and we're the only ones who know about it," Sara said. "Except, of course, for whoever's responsible." She reached for the phone on Wendy's desk.

"No," Wendy shouted. She grabbed the receiver out of Sara's hand and slammed it back into its cradle. There was nothing unsure or indecisive about her now. "I'm the one who told you about it, so it's up to me. I say we forget about the whole thing and wait for somebody else to find him."

"Wait for somebody else?" Sara was incredulous. "Rick is dead. It could take days for anybody to find him back there. We can't wait make believe we don't know about it."

"Why not? It could be an accident. You don't know for sure what happened and it doesn't matter because it's not your decision to make. This has nothing to do with you. You're nobody here. You're just a temp. It's not up to you to do anything and I don't even know why I told you about it except that I was scared."

Even from Wendy, Sara would not have expected such callousness. "You got over your tears pretty fast, didn't you?" she said as she turned away. She went to her own desk, picked up the phone, dialed for the operator and explained there was an emergency. She asked for the police.

"You're trying to ruin my life," Wendy screamed. "It's none of your business and if you tell anyone I had a date to meet Rick last night, I'll tell them you're a liar."

"Tell them whatever you want," Sara said. She held on to the phone, and gave the police information about the body in the warehouse as clearly and succinctly as she could.

"I'm leaving," Wendy said. She had grabbed her handbag and was already halfway out the door.

"You can't run away," Sara said.

"I'm not running away. I feel sick and I want to go home."

"What are you going to do, walk?"

"Don't worry about me. And don't say anything about me and Rick to the police...or to anyone else. I'm warning you. I'll tell everybody how you're the one who found him and how you were always coming on to him and how he rejected you and that I don't have anything to do with it."

Sara sat at her desk, to wait. She wasn't worried about stories Wendy would tell about her. Her lack of involvement with Rick was obvious. Her doubts were about having been the one to make the phone call. Why had she so quickly assumed it was her responsibility? She was a temp, like Wendy said. This affair was none of her business.

In the silence that had become oppressive the image of Rick's body haunted her. If only Sheila would get back from lunch early along with Gerry and Mark. She wouldn't feel so isolated. There would be somebody to tell about what she'd seen. Other people to meet the police and answer their questions.

Now that it was too late, she could see the choices she hadn't made. She could have delayed calling the police for just a little while, until Sheila or Mr. Maruri or anybody else came back from lunch. There were the men on the loading dock. She could have told one of them what had happened. Instead, she was on her own. A temporary employee waiting to show the police a body somebody else had discovered.

Chapter 30

"**A**re you the lady who called about a body?"

The uniformed police officer's voice was stern. This was, after all, Hollywood, where almost everybody was in show business and screwball phone calls came with the territory. He was accustomed to the extraordinary lengths people went to for some attention, a little publicity, a name in the newspaper and his guess was that this summons would turn out to be, like so many others, a hoax.

"Yes," Sara said. "I called. My name is Sara Fisher. And I--"

"You called about a body?" he said, in no mood to waste time. His partner, a few years younger, stood off to the side and remained silent.

"It's...he's back there...through that door...in the warehouse. I'll show you--" Sara hesitated. The front office couldn't be left unattended, especially considering what had happened to Rick.

"Somebody should be in here," she explained. "And I'm alone." She looked from one impassive face to the other. "Everybody else is out to lunch. Could one of you stay?"

The first officer walked into the accounting office, looked around and checked the corridors. Satisfied that Sara was telling the truth, he signaled his partner to stay in the reception area. Then, his hand having gone to the holster on his hip, he motioned Sara toward the warehouse.

He stopped her before she reached the door. There was a reddish-brown spot near the hem of her skirt. More than one, he saw, when he knelt to examine it more closely.

Sara's hand went to her throat to keep the nausea at bay. Traces of Rick's blood had clung to her clothing. "My God, I didn't know," she said.

The police officer stood. "Let's go." His voice grim as he once again motioned for Sara to precede him into the warehouse. Maybe there would be a body after all.

With a quick and practiced eye, he took note of the glass paneled office on the other side of the door, the work benches, a section of employee lockers and, against the wall to his right, a heavy metal door that he assumed led to the underground parking area. There was no apparent sign of disturbance. The place was deserted except for a group of men who were visible outside, sitting on the loading dock.

"Who are those people?" he asked, pointing an accusatory finger toward the other end of the warehouse.

"They work back here," Sara said. "They're on their lunch break."

"You told us you were alone."

"I was...I mean...I was alone on the office side of the building. You see I'm a temp here and I have nothing to do with the people in the warehouse so...I guess...for the moment...I wasn't thinking about them." She paused, angry with herself for not having mentioned the men from the warehouse and waiting for him to assure her that her reaction was understandable.

No such assurance was forthcoming. "You found a dead body and you didn't tell them about it?" he said.

"I didn't find the body," Sara exclaimed. "It was Wendy. Wendy Solomon. She was the one who found him."

"Who is this Wendy Solomon? Where is she?"

"She works here. Out front. A secretary. But she left and I don't know where she went."

"She found a body and she left?"

"Yes," Sara said. "She told me about it and at first I didn't believe her. But then I saw it. The body. And I called the police. Then she left."

"Okay. This Wendy who isn't here found the body," he said. "And neither one of you bothered to tell one of the men about it?"

"I told you, I'm a temp. I don't know anybody back here," Sara said, with growing impatience and...I guess I didn't want to get everybody all excited. It seemed better to call the police myself before telling anybody else...back here...I mean. Is that so hard to understand?"

Sara could tell he was skeptical. Was it because she'd called the police herself instead of asking a man to do it? Maybe she was supposed to have screamed or fainted or gotten hysterical or all three. Maybe it would have been better to have the warehouse people tramping all over the place before the police got here. She glared at him. Instead of doubting her, he should be grateful.

"People will be coming back from lunch around one o'clock," she said. "Wouldn't it be a good idea to check things out before then?"

She saw his jaw tighten. Clearly, he didn't take kindly to having her tell him how to do his job.

"Let's get going," he said.

Sara didn't hesitate. She moved quickly, anxious to get this over with. Anxious get away from the warehouse and the policeman.

"He's back there," she said, when they reached the bank of cartons behind which Rick lay. She trembled again as she pointed to the passageway.

The police officer didn't ask her to go with him and it wouldn't have done any good if he had. He would have had to use force to get her to witness that scene again. Her help wasn't needed. He would see Rick's body for himself, covered with violent wounds that could not have been accidental or self-inflicted. Maybe, after he'd seen the blood and raw flesh, he would treat her with more understanding.

It didn't work that way. His attitude was even more hostile than it had been when he'd left her, as if he was angry that she'd been telling the truth. They went back to the front office in silence.

"There is a body," he said to his partner before reaching for the phone on Wendy's desk. He turned to Sara.

"How do I get an outside line?"

Sara told him and listened as he called in to report what he had found and to ask for the homicide team.

"You wait in here, with her," he said to the other officer. "She wasn't alone, like she told us. There are a bunch of men who work back there. Out on a loading dock. And I'm going back to make sure they stay put."

He would be happier in the warehouse, Sara thought. He could feel more important back there, watching the men to make sure no one went near the body, as opposed to being left behind to look after a woman.

She was past caring. Back at her desk, she determined to sit quietly while waiting. She looked down at the stains around the hem of her dress and remembered what she'd seen in the ladies' room that morning. The traces of blood she'd cleaned away. Once again, the good girl had emerged, and unable to mind her own business, had probably washed away the evidence of a crime.

She considered telling the police officer what she'd remembered and decided against it. Better to wait until the appropriate people arrived. They would be here soon enough and might listen to her with more open minds. She just wanted them to understand that she was nothing more than a bystander who had been pulled into this situation by accident. She looked at her watch.

Sheila should also be here very soon. She would lead the way through the door followed by Gerry and Mark. Sara wanted it to happen that way. For the three of them to get back first, before Mr. West or Mr. Maruri. She wondered if they would arrive soon enough to save her from having to face the homicide team alone.

The answer came almost immediately. She could hear their voices outside, discussing something...maybe arguing. She stood, waiting for the door to open, amazed at how impatient she was to see them. They would have so many questions for her but she wouldn't mind. She would answer them gladly.

CHAPTER 31

"**W**hat's going on? There are police outside but no one would tell us what's happening. Was there a robbery?"

Sheila was bursting with curiosity. She looked around, her blond curls in motion, her eyes growing wider when she saw the man in uniform just inside the door.

"Where's Wendy?" she asked. "Was it Bert? Did he come back?"

Gerry and Mark crowded in after her. They repeated Sheila's questions and added some of their own

"What did they take?"

"Was anybody hurt?"

"It's horrible," Sara said. "It's--"

"That's enough." The police officer held up his hands for silence and, before Sara realized what was happening, he had placed himself between her and the others.

"Your questions will be answered soon," he told the new-comers. "In the meantime, I need to know where you belong."

Sheila pointed to Gerry and Mark. "They work in the next office," she said. "My desk is in here"

"You go with them," the officer said, directing her into the accounting office. "You," he told Sara, "stay here."

By now, Sara knew it would be pointless to argue. Sheila, having just arrived on the scene, still thought she could get her way if she stood her ground.

"Why can't you tell us what's going on?" she demanded, even as the group was being herded into the next office. "And why can't Sara come with us? She's only a temp. I'm the one who belongs out here?"

The policeman didn't answer and Sheila was forced into exile with the others, her resentment growing. Her complaints carrying into the front office.

Sara was tempted to call out that Sheila didn't realize how well off she was. She wasn't being kept incommunicado, like a prisoner. All Sheila had to do was wait for a little while and her curiosity would be satisfied which, as it turned out, took less than half an hour. By then, everybody had returned from lunch, people were allowed back to their desks and the news about Rick was no longer a secret.

Impossible as it seemed, he was dead. More shocking, they couldn't bring themselves to believe there had been an accident. Too many policemen were swarming all over the place for it to have been an accident. They wouldn't be stopping people from leaving the building or preventing phone calls to the outside.

And, what about Sara? That she was the one who called the police seemed obvious. It was also assumed that she had discovered the body in the warehouse. Was that why she was being treated like a privileged character? Were the police aware that she had no business having been back there?

And, by the way, where was Wendy?

Sara could hear the discussions swirling around her. The resentment. People believing that she was the one who had found the body. Acting as if she was invisible. It was maddening. The police had turned her into an outcast by insisting she remain silent, unable to defend herself. They had even supplied a police officer of her own to make sure she complied.

And it was her own fault. If she'd gone to lunch with the others Rick's body would still be hidden away in the warehouse. Of course, Wendy would have found him. But she would have gotten over the shock soon enough. Sara had witnessed her powers of recovery. She would have figured out the wisdom of keeping her mouth shut and made a quick get-away. Sara could picture her washing away the tears while coming up with a self-serving tale of woe, one that necessitated quitting her job that very afternoon.

The police wouldn't be here and Rick would be lying in his secret space until putrefaction made discovery unavoidable. Or, until somebody else went looking for him. Somebody who knew about that hidden place and was willing to admit it.

Sara tilted her head in concentration, her hand massaging the nape of her neck. It was an interesting question. Who else knew about the secret little room? Did any of the men who worked in the warehouse know? Did Ed Walsh know? And what about the traces of blood in the ladies' room?

Sara looked up. One of the more recently arrived policemen, a detective in plain clothes, was speaking to her.

"Miss Fisher?" he asked, with more politeness that the others had shown.

She nodded and smiled.

"Would you come with me, please."

Chapter 32

Sara expected better treatment from the detectives than she'd received from the uniformed officers who had answered her phone call. They had reacted with suspicion. The job of the detectives was to listen. They would be appreciative of what she had to tell them. And, of course, they would believe her.

It wasn't until they'd finished the first round of questions that she realized how naïve she had been. At first, both men had seemed sympathetic, especially Detective Roarke. He had taken the lead while his partner, Detective Spivak, stayed in the background. They took notes, listened to her carefully and nodded at the appropriate moments, especially when she told them how horrible it had been to see Rick's body, how she'd felt at being left alone to deal with the situation. When it was over, it came as a shock to find they hadn't accepted her story at all. Once again she was being treated like a suspect.

"Why don't we start again. From the beginning," Roarke said, his tone less friendly. "And, this time, why don't you tell us everything you know about Rick Hanson."

"I already told you. I came here through a temporary employment service," Sara said. "I don't know anything about him. Any of the other people who work here can tell you more than I can."

"But he wasn't a stranger to you," Roark insisted. "You've worked here before. Surely you must know something about him."

"He worked in the warehouse. What else could I know?"

Sara paused. She did remember a time when she had been alone in the front office and Rick had come in and started flirting with her.

"He did once tell me some story once," she said. "About how he didn't get along with his father who was a famous movie producer. He said he had left home and changed his name because he wanted to prove his independence." She saw the two men exchange glances and wondered if she'd misjudged the situation again.

"Did he say what studio his father worked for or what his real name was?"

"Of course not. And I didn't ask."

"Weren't you curious? You did say you were an actress. Rick could have been a valuable contact."

Sara looked at him in amazement. "I'm an actress, not a fool. I didn't believe him," she said. "He was just a kid and, although it might be difficult for you to believe, he was trying to impress me."

The expression on his Roarke's face didn't change, still it conveyed triumph. "So there was a relationship," he declared. "You knew him well enough to believe he was a liar."

"I ran into him a few times. That's all. I worked on this side of the building, he worked in the warehouse. I've never even been back there until this morning."

"Yet you were willing to go into an area with which you were unfamiliar, all by yourself, to check out a dead body?" Roarke asked.

"I told you, Wendy was almost hysterical and I thought I'd better do what she wanted. It seemed to be the only way to calm her down."

"You could have called the police. Why didn't you do that instead of going back there alone? Weren't you afraid? Didn't you think that you might be in danger?"

"I didn't believe her. It didn't seem possible that Rick could really be dead."

"This Wendy is also a liar?" Roarke asked.

Sara was careful before replying. The detective seemed to be implying she was a neurotic woman who thought everybody was lying to her and she evaded giving him a direct answer.

"Wendy can get carried away," she said, "and I was sure she'd made a mistake. I kept thinking, because she was so worried about Rick, that she must have imagined it all."

The detective nodded, although Sara didn't think he looked convinced. "I want to make sure I have this part right," he said, looking down at his notes. "After you saw the body for yourself, you didn't ask the men out back for help. Instead you went to the front office and told this Wendy, who you say was the one who discovered the body, that you were going to call the police. She argued with you and when you insisted on making the call, she disappeared."

"She did discover the body and I didn't say she disappeared," Sara contradicted. "I said she left."

"She left," the detective repeated. "And, you have no idea where she's gone."

"It isn't as if she's a friend," Sara exclaimed. "I'm a temp. I don't even know where she lives. I've never had anything to do with Wendy other than when I've been assigned to work here. If she didn't go home, I have no idea where she is."

"You were close enough to invite her to spend the night at your apartment," Roarke pressed.

"I didn't invite her. She invited herself. How many times do you want me to say it? She wasn't going to spend the night with me. She was going to spend the night with Rick."

"Well, let's hear it again," the detective said. "From the beginning."

By the time they were finished, Sara no longer cared about whether the police--or anybody else--believed her. She wanted to get way. To grab her things, walk out of the building and never look back. But Detective Roarke had other ideas.

"We might need to question you again," he said. "We'll let you know when you can leave."

She walked out and went straight to Mr. Maruri's office, to let him know that once the police gave her permission to leave she would go and she wasn't coming back. He would have to get somebody to replace her and if it was too late to get a secretary for Mr. West by the next day he would just have to do without. Unfortunately, his door was closed. Martin West was with him, the last man in the world she wanted to encounter. Once again, declaring her exit plans would have to wait.

CHAPTER 33

Martin West paced from one side of Haru Maruri's office to the other. The situation was intolerable. A dead man in his warehouse. Police refusing to give him any meaningful information. Being told where he could and couldn't go in his own company.

"What the hell is going on here?" he growled. "I don't understand any of it."

He had posed the question several times before and no longer expected a satisfactory reply. Maruri, who he relied on to know what was going on in every corner of his company, didn't seem to know any more than he did which, even in his frustration, was understandable. How could anybody come up with a reasonable explanation for this extraordinary situation? It was beyond his imagination.

"Please Martin, sit down," Maruri begged.

The pain in his stomach nagged and he felt increasingly queasy as he watched West go back and forth along the same narrow band of carpet. From his pocket, he took an almost empty roll of antacid tablets.   He also had questions, but they couldn't be spoken out loud. Not to Martin. He wanted to understand how events could have spun so far out of control between yesterday and today.

"Why is this happening at my company?" West asked, raising his voice. "That's all I want to know. The other day it was missing merchandise. This morning an insurance investigator was spending half the day nosing around in the warehouse. And this afternoon, we have a dead body back there. What's going on around here?"

Maruri put the last two antacid tablets into his mouth. It was disturbing to see Martin, who could maintain his equilibrium under the most difficult of circumstances, lose his control. He was acting as confused as everybody else, repeating questions and getting angrier every time he asked them.

West had stopped pacing. He stood in front of Maruri's desk and continued to speak, not waiting for Maruri to reply.

"For days, the people who work here have been doing whatever they want. Coming and going as they please. I won't put up with it," he declared and banged his fist on Maruri's desk.

"Please Martin, I understand why you're upset, but getting angry will only make things worse. It's important that we stay calm." Maruri paused, waiting to see how West would react to the implied rebuke.

"We have to discuss this rationally, he continued, when he felt assured that West hadn't taken offence. "The situation is bizarre, I agree. But we must find out what the circumstances are before we can figure out how best to handle the situation. Until then there is nothing we can do."

West stared at his subordinate then relaxed his fist until his hand was flat on the desk. With that gesture, the anger and frustration seemed to have dissipated.

"You're right," he said. He smiled at his own unreasonable behavior, displaying the charm which, ever since he was a child, had drawn people to him. He pulled the chair that was next to Maruri's desk around to the front and sat down. "Thank God, I can still rely on you to be sensible."

Maruri had watched West's fist loosen and felt himself relax with it. He didn't want to see the side of his employer that was vulnerable to the same doubts and fears that preyed on more ordinary mortals, the doubts and fears that were preying on his own gut right now. He nodded his appreciation of the compliment as he took yet another roll of antacid tablets from his desk drawer.

The calm strength and leadership that West had displayed during the early days of American occupation of his country had awed the young Maruri. In the aftermath of the war, when he had felt so vulnerable, those were the qualities that had inspired confidence and respect. When opportunity beckoned, those were the qualities that had prompted him to follow West to the United States.

Eventually, the awe had dissipated and disillusionment had set in. Still he thought of West as someone with special powers, someone who could take care of himself and others in any situation. He had come to resent the icy control of the man. He chafed at the subordinate position from which he saw no possibility of escape. But he didn't want anything to impair the image of invulnerability, especially now. This wasn't the moment to see what lay beneath the icy control, the flaws he had come to recognize that few others suspected.

Almost everyone who knew Martin West looked up to him, including the men who had financed his electronics company. People who worked for him wanted to please him and coveted his praise. Only his wife, who drank too much, and his children, who spent as much time away from home as possible, realized that his indisputable charm masked a lack of warmth and his impeccably correct behavior hid an inability to truly care about anyone other than himself.

The complete truth, unsuspected even by Maruri, or anyone else outside of West's immediate family, was that his interest in that family was no more than perfunctory; the lives of his associates, business and otherwise, didn't involve him beyond the necessary social amenities; and any concern he displayed for the people he worked with directly was minimal, limited to maintaining useful relationships.

For the people on the lowest rungs of the company hierarchy, he had no time at all. He barely knew their names. He expected that, under supervision, they would do their jobs well. In return, he held the reins of authority lightly and did not interfere with the details of how the company was run.

Now, the personal lives of the people who worked for him were going to be intruded upon his consciousness. For a start, he would have to ask questions about the one who was no longer among them.

"Tell me about the man who was killed," West said, his distaste for the subject obvious. "Tell me about Rick Hanson."

"There's not much to tell," Maruri said, smoothly, having prepared himself for the inevitable questions. "It's very sad, of course. He was just twenty-three years old.

"When did he start working for us?"

Maruri had already pulled out Rick's personnel file, a duplicate of the one he had made for Ed Walsh to give to the police. It was very slim, containing only his original application for employment, two short employee review forms, and an application for the company supplied health insurance. But Maruri made a show of looking through the contents, as if examining them for the first time.

"A little more than two years ago," he said, declining to mention Rick's recent promotion to manager of the loading dock over the heads of men who were older and more experienced.

West nodded. "That's pretty much what I remembered. I've seen him around, of course, and I did think his attitude bordered on insolence. But, for as long as it didn't bother Ed, I didn't want to interfere."

"Ed never had any problems with him and he showed capability beyond his years," Maruri said. "He was responsible and he certainly wasn't a troublemaker. He never got into fights or anything like that."

West withdrew into himself to think about what he'd been told.

On the opposite side of the desk, Maruri once again made a show of looking through the papers in Rick's folder. He hadn't thought this through well enough. It was a mistake to have painted such a positive picture of the victim. Although he didn't want to cast doubt on Ed's judgment in hiring Rick, he should have hinted at some flaw in Rick's character, some negative trait that would explain the existence of an enemy, somebody outside the company, who might have wanted to kill him.

"What about the girl who found him?" West asked. "The one who took it upon herself to call the police. The one from the temporary agency who seems to be running things around here?"

"Be reasonable, Martin. She's not running things. She had to call the police. You could hardly expect her to sit around... knowing that Rick's body was in the warehouse... and wait for one of us to come back from lunch."

"What was she doing in the warehouse? Why is she involved in this at all? She just got here yesterday and today she'd finding bodies."

"I haven't had a chance to speak to--" Maruri broke off mid-sentence.

Behind West, through the glass panel on the upper half of the office door, he could see Ed Walsh. He shook his head very slightly, then picked up the thread of what he'd been saying, hoping that Ed would understand the warning sign and go away.

He dropped his eyes and fiddled with a pencil on his desk. When he looked up, he saw that Ed had understood the signal and was gone.

"My understanding is--" he went on, falteringly, "that she didn't find the body. It was Wendy Solomon who found the body, but Wendy left before the police arrived"

Okay," West said. The dark haired one, the one who works for Ed, finds a body-- then picks up and walks out of here. What was Wendy doing wandering around the warehouse and finding bodies? Why didn't she call the police? What kind of an operation is Walsh running back there?"

"Ed does a good job," Maruri said, quickly. "You know that. So, there's no point in jumping to conclusions." He paused and wondered if he should tell Martin about Wendy's boyfriend and the argument he'd had with Rick last night. A bad idea, he decided. It would only raise more questions about how well he and Ed were handling the employees. He would go in another direction.

"My guess is this has nothing to do with West Electronics," he said.

West nodded. "I suppose that's possible."

"Not only is it possible, I think it's likely," Maruri said. "Rick must have gotten himself into some kind of trouble that has nothing to do with the company and somebody came looking for him. Or, maybe a thief got into the warehouse and Rick tried to stop him."

"Well, whatever is behind all this, the timing is terrible," West declared. "I don't need more problems, right now. Not with the rate of exchange going against us and the factory in Japan saying they can't meet specifications on the new model tape recorders. They're expecting me in Tokyo next week, but I suppose I'll have to change my plans. Spend some time concentrating on what's been going on right here. I should have started looking into it a long time ago."

"There's no need to cancel the trip and there's nothing to look into. I was all over the warehouse this morning with the insurance adjustor. Everything was in order."

"If you were all over, how come you didn't find the body?" West asked. "It must have been there."

It was a reasonable question and Maruri cursed himself for leading into the subject so carelessly. "We still don't know exactly when Rick was killed. And I assume the body was hidden," he added, defensively. "Until we know more about it, we're only guessing. So, why not let the police do their job and see how it develops before you change your plans."

"Maybe," West conceded, "but I still want to get into the warehouse and look around for myself. I'd be back there now if that damned fool of a policeman hadn't stopped me."

"It's a murder investigation. They said they'd be finished back there in a couple of hours."

"The temp was back there. I saw her."

"Martin, her name is Sara. And she's the one who showed them where to find the body. They probably wanted to walk her through it again."

"I know what her name is," West said, impatiently. "Sara Fisher. I also know that I don't want her around here anymore. Tell her not to come in tomorrow and, if Wendy ever shows up again, tell her she's fired. I want them both out of here."

"That's not a good idea," Maruri said, horrified at the thought of making any changes while the police were still around. "It might look as if we were trying to hide something, cover things up. And finding replacements in the middle of a murder investigation might be difficult. After all, we still have a business to run."

"Okay," West said, unable to deny the logic of Maruri's argument. "For the time being, we'll let things stay as they are."

"Good. It won't be for long. As soon as this is over, we'll make whatever changes are necessary."

West stood. "Now, I want to see what the police are up to. It's bad enough that they're keeping me out of the warehouse. They won't let me get out of the building either, not until they're finished looking around and asking questions."

"I wanted to talk to you about that. I thought we could let people go home, as soon as the police allow it. There isn't any work that's going to get done and, naturally, everyone is upset. Sheila," he added, "will stay to cover the front office and answer the phones. And, of course, I'll be here."

"Of course, and as usual, you've covered all the bases," West said, with a return to the easy charm that made people want to please him.

"I do my best," Maruri said, quietly, conscious of the shame which had been with him for so long, he barely noticed it anymore. In the beginning, he had convinced himself what he and Ed were doing wasn't really harming anyone, but he couldn't believe that any longer. He had betrayed Martin West and the knowledge stayed with him. He didn't think it would ever go away.

"Well, I'm going to insist that they let me go back into the warehouse. I want to see where they found the body."

"I have great faith in your powers of persuasion," Maruri said, with a faint smile. "But, I still don't think they'll let you do it."

West grinned. "The way I feel right now I'd like to see them stop me."

"By the way, I told them they could use Ken's office," Maruri called out, before West was out the door.

"The police? In Ken's office? What for?"

"They need a base of operations while they're still in the building and Ken doesn't spend much time in the office. He can use one of the desks in the accounting department while they're here. It won't kill him."

West shrugged. "Like I said, you're in charge."

Maruri watched him leave and wished he had just some of Martin's self-assurance. He, too, resented the restrictions put on him by the police. He was more anxious than Martin to go back into the warehouse. But he knew he would wait for permission. He would follow the instructions the police had given him and wouldn't make trouble. In the meantime, he would prepare as best he could to answer their questions.

But before they came for him, he needed to find out where Ed had gone to. He needed to know what the police had asked him and how he had answered. It was important they tell the same story.

Chapter 34

"**C**ome on in," Maruri said. "And we don't have to worry about being interrupted. Martin is gone for the day."

"That was quick." Ed Walsh closed the door and looked at his watch. "Did he say how the questioning went before he left?"

"He left before they questioned him."

"How did he pull that off?" Walsh asked with a mixture of envy and reluctant admiration.

"It started because he wanted have a look around the warehouse and you know how determined Martin can be when he wants something. I was in the front office when one of the police officers stopped him and explained that the forensic team hadn't finished investigating. The warehouse was still off-limits. To everybody."

"I'm sorry I missed it," Walsh said. "It isn't every day that somebody says no to Martin West.

"Martin had to back down, but when he was told that he couldn't leave the building without permission, he exploded.

"You can't force me to stay," he said. "If you won't let me into my own warehouse, I'm leaving."

"That was it? The cops stood back and let him walk out?"

Maruri nodded. "It was a wise decision. Better than a physical struggle with a chief executive who had no obvious connection with the victim. I'm sure the officer in charge was informed and, if he'd ordered it, they could have stopped Martin before he was out of the garage."

"You're probably right. Anyway, I'm glad he's gone."

"Who else have the detectives talked to?" Maruri asked. "Do you know?"

"While Martin was in here with you, they talked to Oliver Blakely and let him leave. It couldn't have taken long to figure out that he had nothing much to do with Rick and he wasn't in the building when Wendy's boyfriend showed up.

"Have they talked to anybody else? I know Gerry was in there."

"I kept an eye out," Walsh assured him. They spent a good bit of time with Gerry and Mark is in with them right now. I get the impression that they're mostly interested in the people who were around for the fight with the boyfriend."

"I was here but there's not much I can tell them. You know that. I was in my office the whole time. Didn't see or hear anything."

Walsh grunted. "Don't worry. I already made that clear to the detectives."

"Maybe that's why they're not in a hurry to talk to me," Maruri speculated. "What about your men out back".

"A couple of detectives went out to the loading dock to get their statements. It didn't take long. I let them all go and they won't be back until the police are out of the warehouse."

"On this side, work has to go on," Maruri said. "But, for today, everybody can leave as soon as the police are finished with them. Sheila will stay and answer the phones."

"What about the temp. Why is she still hanging around?"

"The police. They won't let her go yet."

"I'd like to see her out of here right now," Walsh said. "And for good."

"Martin agrees with you. He's also fed up with Wendy. Wanted me to fire her if she shows up here again or calls in. I had to talk him out of it."

"Why? It sounds like a damned good idea to me. Neither one had any business wandering around the warehouse."

"That's all we need," Maruri said, the anger he'd kept hidden while talking with Martin West, rising to the surface. "Let's start firing people. That would be smart, wouldn't it? What would the police think if employees start disappearing? Get it through your head that we must act as normal as possible. No changes until they're out of here. We don't want to do or say anything to raise suspicions."

"Okay," Walsh said. "Calm down. I get the picture."

"And we have more important things to worry about," Maruri said. "Martin wants to put off his trip to Japan so he can keep an eye on things here. He especially wants to check into the warehouse operations."

"Oh, my God," Walsh said. He seemed to collapse in on himself. "What's going to happen to us?"

Maruri watched him and swallowed hard. There was a question that had to be asked and there was no point in putting it off. "Before the police call me in, I need to know what happened here last night."

Walsh kept his head lowered. "What do you mean? I told you everything. Right now, you know as much about last night as I do."

"I don't know how Rick got back into the building. When Mark dropped him off there were no other cars in the garage. Just Rick's motorcycle. And I know the door to the loading dock was locked. I checked it myself before I left. If Rick didn't have a key, how did he get in?"

"Alright. Rick did have a key," Walsh said, speaking so softly Maruri could barely hear him. "He had keys...to all the doors."

"I see," Maruri said. "You gave him the keys after we made a decision not to do it. After I made clear my opposition. After you knew how strongly I felt that he shouldn't be trusted with them."

"That's why I never told you. Because I knew you would never agree. But he said he needed them and I couldn't see the harm in it. He was being cooperative back then. Helping us out. You know how good he was, in the beginning."

Maruri wasn't surprised. This had been his suspicion all along. But it was too late for recriminations. He had to think clearly. Maybe this key business could be turned to their advantage. If Rick had a key, he wouldn't have needed anyone from the company to let him in and a case could more easily be made for an outsider. He leaned forward.

"What did you tell the police?"

"That Rick needed the keys because he often assisted me by coming in early or staying late."

"That sounds good," Maruri said. "What else?"

"Nothing," Walsh exclaimed. "Except...of course, I told them about Wendy's boyfriend showing up and the scene he made with Rick."

Maruri nodded. "Very good," he said. "There was a fight with Wendy's boyfriend and Rick could get into the warehouse on his own. He could have let Wendy's boyfriend back in or it could have been someone we've never heard of. There are all kinds of ways Rick could have been killed that have nothing to do with us or our business. It all begins to make sense."

Walsh looked like a man who had been pulled back from the edge of a precipice. "Do you really think so? Do you really think the police will believe it could have happened that way?"

"Why not," Maruri said. "That's probably the way it did happen and I think this could be over with very quickly."

"Before anybody has a chance to ask too many questions," Walsh added, reinforcing the spoken hope with a silent prayer. He smiled. "And with Rick out of the way...our troubles are over."

"That's right," Maruri said. "That's exactly right."

CHAPTER 35

Ed Walsh left Haru Maruri's office buoyed by a surge of optimism. His head was held higher. His barrel chest had expanded, not unlike a balloon getting a helium fix. The Rick who had deceived him was dead and, if Harry was right, and the police started to look for the killer outside the company, his murder could turn out to be a blessing.

Untroubled by the sacrilegious thought, he smiled benignly on Gerry Fineman. If he had looked back at the man he'd left behind, some of his newly aroused self-assurance might have seeped away. Maruri did not look like a man who had gained confidence from their encounter. On the contrary, he seemed somewhat diminished, the energy sucked out of him. He looked like what he was, a man who, in the depth of his aloneness, had no other human being to turn to for support. If Haru Maruri was hopeful for a positive outcome, it didn't show.

⋏

Resisting Ed Walsh's anxieties had taken a lot of effort, more effort than Maruri could afford. He needed every ounce of strength to fight his own anxieties, to avoid falling into the pit of depression that yawned ever closer. He needed to decide if the time had come to put his wife and children on a plane to Japan. He needed to prepare for questions from the police. He needed to keep himself strong until all this was over, until the police went away, until he was safe, although he couldn't imagine ever feeling safe again. He fought to believe that the outcome he'd predicted to Ed would come true, that the police would look outside the company and never uncover Rick's link to the two of them. But he wasn't nearly as sanguine as he'd allowed himself to appear.

He forced himself to concentrate. He leaned forward, his elbows on the desk, his forehead supported by his hands and tried to think about what was ahead of him in the police interview. What questions would they ask? How should he answer? Had anyone said anything to raise suspicions about the relationship between Rick and Ed and himself? Startled by a knock on the door he raised his head to find that Mark Cranston stood in the doorway. For a painful moment, he found himself embarrassed, unable to speak, as if he'd been discovered in some shameful act.

"The police are finished with me and with Gerry too," Mark said, confused by the awkward silence.

Maruri cleared his throat and gestured to the chair by his desk. "Come in," he said. He reached again for the little roll of antacid tablets. His mouth was dry and he wished he had some water. "Did everything go alright?"

"Fine," Mark replied. "It went fine," he added to fill what was becoming another uncomfortable silence.

Maruri fumbled as he worked at extracting a tablet from the packet. He was trying to find the right words. He wanted to find out what questions the police had put to Mark and, more to the point, what the answers had been, but he wasn't sure how to do it without appearing to show too great an interest.

"The police didn't give you a hard time...or anything like that?"

Mark shrugged. "It wasn't bad."

"That's good, very good," Maruri said. "I don't want them badgering anybody. After all, there's not much you could tell them, is there?"

"They just wanted to know about how Rick got along with everybody."

"What did you say?"

"That as far as I know he got along with everybody fine."

"Of course, of course. After all, the people in the front office don't mix much with the people in the warehouse."

"Right," Mark said.

"Anything else they wanted to know?"

"They asked about what happened last night," he replied. "You know, about Wendy's boyfriend showing up."

Mark paused, unwilling to go any further. The detectives hadn't asked much about his relationship with Rick and they seemed satisfied with the lies he told them, but he was afraid of how quickly that could change. He was, after all, the last person known to have seen Rick before he died and he didn't want to talk about it or be forced to give explanations to Mr. Maruri who might be more curious than the police.

"Well, I guess that's it," Maruri said. Except...would you happen to know who the detectives are questioning now."

"Sheila was called in after I left," he replied.

"Well then, if the police are finished with you there's no reason why you can't go home."

"And Gerry?"

"Of course. I don't know why she is still here. I told her she could leave after the police questioned her. I appreciate her good intentions but, with what's happening around here, there's no point in trying to get any work done today. If the police say it's alright, you can both go."

Mark nodded and, still feeling awkward, left Maruri's office.

⅄

Once outside he tried to relax but found that the silence in the front offices made him uneasy. It was too quiet. Even the phones had stopped ringing, as if some subliminal message had gone out telling people to keep their distance. He turned, glanced through the glass panel of Maruri's office and saw that the man was once again in deep thought, his forehead supported by his hands.

What a strange interview that had been. Mr. Maruri had seemed so uncomfortable. What was he so nervous about? He wasn't the one that needed to worry. He hadn't had any arguments with Rick--and he hadn't been dumb enough to go out for a drink with him either.

And why had he questioned that Gerry was still there? Of course, on a day like today, Gerry would be waiting for him. They never tried to hide that they had become close friends. People even believed they were a couple. It was natural for them to wait for each other. Mark shrugged. It didn't matter. She was ready to leave and so was he.

"Let's go," he said and looked back once more, ready to wave if Maruri saw him, but relieved that the man was still looking down, absorbed in his own thoughts.

⋏

Mark had no idea how far he and Gerry Fineman were from those thoughts. The two of them had floated out of his consciousness and were completely gone with the sound of the door closing. More pressing was the ongoing pain in his gut. The antacid tablets were no longer helping, but he reached for another one anyway before dropping his head back onto his hands. He had returned to the position he'd been in when Mark entered the office, gone back to the rehearsal in his head. "I hardly knew him," he prepared himself to tell the detectives.

And it was true. Ed was the one who had dealt with Rick and who had claimed to understand him. Of course, he wouldn't share that with the police nor would he confess that he'd never had faith in Ed's assessment of Rick's character. It was against all his better instincts that he'd allowed himself to be pressured by Ed. From the beginning, he'd been afraid that Rick meant trouble. But, with all his doubts and reservations, he could never have imagined it would end like this.

CHAPTER 36

Training for the Homicide Division had taught Michael Roarke to hide his feelings and his face gave nothing away as he sat at Ken Ichiwara's desk, questioning Sheila and listening carefully to her replies.

"You said Mr. Rudner arrived at around five o'clock?" he confirmed, while Detective Spivak, the more junior of the two, sat in a corner of the office trying to be unobtrusive as he noted the question and prepared to write down the response.

Sheila nodded vigorously, blond curls in motion. "I was clearing my desk getting ready to leave, when he barged in through the front door. It must have been very close to five."

Roarke's initial appraisal of her was proving correct. A pretty girl, eager to cooperate who, instead of being nervous, as most people are when being interviewed by the police, appeared to be enjoying herself. He wasn't at all put off by her partiality for gossip. On the contrary, it could be useful to get at relationships and antagonisms within the company more quickly. If he was careful to sift reality from the swamp of speculation.

"Did you happen to notice what time Mr. Rudner left?" he asked.

Sheila nodded again, pleased to provide another tidbit of information. "I walked out right after he did and I looked at my watch." She held up her left wrist to display the gift she'd received upon graduating from high school. "It was only ten minutes after five," she said. "I remember because it seemed like so much had happened and such a little bit of time had gone by."

"And you saw him again when you drove out of the building?"

"I did. He was sitting in his car. You can't miss it. It's a red Thunderbird and it wasn't in the garage. It was parked on the street. Right in front of the building. I remember thinking how strange it was. I mean--" Sheila lowered her voice before asking the question. "What he was waiting for?"

She shifted in the chair so she could have both policemen in her line of vision, trying to decide which of the two was more attractive. Either could fit the description of the ideal man that she had carried in her mind since she was a child. Detective Rourke was older, slimmer, with dark hair and a wedding band on his left hand. The fair haired Spivak was taller, his shoulders broader and his fingers unadorned. The sort of men her mother would call "the strong silent type." Sheila looked from one to the other and decided that, in any fair-minded contest, it was the younger man...the one without the ring...who would have the advantage.

"You're sure Mr. Rudner was still in front of the building when you drove out?" Roarke asked, carefully. He didn't want to be accused of having put words into anybody's mouth.

"I told you what I saw," Sheila said, indignantly. "He was sitting in his car. After the way he came busting in here, I was paying attention. And I'll tell you something else. From the first minute I saw him, I knew something terrible was going to happen. I could feel it."

"I understand, but did you actually hear him make any threats?"

"Not exactly. But I could see what he was thinking," she insisted. "I could tell what was on his mind just by looking at him. He didn't believe the story Wendy had told him anymore than the rest of us did. And I don't blame him. The only thing is, he should have figured out what was going on a long time ago. The rest of us sure did." She lowered her voice again, not wanting to speak the shocking words too loudly. "We all knew that she was having an affair with Rick."

"But, you didn't hear Mr. Rudner make any accusations or threats?"

"I didn't have to," Sheila said. "It was obvious that he was capable of anything. That's why we were all so scared. And you don't have to take my word for it. Gerry and Mark were there. They must have told you. What did they say?"

The detective ignored her question. Their stories all matched, but it was Sheila's vivid description that brought the events of the day before into clear focus. He was feeling optimistic. The way things were going, there was a good chance they would be able to make an arrest within twenty-four hours.

"Thank you for your cooperation," Roarke said, allowing a degree of warmth to creep into his voice. "And you're free to leave whenever you like."

"I'll be here until five o'clock." She glanced at the man taking notes, hoping to see a sign of interest. "Somebody has to answer the phones and I don't mind. But I'm sure Sara would like to go home. She's only a temp and I don't need her hanging around. Do you want me to tell her?"

"That's not necessary," Roarke said. "We'll take care of that when we're ready."

"Well, I supposed you might have more questions for her. She did leave with Wendy last night and she is the one who found the body."

"We'll let Miss Fisher know when she can go," he told her. He didn't think it necessary to explain that there was still a question as to who, exactly, had found the body.

Sheila stood and once again glanced over at the detective who had closed his notebook. "Well...if you think of any more questions for me, I'll be in the front office."

Roarke thanked her again and waited for the door to close before speaking.

"It looks like we'll wrap this one up pretty fast," he said. But before head out to Hanson's apartment, let's have the temp in again. I still can't see how she fits into all of this, but wherever I look Sara Fisher is in the picture. She claims she hardly knows the prime suspect's girlfriend but Wendy Solomon spent the night with her and disappeared after pointing her to Rick Hanson's body. She's the one who makes the phone call to the police and the one who, coincidentally, finds traces of blood in the ladies' room earlier in the day and cleans them up without, by the way, mentioning it to anyone else.

"She must know more than she's told us," Spivak said. "And how come she missed spotting the weapon? I know it was buried under paper towels in the trash bin when our guys found it, but were all those paper towels there before she cleaned up?"

Roarke went back to Ken Ichiwara's desk and took a crowbar from the top drawer. It was one of several used in the warehouse, exactly like the murder weapon that was now at the forensics lab where it was being scanned for the fingerprints of which it had, most certainly, been wiped clean. He laid it on top of the desk where anyone coming into the office couldn't miss seeing it.

"Okay. Let's get her back in and see what she has to say about this," he said.

CHAPTER 37

"This has to blow over fast," Mark said. "Really fast. I don't think I can handle talking to the police again."

He and Gerry Fineman sat in the same luncheonette Ed Walsh and Haru Maruri had eaten at a few hours earlier. They were, however, at a different table. The one Mark had chosen was in a dimly lit corner near where the counter ended, as far away from daylight and the window as he could get.

"This is depressing," Gerry, objected. "Can't we sit over there, where it isn't so dark?"

Mark, who had taken the seat facing the wall, turned to get her perspective. The only other customers were a grizzled old man, sitting at the counter, and two old women who sat in one of the booths Gerry was suggesting they move to.

"This is okay," he said. "It fits the way I feel."

"I don't know what you're so worried about," Gerry declared. "The police are concentrating on Bert. I could tell. They asked you about him too, didn't they?"

Mark nodded.

"You see? They're not interested in you. When they questioned me, they didn't even mention your name. Mostly it was about Bert and Rick. About their argument."

"But I came into it. You told them that Rick left with me."

"Of course I told them! Did you want me to lie? I wasn't the only one who saw the two of you leave together. Try to relax. They don't know anything about what happened between you and Rick and I don't see how they'll find out. You know I won't say anything."

"He's dead," Mark said. "I'll never see him again."

Gerry sighed. She knew too well that people didn't always give their love to those who deserved it. "I'm sorry," she said, reaching across the table to pat his arm. "I know it's hard."

"The whole thing feels like a bad dream and I can't wake up."

"You've got to keep control of yourself. You don't want people to see you being nervous or scared."

Mark nodded. "I know, but I keep thinking of him being back there in the cold dark warehouse all by himself."

It would have been unkind for Gerry to point out that Rick hadn't ended up by himself. He had chosen someone other than Mark to be with and, most probably, when that person left, Rick was dead. Never again to be troubled by a need for heat, light or companionship. It would be better to turn Mark's attention to a less morbid direction.

"Are you sure you didn't see anybody hanging around the building last night, when you dropped him off?" she asked.

"I told you. There were no cars in the garage and there weren't any in front of the building. I would have noticed."

"And you didn't go back into the building with him?" she asked, tentatively. "You know you can tell me about it if you did."

He drew back from her. "You don't believe me."

"Of course I believe you. I just thought you might have gone in and didn't want to tell me. I would understand."

"I didn't go in with him. He was standing near his motorcycle when I drove out. The truth is, he brushed me off." Mark hadn't meant to tell her how Rick had humiliated him but the words came rushing out.

"While we were in the bar he kept acting like he wanted to be with me and then, when we got back to the building, he treated me like I was dirt and he wanted to get rid of me. Like maybe he was expecting somebody else to show up and he didn't want me hanging around. I don't know what happened after I left."

"I'm sorry," Gerry said. "I always told you not to trust him, but I didn't think he was that bad."

"You don't know," Mark said. "I didn't tell you the worst thing."

Gerry waited, curiosity at war with the fear of finding out what terrible thing Mark was going to tell her, something so terrible it might give him a motive for murder.

"I gave him twenty dollars."

Gerry looked relieved and puzzled. "So you gave him twenty dollars. What for?"

Mark looked away. "He said it was a loan, but I don't think he meant to pay it back."

"You mean it was like a business deal. If you gave him money...then he would--"

Mark nodded. "That's what he acted like. If I gave him money then we could be together."

"You should have waited till afterwards to give him the money," Gerry said, in a practical tone of voice. "That's what you did the last time."

"The only time," he said, sadly. "That time we didn't go for a drink and he didn't ask to borrow the money until...you know... it was over...and we were on our way out of the building." Tears filled his eyes, remembering how happy he had been that night. "It was wonderful being back there with Rick, in that little room."

"The important thing is that nobody else knows about you and Rick," Gerry said. "And I won't tell. So you have nothing to worry about."

"They'll suspect," he told her. "I think they're suspicious already. They recognized the name of the bar we went to. I could tell."

For the first time, Gerry looked worried. "Just don't tell them anything you don't have to," she said. "Answer their questions but don't volunteer anything. Okay?"

"Okay," he said, "but there is something more about Rick that I could tell them. It might be important."

"Is it something about sex?" she asked, her face turning bright red. "I don't think I want to hear about it."

"No. Nothing like that...that I know of. I think he had ways for making extra money on the side. Like selling drugs. Marijuana."

"Wow," Gerry exclaimed. "That changes the whole picture. If he was mixed up with those kinds of people...with dope dealers…criminals…maybe the police won't be looking at anybody from West Electronics."

"You think I should tell them?"

"No! Like I said, don't volunteer anything. Don't say anything drugs unless they start suspecting you. If that's what he was doing, they'll find out on their own and leave you alone."

"I hope you're right," he said. "But you can't say anything either. Especially about me and Rick. And it isn't just the police," he reminded her. "You won't say anything to anybody, will you?"

"Of course not," she assured him. "Don't worry about me."

He smiled weakly. He believed her, but sometimes, secrets slipped out. If only Rick Hanson had never come into his life. If only he had never set eyes on the man.

Chapter 38

West Electronics might be a small company today, but Oliver Blakely's wife had no doubts about its future. It was on the way to becoming an important player in its field and she was pleased that her husband, Vice President of Sales and Marketing had, with her encouragement, hitched his wagon to that particular star. It was, as she had told him, cheerfully scrambling her metaphors, a gamble worth taking.

She was a tall woman, large-boned and lean. Her brown hair, bleached blond by the sun, was cut short in a look easier to care for than it was stylish and she took care of her home and children with a no-nonsense combination of grace and efficiency that was the envy of her friends. She also prided herself on being impervious to shock.

"It's almost impossible to get a rise out of her," her husband often bragged. His efforts to do so and her efforts to resist had become a good-natured game between them. Today, he thought, he was going to succeed.

"I don't believe it," she exclaimed.

The surprise of having him come home from the office in the middle of the afternoon hadn't been enough to stop her from chopping the vegetables she was preparing for a stew. Now, however, as her hands rested on the chopping block, she searched her husband's face for some sign he had made up the story.

"Are you really saying that the little rat is dead?"

Blakely grinned and grabbed some slices of raw carrot. "That's right," he said. "Somebody killed him."

"Tell me about it." Her strong and capable hands, tan from hours spent on the golf course, took up the knife and went back to work while she listened.

"I don't know much," he admitted and went on to tell her what little he had gathered from questions the police had asked and from his secretary. Sheila had been eager to tell him what she knew and what she surmised.

"So it's not going to be one of those open and shut cases," Marilyn Blakely said.

He shrugged. "Sheila seems ready to pin it on Wendy's boyfriend and that makes sense to me."

"Don't be silly," his wife said. "People like that, ordinary people, don't go around murdering each other."

"Maybe not. But somebody did it. Who would you suggest?"

"I'd start with the little rat's gambling friends. It's the most obvious place to look, don't you think? You did tell the police that he had placed some bets for you and that he threatened you with blackmail?"

Blakely frowned. "Of course not," he exclaimed. "What would I do a silly thing like that for? Why get involved when I don't have to?"

"Civic responsibility," was her firm reply.

Oliver Blakeley's occasional wagers on a horse race or a ball-game were not something he kept hidden from his wife. His bets were small and it would no more have occurred to her to object than it would have occurred to him to keep it a secret. That was why Rick's attempt to extort money had seemed so ridiculous and why he hadn't hesitated to tell Marilyn about it. Telling the police was something else. Although he considered this to be an altogether harmless vice, he didn't see any reason to share it with them. It was doubtful that Rick kept records of such petty transactions so why raise the subject. But the police might take a less benign view of the matter and might even take it into their heads that his having used Rick to place illegal bets made him a suspect.

"We're talking about murder," he said. "It doesn't make sense to get involved in something like that without thinking it through very carefully."

Marilyn Blakely transferred the chopped vegetables into a large stew pot then, using her apron to dry her hands, turned back to her husband. "I'm not trying to tell you what to do," she said. "But, since you had nothing to do with this man's death, you have nothing to be afraid of. They aren't going to hassle a man in your position over such a minor matter and I think it's your duty to give the police any information that will make their job easier."

"I'm going to have a drink," he said, going to the refrigerator for ice cubes trays that he emptied into a handsome chrome bucket. He glanced back at his wife. He loved and respected her but this was one of the times when he wondered what it would be like to be married to a woman who held less rigorous standards.

"Will you join me?" he asked.

"Yes," she said. It was time to change the subject. "Scotch. I'm not ready for a martini. We can take them into the living room. I'm finished in here, for the moment."

She took off her apron and followed him out of the kitchen. Seated in a comfortable armchair by a bay window, overlooking a perfectly manicured lawn, one of the many in their cul-de-sac, she watched as her husband poured the drinks. An enjoyable ritual for them both. As for telling the police about the piddling bets he'd placed through Rick's bookie connections, it was a minor infraction and she had confidence he would do the right thing. Sometimes, of course, he needed to have it pointed out to him but, that done, he had never yet let her down.

She sipped her drink and listened to the gentle rattle of the ice cubes in her glass. There was a more pressing reason to be forthcoming with the police, one having to do with self-interest. It was possible, even probable, that Rick had mentioned his gambling sideline to others. If so, he might have mentioned Ollie's name as well. Or, he might have kept a written record of the people he placed bets for. In that event, it would certainly be better for the police to hear about it from Ollie than in some other way. She would mention this to him, but not right now. Right now, he was relaxing and she would allow him to enjoy his drink.

Chapter 39

Sheila had forgotten about Ken Ichiwara. Her head had been too full of theories about Rick's murder to be thinking about somebody who wasn't even there. Now he was calling to find out if there were any messages for him. What to say?

She put him on hold and called Detective Roarke.

"Remind me," he said. "Where is Mr. Ichiwara?"

"Santa Barbara. On a sales trip. Shall I connect you?"

"Not necessary. Tell him we'd like him to be back in Los Angeles tomorrow."

"Can I tell him what's happened? About Rick?"

"Sure," he said. "If you don't tell him, he'll call somebody else who will."

He replaced the receiver, and went back to questioning Sara Fisher, trying again to find out where she fit into this puzzle and how much of her story could be believed.

A

"You have to come back to Los Angeles," Sheila told Ichiwara, pleased to be the conduit for the policeman's message. Being involved in a murder was the most exciting thing that had ever happened to her and she enjoyed explaining why he was being summoned back to the office with as much alarming detail as she could provide.

"Detective Roarke will want to see you first thing in the morning," she added, although he hadn't said anything of the sort. But she was sure that's what he expected and there was no harm in using her own initiative to let Ken Ichiwara know the seriousness of what was going on here at the office.

"I'll be there," Ichiwara said.

"Shall I cancel the rest of your appointments in Bakersfield and Fresno?" she asked.

There was no reply. Ken Ichiwara had already hung up the phone. He remained motionless, his hand still on the receiver.

⋏

"Ken? Is anything wrong?" Mel Bernstein asked. He was the electronics buyer for a small group of California stores head-quartered in Bakersfield. While Ken called West Electronics to check for messages he had gone to tell his secretary that he and Ichiwara would be going out to visit one of the stores.

Ichiwara ran his tongue over his lips and realized his mouth was dry. "Just some problems back at the office," he said. "Nothing to worry about."

"Are you sure? It was obvious to him that Ichiwara had experienced a shock and he was concerned. He always looked forward to being called on by this salesman and couldn't remember ever seeing him look worried or distressed over anything. Something must be very wrong. "Is there anything I can do to help?" he offered.

"Hey, I appreciate that," Ichiwara said, trying to laugh and failing. He wished he hadn't made the phone call from Mel's office and now he wanted to get away. He needed to think.

"It's nothing to do with me," he said. "There's been an accident...one of the people in the warehouse...and they want me to drive right back."

Bernstein didn't believe it was that simple and he hoped his friend wasn't in any trouble. He was also disappointed. The story he had told his secretary, about going to check the West Electronics display at one of the stores, was an excuse for leaving the office early and going out to have a few drinks, the usual routine that went along with a sales call from Ken Ichiwara.

"I am sorry," Ichiwara said, trying to pull himself together. "I'll make up for it next time I come through."

"Nothing to worry about," Bernstein said. "And don't forget. If I can be of help--"

Ichiwara made his way from the buyer's office to the solitude of the men's restroom where he pulled a small amber-colored glass vial filled with white powder from his pocket; the cocaine he had so foolishly driven back to Los Angeles for on the night before, anxious to have it for a new girlfriend. A redheaded stripper in Bakersfield. He unscrewed the top, and using a small silver spoon, drew a generous amount into each nostril. If ever he needed it, he needed it now.

CHAPTER 40

Sara held on to the railing at the top of the steps, grateful for the cool breeze and the soft afternoon sunshine. At last she was free from Ken Ichiwara's cramped and windowless office where it had felt as if the police interrogations would never be over. By the time Detective Roarke told her she could leave, she'd almost given up hope.

Getting away, however, might take longer than she'd expected. The echoes of all she'd been through during this long and painful day still reverberated. When she got into her car, she was trembling, having difficulty with the simple act of fitting the key into the ignition. It wasn't just her hands that seemed to belong to somebody else. Her entire body was shaking, as if in the grip of a fever.

She let the keys drop into her lap and sat very still, forcing herself to take deep breaths, willing herself to be calm. It was no use. She would have to wait until she felt better. She laid her arms on the steering wheel, lowered her head and surrendered herself to the inevitable regrets.

She wanted to put all the blame on Wendy but, even now, in all her anger and frustration, she had to admit she had contributed her own share to the mess she found herself in. There had been choices. She could have gone to lunch with the others or taken a solitary walk around the neighborhood. She could have gone out to eat by herself. Instead, she'd chosen to stay in the office alone with Wendy.

Even after that, there could still have been a way out. It was the next decision that made escape impossible. But had there really been a choice? Wendy was terrified, stammering out an incredible story about finding Rick dead in some secret hiding place. How could she refuse to go back and look? It was the only way to get Wendy to calm down and to prove to her that she was mistaken. And if Sara was sure of anything it was that Wendy, in her anxiety to find Rick, had imagined the whole thing.

How could she have been so blindly sure of herself? Why had she been so adamantly insistent that Wendy was mistaken? More to the point, why did she have to interfere? Even if she didn't believe Wendy she could have called the police and asked them to check it out. The decision to go into the warehouse had been hers.

Sara lifted her head from the steering wheel. The trembling was still with her but much less. She reached for the keys in her lap and this time succeeded in starting the car. Concentrating, as if she were learning to drive all over again, she put her hand on the gear shift lever and considered the rear-view mirror. She wasn't alone. A uniformed police officer was back there, by the warehouse entrance, standing where Rick had been just the day before. He was watching her, spying, like a peeping tom.

Furious, she wanted to call out and ask what he was doing there. Did the police believe she could be a murderer? Did they think she was planning some criminal act in the garage? Her car had already been searched, so they couldn't believe she was a radical hiding a bomb in the trunk. She felt violated by his presence and wasn't going to make a move until he looked away. When, finally, he averted his eyes, she was pleased to find the trembling had stopped.

Even though she had answered their questions completely and honestly, the police were still treating her like a criminal. When they'd asked for her car keys, she'd handed them over without a murmur of protest although they had no reason to suspect her of anything. She could have insisted they get a search warrant, but she'd been trying to cooperate. That was over. She had allowed them to intimidate her for the last time.

They had been skeptical of every word that came out of her mouth. While the first round of questioning was difficult, the second was even worse. They started off by showing her a crowbar--like the weapon used to kill Rick. They told her that the actual weapon, the one used by the killer, was discovered in the ladies' room, buried under dirty paper towels in the trash bin. That she hadn't found it when she was cleaning up seemed to amaze them.

"Of course I didn't see it," she'd answered to their repeated questions. "I would have told you if I'd seen it. I would have told Mr. Maruri or somebody else in the office that there was a bloody crowbar in the trash if I had seen it."

Finally, after several more rounds of questions covering the same ground as earlier in the day, they gave up and granted her permission to leave. It was over. After informing Mr. Maruri that she wasn't coming back, she would put West Electronics behind her. If the police wanted to question her again they could damned well come to her.

"The police have given me permission to leave," she told him. "And I won't be coming back. I tried to tell you earlier but--"

She should have been better armed to face his objections, but she was exhausted and he was convincing. She could understand how upsetting it would be to have someone new come in during a police investigation. And he was the only person at West Electronics who had shown her any consideration. How could she not sympathize? In the end, found herself agreeing to stay on until the end of the week.

CHAPTER 41

There were noises in the background. Haru Maruri could hear people talking, laughing and music sounding like it came from a jukebox. Ed, with no wife or family to go home to, must have taken refuge in a bar, perhaps one in his San Fernando Valley neighborhood. In a way, Maruri envied him. Since the discovery of Rick's body, he could no longer take comfort in going home to his wife and children, from whom all his insecurities must be hidden. Tonight, he would rather be like Ed, on his own.

"Have they finished with you?" Ed Walsh asked. The renewed self-confidence with which he had left the offices of West Electronics was gone. It had evaporated in just the short time it took to cross the Cahuenga Pass from Hollywood into the Valley. Anxiety was back.

"How did it go with the police? "What did they ask about?"

"It was easier than I expected," Maruri said. "Mostly, it was questions about problems Rick might have had with people at work. If he had any enemies. Of course, I denied knowledge of anything like that. Otherwise, they seemed focused on what went on last night, between Rick and Wendy's boyfriend."

"That's good. Very good. Did they say you could leave? Are you going home?" There was an unusual note of loneliness in his voice. He was, as Maruri had assumed, in a bar not far from where he lived, an unpretentious watering hole, where he spoke from the wallphone in a dimly lit corridor, next to the men's toilet.

"I can leave whenever I want to," Maruri said. "But somebody has to stay until the police finish up for the night. Somebody has to be here to keep an eye on things and lock up."

Walsh knew he should have stayed in the office even though Harry had told him it was alright to go, even though Harry had said he didn't mind being there on his own. But the need to get away from the warehouse and the office and the police and from Harry as well, had been overwhelming. He couldn't explain it and even if he'd been able to find the words, he wouldn't have admitted his weakness.

"Who else, beside the police, is still there?" he asked.

"Just Sheila. She volunteered to stay and answer the phones. I didn't have to ask."

"At least one of the girls is reliable," Walsh said.

"Yes, and I should be grateful, but I wish she wasn't enjoying herself so much."

Walsh barely heard him. There had been only one reason for calling the office and now that he knew how Harry's interview with the police had gone he had run out of things to say. He felt as if he was suffocating in that narrow corridor.

"I have to go," he said. "There's somebody waiting to use the phone. But I'll be back in my place soon. You can reach me there if you need me or if anything changes."

 ⋏

In the front office, Sheila saw the light for the call go out and wondered what they had been talking about. She had been surprised to see Mr. Walsh leave so early. She would have expected him to wait around to see if there were any developments. After all, Rick had worked for him and had been killed back in the warehouse, the area that was his responsibility. It wasn't right for him to run off like that. What must the police think?

She turned her attention to her shorthand notebook, ready to go back to her job while the police went about theirs. She assumed that the two detectives in Ken Ichiwara's office had finished their interviews for the day and must be discussing what they had learned and what their next steps would be. Meanwhile, in the warehouse, she could imagine the forensic team continuing their search for any trace of evidence the killer might have left behind.

She shuddered to think of what had happened to Rick and was glad that an officer was still on duty in the front office, ready to make sure the team in the warehouse was not disturbed and to keep an eye out for suspicious activity. She didn't think she'd feel safe if he wasn't here. Mostly, he stationed himself by the windows or the front door with occasional forays into the accounting department where he would glance through the glass panel into Haru Maruri's office before returning to his post.

He was nicer than the original police officer, the one who'd been there when she'd come back from lunch, and she'd offered to get him a cup of coffee which he'd accepted, expressing gratitude. She did not, however, attempted to engage him in conversation. The knowledge of all the police activity going on around her was enough to provide a warm feeling of belonging and there was plenty to keep her busy. There was always work to catch up with for Mr. Blakely.

She was in the middle of transcribing a letter to an important chain store buyer, when the phone call came. It was him. She recognized the voice immediately.

"I want to speak to Wendy," Bert Rudner said.

"Hold on a minute," Sheila said, breathless with excitement. "Don't go away."

"Is she there?"

"Hold on. I'm going to look for her."

⋏

Bert Rudner's apprehensions were multiplying. Sheila didn't sound like herself. Maybe it had been a mistake to call. Maybe he should have followed Wendy's instructions. Maybe he should hang up.

He couldn't think clearly. The night before had been sleepless which hadn't made this morning's meeting with a difficult client any easier, especially since it was followed by an alcohol-fueled expense-account lunch that had left him with a throbbing pain over his left eye. And, when he called his secretary to ask for messages, her response made the headache worse.

There had been curiosity in her voice when she'd told him a policeman called several times but declined to leave a message. Had something happened to Wendy or to Mikey? But Wendy had also called and her instructions were very clear.

"I'll call you later," she'd said. "In the meantime do not try to reach me at the office."

"She was very emphatic about that," his secretary added. "You're not to call her at work."

He probably should have paid more attention but had convinced himself that Wendy was being melodramatic. What harm could there be in making a phone call? He needed to find out what was happening.

"What's going on there?" he demanded.

But he was still on hold.

"Bert Rudner is on the phone," Sheila told Detective Roarke. "Wendy's boyfriend. I told him to hold on because I thought you'd want to talk to him."

"Does he know about Rick Hanson?" Roarke asked.

"I don't think so and I didn't tell him. I didn't even tell him that Wendy isn't here. I just asked him to hold while I looked for her."

"Very good," Roarke said. "Put him on this line."

It was too late. A few moments later, Sheila had to admit that she couldn't deliver her quarry. Bert had hung up.

"It's not your fault," Roarke assured her. "Did he leave a number where he can be reached?"

"No. But he works for his father's public relations company and the name of the company has "Rudner" in it. Would you like me to try looking it up in the phone book?"

"That's an excellent suggestion," Roarke said. "But, we'll take care of it."

Disappointed that she wasn't allowed to help, Sheila took pity on the young policeman, who could have no idea about what was going on. She explained a little about Wendy and about Bert Rudner and who he was, but resisted the temptation to go any further. She didn't tell him that she was sure Bert was the one who killed Rick, and that she believed the homicide detectives, if they had not yet arrived at the same conclusion, were well on their way to getting there.

"Would you like more coffee?" she said. "I can make a fresh pot."

CHAPTER 42

Sara was finally on her way home, ready to soak in a hot tub and wash away the images of what she'd seen that day. She wanted to get rid of the clothes she was wearing, rip them off and throw them away, although the police had insisted she hold on to the blood-stained dress. She wanted to forget the people at West and the way they'd treated her--like an enemy from a foreign camp.

The home she was heading to, the one Wendy Solomon had looked upon with so much contempt, had no swimming pool or garage. It was also, by Los Angeles standards, old. Her apartment, however, was spacious, gracious and comfortable while the rent was easily affordable even given her erratic income.

The building dated back to the early nineteen-thirties and for Sara it was a glamourous place to live. The roof was covered by warm orange colored tiles, each apartment had a heavy wooden balcony and the entry way courtyard was sheltered from view, in the Mexican colonial style. It was easy to imagine secret love affairs taking place behind the pink stucco exterior while the street outside gave off an odor of quiet respectability.

This was very different from the crowded, rowdy neighborhood in the Bronx where she had grown up or the street in Greenwich Village where she'd lived before coming to Los Angeles. She still missed those places, the excitement and wonderful mix of people in New York. She continued to insist that she would return there sooner rather than later but those feelings did not stop her from taking pleasure in her current home. She liked living here and it was with a sigh of relief that she pulled into one of the parking spaces directly in front of her building.

Still wary of the police and their suspicions, she checked the street in both directions before getting out of the car, reassuring herself that she hadn't been followed. She would be able to relax completely if only she could forget the commitment she'd made to Mr. Maruri. He'd been so convincing, explaining the problems he would face trying to replace her in the middle of a murder investigation, that she'd agreed to return on the next day, even though the thought of it made her stomach turn.

She would have to face it all again: the police with their suspicions; Sheila with her resentment; Martin West with his supercilious attitude. It was enough to make a person sick. She paused before locking the car door. That was it. In the morning, she could call in and say she was sick. It was almost true. And Mr. Maruri couldn't argue with sickness. She felt better immediately. Tomorrow morning, if she decided to go back, it would be her choice. And maybe it wouldn't be so bad.

Maybe she would find out what Sheila told the police. She will have had to confirm that Sara told the truth about staying behind with Wendy when the rest of them went out to lunch. She will also have given them her version of how Wendy went home with Sara on the night before, with as much lurid conjecture as possible. But about the murder. What could she possibly know about Rick's murder?

Did Sheila know about Wendy's relationship with Rick? Did everybody in the office know? Or, was it a secret, as Wendy believed? The flicker of interest that had been there from the beginning could no longer be ignored. Maybe, when she'd agreed to go back to West Electronics, it had been more than a simple humanitarian desire to help Mr. Maruri. Maybe it was morbid curiosity and a congenital inability to stay out of other people's business.

She would sort it out later. At the moment, all she was prepared to deal with was a nice bath and a quiet evening at home, both of which were within reach. The tension drained away as she walked into the narrow courtyard on the other side of a pink stucco archway. She was more than usually aware of it was the stillness in here, a stillness to which she'd become so accustomed she hardly appreciated it anymore.

To her right was a narrow verge of grass and a thick hedge that separated the enclave from the cottage next door. On the left, along the length of the building was a wider stretch of grass with flowering bushes and palm trees that seemed to lean against the pink stucco walls. It all worked together to create a feeling of privacy, heightened by there being only eight apartments in the two-story building, four in the front section and four in the rear, each with its own arched entryway.

She walked up three steps into the hallway of the front part of the building and paused in front of a row of mailboxes. Her senses seemed to be especially acute. She heard birds chattering as they flew back and forth between the palm trees to the hedge and felt comforted by the sounds. From upstairs, there was the murmur of voices. Marissa was home, her door open to any friend or acquaintance who cared to drop by. The sounds were warm and familiar, woven into the stillness of the late winter afternoon.

It was nice, Sara thought, as she pulled some bills and advertisements from the letterbox, to find that, here, life was going on as if nothing out of the ordinary had happened. The birds were keeping busy and Marissa was still offering a cordial welcome to all comers, whether they deserved it or not. Sara shoved the mail into the large bag slung over her shoulder. Perhaps, when Marissa called out to her, as she undoubtedly would, and offered a glass of wine from one of the half-gallon bottles of white or red that were always available, she would accept the invitation. Maybe a short visit across the hall would help her to unwind.

She started up the steps and stopped. She listened then moved more quickly to the first landing and paused where the staircase angled sharply to the left. It couldn't be. She listened carefully, waiting to hear the voice again.

"Damn," she muttered and climbed the rest of the steps, still hoping that her imagination was playing a cruel trick on her while, at the same time, preparing for the worst. Yet another encounter with the inescapable Wendy.

Chapter 43

It made sense when Sara thought about it. Of course Wendy would be here. By running away from the office, she'd gained time to come up with her story and by showing up on Sara's doorstep, she would find out what had happened at West Electronics after she left. Where else would she go?

Wendy had even found a comfortable place to wait. Marissa's apartment. That they were strangers to each other wouldn't have deterred either of them. Marissa Turner, née Maria Jankovic, had never been known to turn anyone away from her door and Wendy couldn't resist taking advantage wherever she could.

Had Wendy rung the bell or was Marissa's door open when she arrived? It didn't matter. That was where Sara found her, curled up on one of two overstuffed loveseats, making herself at home as she and her hostess faced each other over a large circular Spanish oak coffee table that was strewn with fashion magazines and the romance novels to which Marissa was addicted, chatting away as if they'd been friends forever.

"Come in," Marissa called out, when Sara reached the top of the stairs.

Sara stopped in the open doorway, unsure of how to respond. Marissa looked so pleased with herself, and as usual, very pretty. Her blonde hair fell in soft waves to her shoulders and her carefully made-up face couldn't hide her faith in the essential goodness of everyone she came across.

"I've got your friend here," she declared. "We've been waiting for you."

"I see." Sara said. She remained standing in the doorway, still hoping that the scene was some terrible figment of her imagination. She'd rather believe she was having a nervous breakdown than accept that Wendy Solomon was sitting in Marissa's living room, drinking from a glass of red wine.

"What are you doing here?" Sara said, with a hostility that was only thinly veiled for Marissa's benefit.

Wendy laughed. "I told you," she said to Marissa. "Sara forgot all about me."

"We all forget things sometimes," Marissa said. "And, luckily, I was home. So, no harm done." She smiled, happy to have such nice company and convinced she had poured the necessary oil on what had begun to look like troubled waters.

"Wendy has been telling me about her boyfriend and the problems she's been having with him," she continued as she went through the small adjoining dining room and into her kitchen. It was a subject Marissa enjoyed and one with which she'd had a great deal of experience. She kept dreaming about Mr. Right, but she'd been bringing home a series of Mr. Wrongs ever since Sara met her. "Men are all alike aren't they? Nothing but trouble," she declared.

"Especially when they turn up dead," Sara said, the words louder than she'd intended.

"Dead?"

Marissa came back into the living room carrying a wine glass for Sara in one hand and a replenished plate of cheese and crackers in the other. "Is that what you said?" She looked first to Sara and then to Wendy, unsure if she was supposed to laugh or if there was a tragedy not yet revealed that would demand a more serious response.

"Sara's sense of humor," Wendy told her quickly.

Marissa looked at Sara more closely, beginning to sense that the situation might not be as simple as she'd been led to believe. "You'd better have some wine," she offered, gesturing with the empty glass. "You look like you need it. Red or white?"

"Thanks, but something stronger is called for. Anyway, I can't stay. I have some things to take care of. I'll take a rain check." She turned towards her own apartment, ignoring Wendy although she knew it wouldn't make any difference.

"I've got some Scotch here," Marissa called after her. Whiskey was too expensive to leave out for just anybody who might drop by and it showed her high regard for Sara that she made the offer.

Wendy was already on her feet. "Sara and I are going across the hall," she announced, as she gathered her belongings from the sofa.

Sara turned back. "No!" she said. "I've had one hell of a rough day and I'm not about to play hostess. You're on your own."

"You don't understand. We have things to discuss before Bert gets here."

"Bert?" Sara said. "Bert is coming here?"

"Of course," Wendy declared. "I couldn't take the chance that he'd try to pick me up at work, could I? I left a message at his office letting him know this is where I would be. I didn't think you'd mind."

"Of course she doesn't mind," Marissa interjected with a reproachful look at Sara. "And if Sara isn't feeling up to having company you can wait for Bert right here."

Wendy had almost forgotten that Marissa, for whom she foresaw no further purpose, was there. "You don't understand," she said, dismissively. "There are some things I need to talk to Sara about in private."

"There is nothing for us to talk about," Sara said. She knew Wendy was going to stick like glue until she got what she wanted, but there was no reason to make it easy for her. "You can wait for Bert out here, in the hallway," she said. "Have a seat on the steps. Marissa won't mind."

"Like I said, you can wait in my living room," Marissa said, gesturing toward her loveseats.

"I need to talk to Sara," Wendy said. "And it's personal."

She brushed by both women and crossed the few feet of hallway to stand at Sara's door, not bothering to respond to Marissa's offer that she take her glass of wine with her.

"Well then...see you later," Marissa called out, hopefully.

Sara went back to Marissa and hugged her. "I'm really sorry for getting you mixed up in all this," she said.

"Don't be silly," Marissa assured her. "It's no big deal. Besides, I like your friend. She's just got some problems right now. I can understand that."

Sara smiled. Marissa's insights into human nature were invariably mistaken but this wasn't the time to straighten her out about Wendy, nor was it the moment to deliver yet another lecture about allowing strangers into her apartment, even strangers who claimed to be friends.

Thanks again," she repeated while Wendy, who hadn't found it necessary to show any appreciation for Marissa's hospitality, waited impatiently for Sara to open her door.

Chapter 44

Sara left the door to her apartment open as a kind of apology, a way to make up for Wendy's unpardonable rudeness. But even that small gesture was more than her uninvited guest would allow.

"I thought we'd never get out of there," Wendy complained, as she compounded the insult to Marissa by slamming the door shut and turning the lock. "Bert could show up any minute and before he gets here I need to know what happened after I left work."

Sara, who had been on her way to the kitchen, turned back. "I left the door open on purpose," she said, her voice tight with anger.

"I told you, I'm not sure when Bert is going to get here. We have things to discuss and I don't want him or your nosy friend across the hall to hear us. So you'd better hurry up and tell me what happened."

Sara was too angry to reply. She didn't want Marissa involved in a discussion about Rick's murder any more than Wendy did and if Wendy had been willing to wait she would have gotten around to closing the door herself. But Wendy was too cocooned in her own universe to allow anybody else's feelings to penetrate.

"I need to know what happened after I left," Wendy repeated.

"I don't give a damn what you need," Sara said. She wasn't going to argue about the door, but the decision about how and when to answer Wendy's questions was hers to make. She turned back toward the kitchen.

Wendy followed closely behind. "What happened after I left?" she insisted.

Sara opened the antiquated refrigerator, that she liked to joke was older than she was, and took a metal tray of ice cubes from the tiny freezer compartment.

"Tell me what happened," Wendy, said.

Sara ran hot water along the bottom of the tray and gathered several of the loosened ice-cubes into a squat glass. From one of the wall-mounted cabinets above the sink she took a bottle of Scotch and poured a generous amount of the liquid into the glass. She did not offer a drink to Wendy.

Wendy's eyes followed every move Sara made. "I want to know what happened," she said. "I want to know what kind of questions the police asked. And I want to know how you answered them. Tell me."

Sara added a small amount of water to her drink and continued to maintain her silence. Back in the living room she sat on the sofa, slipped off her shoes and put her feet up on the coffee table.

"I'm not leaving here until you answer me," Wendy declared. She had seated herself in the armchair next to the fireplace.

"Bert's going to be here any minute and I have to know what you told the police. We have to get our stories straight."

"Our stories?" Sara said. "You've got to be kidding."

"Just tell me what you told them," Wendy insisted. "What kinds of question did they ask you? What do you think Sheila told them, or Gerry?"

"If you hadn't run out on me, you would know as much as I do," Sara said. "You dragged me into this then left me to deal with the police and everybody else on my own."

"I was upset and I was scared," Wendy said. "Is that so hard to understand? I needed time to think. So why don't you just tell me what went on."

"If you want to know what the others told the police," Sara said, "I can't help you, even if I wanted to. I'm not very popular at West Electronics right now."

Wendy got up and wandered aimlessly around the living room. "When I think about it," she said, "there isn't much of anything for them to tell. None of the others know anything about me and Rick, so they couldn't have told about that.

"Are you sure?"

Wendy mused. "They might have suspicions, I suppose. But none of them has ever seen us together. What about you? What did you tell the police?"

Sara drank some more of the golden liquid and allowed her body to slide down until her head rested comfortably on the back of the sofa "What do you think I told them?"

"I don't know," Wendy cried, her voice rising. "And there's no time for guessing games."

She paused and dug her fingernails into her palms as the instinct for self-preservation kicked in. She already had the broad outline of a story to tell the police, but she needed Sara's help to fill in the specifics. And she was worried about Bert. He would have questions and she needed Sara to be there, to act as a buffer when he arrived. Swallowing her anger, she went back to the armchair.

"You're still upset because I walked out on you today and I don't blame you," she said, doing her best to sound meek, although the effect was more like that of a child forcing herself to be nice to a teacher she didn't particularly care for.

Sara did not bother to hide her contempt. "You don't blame me? That's good of you," she said. "You asked for my help without giving me a true idea of what was going on. You involved me in lies without asking my permission. You told stories about me that aren't true. Then you found a dead body...asked me to help you deal with it...and left me all alone to cope with the police and everybody else in the office. And you don't blame me. That's very generous of you."

Once again, Wendy restrained herself. She was the one who felt put upon. She, who had put her trust in Sara, was the one who had been betrayed. She wanted to scream and let Sara know how selfish she was. Instead she allowed her very real frustration to spill over in a flood of tears with the requisite accompaniment of heartrending sobs.

"Can't you understand? Rick loved me and now he's dead. You don't know what it's like to have somebody love you so much that it almost makes them crazy. And when I found him like that, all I could think was that maybe it was his passion for me that led to his downfall. That maybe, somehow, it was all my fault."

She glanced at Sara, who showed no sign of having been moved to pity, and allowed herself to be overtaken by yet another paroxysm of tears. "So, how could you expect me to sit there, calmly, and wait for the police? I couldn't," she cried. Nobody could."

"I can't take this anymore," Sara said. "Let's get it over with before I throw up. You want to know what I told the police? Then quit the sob story."

Wendy stopped crying and glared at Sara. "Okay," she said. "What did you tell them?"

"For starters, that you were planning to spend last night with Rick, not with me. That I had no relationship with Rick and don't know anything about him. That you left my apartment to meet him at West Electronics, last night, and that you called from the service station at Cahuenga and Fountain about an hour later and asked me to pick you up. We got back to my apartment around ten o'clock. That's it. Except that you were the one who found the body. Since that was all I knew, that's all I could tell them."

Wendy nodded and, with a heavy sigh, went into Sara's bathroom to wipe away the residue of her outburst.

"I don't know why you had to tell them about last night," she said. "All that business about me going to meet Rick. But it's too late to do anything about it now. What we have to do is to figure out where we go from here."

Sara shook her head in disbelief and went to get another drink.

Chapter 45

Wendy had nursed the hope that Sara wouldn't tell the police about how she'd gone back to meet Rick. It would have made everything easier. If she'd kept her mouth shut, the police would never have known that she returned to the warehouse. And Bert wouldn't have had to find out either. This mess was all Sara's fault.

"What about today?" she wanted to know when Sara returned to the sofa. "What did the police say when you told them I was the one who found the body?"

"What would you expect? They wanted to know why you left the office and where you went. Then there were questions about Rick and my relationship with him. I don't think they believed any of my answers. But they went right on asking as if repeating the questions would change things."

"Did you tell them that Bert went to the office last night, looking for me?"

"No. They didn't ask and since I wasn't there when it happened, there was no reason to mention it. But I'm sure any of the others who were there told them about it."

Wendy nodded. "Well, it shouldn't be too difficult to get the whole thing straightened out," she said. "I'm sure the police will understand that this has nothing to do with me, once I explain."

"Of course," Sara said. "I know they are looking forward to hearing what you have to say. I'm a little curious myself."

"I'll just tell the truth," Wendy said. "I agreed to see Rick last night because I wanted to make him understand that I couldn't return his feelings and that he had to leave me alone. I didn't want to hurt him, but my loyalty had to be with Bert and my son. I'm sure the police will understand."

Sara almost choked on her drink. "That's what you told Rick last night?" she said. "That you wanted him to leave you alone because your loyalty has to be to Bert and your son? How did he take it?"

"Oh, I never saw Rick last night," Wendy said, her eyes wide. "Didn't I tell you?"

"You didn't tell me anything," Sara reminded her. "All you did was cry. All night long."

"I cried," Wendy said, sulkily, "because I was disappointed that I never got to see him. I wanted to get the whole thing over with. Rick was so intense, you know. He was frightening me and I wanted to make him understand that he had to leave me alone."

"I see," Sara said. "Rick was frightening you so you took a cab from here back to West Electronics, after dark, to meet him."

"That's right. Wendy nodded, oblivious to the sarcasm. "You know," she went on, "it's funny about the cabdriver. He was worried about me. It was almost as if he had a premonition or something. If only I had listened to him. He didn't want me to go down into the garage all by myself. Wasn't that sweet," she sniffled. "And I didn't pay any attention to him. I should have let him wait for me."

"You went down into the garage? That's where you were planning to meet Rick?"

"Not in the garage. He was supposed to be waiting for me in the warehouse. That's the way we always did it. And maybe if I'd been on time he would have opened the door," she accused. And maybe if I hadn't had to wait half an hour for a taxi he would still be alive."

"I doubt that," Sara said, declining to point out that waiting for a taxi might have saved Wendy's life. If she'd been with Rick when the murderer struck, she might have been a victim as well. "Anyway," she continued. "Why were you meeting him in the warehouse? I thought you were supposed to go to his place last night. I seem to recall you were all excited because you had never been there before."

"You're trying to confuse me," Wendy declared with a flash of temper. "Maybe we were going to go on to his place. I don't remember."

"Okay," Sara said. "You don't remember. But, help me. I'm just trying to get things straight. Because I sure got the impression that the relationship you wanted to end was the one with

Bert, not the affair with Rick. And, if you were worried about the welfare of your child, you didn't let me in on it."

"You've got it all wrong. And anyway, it doesn't matter what you remember. What's important is that I was going to see him because I wanted him to leave me alone and that I never saw him. And if you say anything different I'll call you a liar!"

"But you believed he was there and you didn't go inside to look for him?"

"That shows how much you know," Wendy said. "Only Mr. Maruri and Mr. West and Mr. Walsh are supposed to have keys to the warehouse. I don't know how Rick got his. He would never tell me. So, all I could do was bang on the door and ring the bell and wait for him to let me in. I did that for I don't know how long, but he never answered."

"Had he ever done that before? Made a date with you and stood you up?"

"Of course not," Wendy said. "And he didn't stand me up. He wanted to see me. He even cancelled his bowling night and anyway, I believed he was in there. I saw his motorcycle."

"His bowling night," Sara recalled. "You told me that's where he had certain connections. Maybe something happened to change his mind and he went to the alley in somebody else's car. Maybe he was late coming back to meet you," she suggested. "Or, by time you got there, I suppose it's possible that he was already--"

"Dead," Wendy said. She was crying again. "Maybe he was laying there, calling out to me with his last breath. Maybe he knew I was outside and couldn't hear him. He couldn't let me know he needed help. Maybe I could have saved his life."

"That's not likely," Sara said. The sight of Rick's bloody body was vivid in her memory. The killer had been determined. "From his wounds," she added, "I would think he died quickly."

Wendy shuddered. "You can't be sure. But what else could I have done? There was no reason for me to think anything was wrong...was there? So, like I said, I kept ringing that bell and knocking on the door. I thought he might be angry because I was late or maybe he was ignoring me," she said. "You know, acting hard to get. He did that sometimes. He used to act like he didn't care and make believe that I was the one who was chasing him. It was like a game."

"Did you see anything else? Anything that looked suspicious, like it shouldn't be there? Were there any cars in the garage?"

Wendy wiped away the tears that she seemed able to stop and start at will. "No," she said, after a moment's reflection. "The garage was empty. I'm sure. Except for Rick's bike. And after a while, I left. I walked up toward Sunset until I found a phone booth in a gas station and called you. It wasn't any fun. It was cold and dark and the streets were empty. I was scared."

Sara couldn't doubt that part of Wendy's story. In a city where walking was considered to be aberrant behavior, the streets were deserted and filled with shadows after nightfall. It could be frightening, especially for a woman alone. She looked at her watch, set her unfinished drink aside and slipped her shoes back on. She was ready to drive Wendy home herself, just to be rid of her.

"There's no point waiting for Bert," she said. "I'll take you home."

"He'll be here any minute," Wendy insisted. "I left a message with his secretary and he always picks up his messages."

"What time was that?" Sara asked.

"I'm not sure. Not long after I left you. I walked up to Hollywood Boulevard and called from The Broadway. I left word for him not to call me at work. He was to wait till I phoned back with instructions. It was very clear."

"You went to a department store?" Sara exclaimed. "You left me to deal with Rick's body and to explain things to the police while you went shopping at The Broadway?"

"You always twist things around," Wendy complained. "Shopping helps me think and besides, I didn't buy anything. I just looked around and then I had coffee in their café while I worked out a plan. Once I figured out that the best thing would be for Bert to pick me up at your place it was simple. I left a second message for him...found a taxi at the hotel...the Roosevelt...and came here so we could get our stories straight while we wait for him."

Sara frowned. "You never talked to him directly. For all you know, he didn't even get the message.

"I'm sure he got it. But I suppose I could call his secretary and double check," she offered. A reluctant concession to Sara's impatience.

"Make that call," Sara said. "And if Bert hasn't picked up the message, tell her to rip it up. Tell her you're on your way home and you'll see him there. I'll drive you."

Wendy nodded, although she had no intention of leaving before Bert arrived. Explaining to him had happened would be tricky and she intended to have Sara there, a third person, to make it easier.

CHAPTER 46

The phone was inches away from Wendy's fingers, on a small pine cabinet between the wall and the armchair, but in spite of Sara's insistence, she had not yet reached for it.

"Make the call," Sara said. "Now. Or I'll make it for you."

Wendy pulled herself out of the armchair. "I don't know why you're in such a hurry," she complained, and once more emptied the contents of her purse onto Sara's much beleaguered coffee table. "Just give me a minute to find my address book. It's in here somewhere."

Sara watched as Wendy returned the objects to her purse, one by one with maddening slowness. "Your keys and your hairbrush," she said, lifting the objects from the carpet to which they had fallen.

The keys looked different from the way they'd looked when Wendy's stuff had been strewn across the table that morning. It was the distinctive T-bird key that made the difference, she thought, almost certain she hadn't seen it there earlier in the day.

She did, however, recall having seen a similar looking key among the collection Rick wore on his belt. But why would Rick have had a key to the T-Bird?

Wendy snatched the brush and keys from Sara's hand and threw them into her purse, the address book forgotten. Like a spoiled child, angry that a grown-up was making her life difficult, she returned to the armchair and began to dial the number to Bert's office without, Sara noted, the benefit of any aid to her memory. At the sound of heavy, hesitant footsteps from the stairway outside Sara's door, she ended the call.

Wendy's anger had melted away. Self-confidence had deserted her. What if those were Bert's footsteps? What if, when he heard her story, he wouldn't believe her? She looked over to Sara.

"Maybe that's him now," she whispered.

"Or it might be a friend of Marissa's," Sara said. She got up from the sofa and paused while Wendy remained seated, pale and gripping the sides of the armchair as if bracing for an ordeal.

"Don't tell him I went to meet Rick last night," she pleaded, her voice low and taut with anxiety. "I'll handle that later."

Sara, who had no intention of telling Bert anything, nodded her acquiescence. She wouldn't lie for Wendy, but if she got drawn into answering questions she would, for the sake of the child, do her best to provide some cover for his mother.

"It's him," Wendy said. "Bert's here."

Sara heard Marissa greeting the newcomer.

"Hi there, I'll bet I know who you are and who you're looking for."

Sara moved quickly and opened the door to find that Marissa had already made a positive identification. She had come into the hallway and cheerfully called out that Wendy's friend had arrived.

"We've been waiting for you for hours," she told him.

Bert stood between the two women, confused and unsure of himself. "Sara Fisher?" he queried, looking from one to the other.

"She's Sara. And I'm Marissa. We're neighbors."

Sara gestured him toward her living room. "Wendy's in there," she said.

Marissa waited until Bert had turned away before grabbing Sara's arm. "He's cute," she said, her lips forming the words without making a sound.

Sara nodded. "I suppose so," she said and, with an apologetic shrug, once again closed the door on Marissa's curiosity.

Wendy, who was crying again, waited until Bert reached her. "Finally," she wailed, as she got up from the armchair and flung her arms around him. She laid her head on his chest. "I was beginning to be afraid that you'd never get here."

Sara remained by the door. What kind of man was he to be taken in by a woman so transparently dishonest? He could be considered attractive, Sara thought, with curly, sandy colored hair and the kind of boyish good looks which, unless he was careful, would fill out and turn florid before he turned forty.

Judging by appearances, which Sara freely acknowledged was as irresistible as it was unfair, she guessed that he'd never gotten past the buddy relationships of his college years. Was drinking

beer and watching the football game still the highlight of his social life? But there was more to him that, something very sweet
and gentle as he awkwardly tried to comfort Wendy. He genu-
inely cared for her. Sara could see it clearly. As clearly as she
could see that the wounds would be deep when she betrayed him
again as she inevitably would.

"I was going into another client meeting when I got your
message," he explained. "And I drove over here as soon as it was
over. Francine didn't say it was an emergency or I would have
come right away. Tell me what's wrong. Are you alright? You're
not sick or anything? Has something happened to Mikey?"

"It's nothing like that," Wendy sobbed.

"Then what is it? Why are you so upset?"

Bert was showing admirable restraint. Instead of demanding a straight answer, he led Wendy to the sofa and, when she
was comfortably settled, sat next to her, keeping a protective
arm around her shoulders. "Now tell me what's happened?" he
coaxed. When the question brought about another paroxysm of
tears, he turned to Sara.

"What's wrong?" he repeated. "Why is Wendy so upset? Did
something happen at work? I called at West Electronics, but--"

"Oh, no!" Wendy exclaimed, pulling away from him. "Didn't
you get my message? I especially wanted Francine to tell you that
you weren't supposed to call me there!"

"She told me, but I didn't see what harm it would do. And
a policeman had called at my office. He didn't leave a message
about what he wanted, but I was worried. Why is everybody acting so strange? Why didn't you want me to call you?"

"Who did you talk to? What did they say?" Wendy wanted to know.

"I didn't talk to anybody...except Sheila. She answered the phone, but she didn't sound like herself and when she put me on hold I decided to hang up. So, tell me what's going on. Did you quit your job, is that it?"

Wendy was crying again. "Sara, you tell him," she sobbed.

CHAPTER 47

Of course. This must be what Wendy was waiting for. The plan she came up with while browsing the aisles of the Broadway Department Store. A way to once again manipulate Sara into taking on a responsibility that should have been hers. What Wendy didn't know was that this time, it was going to be different.

Wendy was giving her a chance to get Bert's story before the detectives questioned him and Sara was ready to grab the opportunity. It would go a little way towards making up for the shabby way the police had treated her. It would also allow her to satisfy her curiosity, something she deserved after the way Wendy had used her.

She moved to the armchair Wendy had vacated and spoke as calmly as she could. "What happened," she said, "is that there was a body found in the warehouse at West Electronics."

"A body?" Bert looked confused. "A dead body?"

Sara nodded. "It was hidden away behind some cartons of tape recorders."

"That's horrible. But what does it have to do with Wendy? Or me?" He paused, waiting for either of the women to respond. "Who was it? Whose body did they find?"

"Rick Hanson," Sara said.

"I...I don't understand," he stammered. He looked at Wendy and back to Sara again. "What happened? Was it an accident?"

"He was murdered," Sara said.

Wendy nodded her head vigorously. Now that Sara had spoken the dreaded word she could join in. "He was murdered. And the police think you did it."

"That's ridiculous!" Sara said. "How can you say such a thing?"

"We have to face facts," Wendy replied. "They know that Bert was in the building last night and he had a fight with Rick. What are they supposed to think?"

"How did you know I was in the building?" Bert said, his suspicions alive again. "You had already left when I got there. That's what they all told me. That you and Sara had gone. Were they lying? Were you there all the time?"

"Don't be silly," Wendy said. "Of course I wasn't there but when Sara and I got to work this morning that's all anybody could talk about. How you made a fool of yourself last night. Now everybody believes there was something between me and Rick and how do you think that makes me feel? So when Sara was going to call the--"

Wendy caught herself in mid-sentence and copious tears flowed again. "It was for you," she cried, picking up the thread of the narrative as she had prepared it.

"When the police were coming, I was so worried about you that I ran away. I didn't even talk to them. But I was sure that Sheila and the others would give them an earful. That's why I didn't want you to call the office. I wanted to make sure you had a chance to prepare."

"Prepare for what? They can't think I had anything to do with it," Bert said. "Rick was alive when I left. Didn't Sheila tell them?"

"How should I know what Sheila told them?" Wendy said, retreating into the cushions of the sofa. "I left the office before the police got there. You'll have to ask Sara."

"I don't know what Sheila or anybody else told the police," Sara said. "But I'm sure they're not going to jump to any wild conclusions."

"How did he die?" Bert said. "How did it happen?"

"There was so much blood, it was hard to tell," Sara said. Although she had seen the weapon, she had no appetite for making explanations. Nor did she think the police would want her to give out specific information.

Bert looked defeated, unable to meet the eyes of either woman. "I must have been crazy to go to West Electronics last night but I was angry and I didn't know what else to do...where else to go. I admit that. But nobody who knows me could believe I would ever do a thing like that. Kill somebody."

Wendy looked doubtful. As if she believed that Bert was capable of "a thing like that"...of having committed a murder. Why, Sara wondered. Did Bert, as Wendy had originally claimed, have a history of violence? Nothing about him gave that impression but the possibility existed. She reached for a pencil and the small memo pad that rested on the cabinet next to the phone and scrawled a note. She wanted to find out more about Bert.

"Then, tell us...what did you do?" Wendy asked, suddenly rejoining the conversation. "After the fight with Rick. Did you go straight home?" And Sara wondered if Bert could hear the doubt in her voice. The suspicion.

"Not exactly," Bert said. "I wasn't sure what to do so I sat in the car for a while. In the street, in front of the building."

"For how long?" Sara asked. "For how long did you sit out there?"

"I'm not sure. Does it matter?"

"It might," Sara said. You could have noticed something out of the ordinary. Somebody who shouldn't have been there."

"I don't think so. I saw Sheila leave. She was carrying the mail and she looked straight at me."

"Of course she did," Wendy said, angrily. She probably thought you were crazy coming there and scaring everybody and then just sitting in the car."

"I told you, I didn't know what else to do," Bert said, looking miserable. "I just knew I didn't want to go home...all by myself."

"Of course. I can understand how you felt," Sara said. "And I think it's lucky you were there. You might have seen something that will help in the investigation. Was there anything else? Did you see anyone else?"

"That guy from the accounting department. I remember him from the Christmas party. He drove out maybe five minutes later. And Rick was with him." Bert paused, his face red with the remembered humiliation. "Rick saw me and he waved."

"Rick left with Mark, from the accounting department?" Sara was puzzled. She had assumed Mark was gay, something she was sure nobody else at West would have picked up on, and wondered why he and Rick would be going out together. "Are you sure? I wouldn't have thought they'd be friends," she said.

"I'm positive," Bert said. I was in the front office when Rick asked him to go out for a drink and they drove out together. He asked me too. As if I would want to go anywhere with him."

"And after you saw the two of them drive off?" Sara said

"I kept watching. I thought maybe--" He looked over at Wendy before continuing. "I thought maybe Wendy was still inside. Or maybe she left and was coming back. I know now it was crazy but I just sat there and waited. I think it was the girl from the accounting department who came out next."

"Gerry Fineman," Wendy said. "So what? It was after five o'clock and people were leaving to go home. There's nothing special about that."

Sara stayed focused on Bert. "You saw Gerry leave?" she prompted. "Do you know what time that was?" Sara asked.

Bert shook his head. "It was before five-thirty because that's when your boss left," he said, looking at Wendy. "Mr. Walsh. He drove out of the garage in his Pontiac. Blue. I looked at my watch."

Sara scrawled another one of her abbreviated notes on the pad and wondered if she'd be able to decipher them later.

"Was that everybody?" she asked.

"Except for the Japanese guy."

"Haru Maruri," Sara said. "Do you know what time it was when he left?"

Bert nodded. "He drove out of the garage about ten minutes to six and the cleaning crew showed up at six o'clock on the dot."

"And you kept on waiting?"

"No," Bert admitted, reluctantly. "I gave up but, like I said, I didn't feel like going home all by myself so I drove to Frascati's and had a few drinks."

Sara nodded and wondered why Bert's reply was so hesitant. She was familiar with the popular restaurant and cocktail lounge up on the Sunset Strip and thought it was a perfectly reasonable place for him to have gone. "And then?"

Once more, his face flushed with embarrassment. "I drove back to West Electronics," he said. "It was like I couldn't stay away. I went back and drove into the garage to see if Rick's motorcycle was still there and it was. I didn't know what to think but I decided to hang around until he showed up. Then I would follow him."

"Where did you wait," Sara asked. She glanced over at Wendy who had pulled away from Bert. She listened intently, pale and motionless.

"There were lots of parking spaces across the street, by the studio wall, where it was dark. I didn't think anyone would notice me there. It was around twenty after seven," he added, before Sara could ask.

"At seven-thirty the cleaning crew's van pulled away and right after, the accounting guy came back with Rick. He drove out a minute or two later by himself and I waited for Rick to come out on his motorcycle but he didn't show."

"I wonder if Rick timed it that way on purpose," Sara said. If he knew what time the cleaning crew came and went." She looked at Wendy.

"What does it matter? That's enough of all these questions. None of this has anything to do with you."

"It's okay," Bert said, assuming her concern was for his benefit. "I don't mind." Sara was easy to talk to and he found himself liking her, thinking she was just the kind of friend Wendy ought to have.

"You still waited?" Sara said.

Bert nodded. "But not for much longer. It was maybe fifteen or twenty minutes later...I wasn't paying so much attention to the time anymore...when a white car drove into the garage. It was a convertible with the top up. It could have been an Oldsmobile, but I'm not sure."

"A *white* convertible?" Wendy exclaimed.

"Whose car is it?" Sara asked.

Wendy was about to claim ignorance but a glance at Sara told her it would be better to admit she knew. "I'm not sure, but it could be Ken Ichiwara."

"I thought he was supposed to be in Santa Barbara," Sara said. "Why would he be back in Hollywood meeting with Rick?"

"How should I know?" Wendy replied angrily.

Sara would be willing to bet that if Wendy didn't know what the meeting was about, she could make a damned good guess. But pushing her would be pointless in front of Bert and she made a note for the next day before turning back to him.

"What then? Did you see the white convertible leave?"

"No. After a few more minutes I gave up. I went home, had a few more drinks and went to bed." He turned to Wendy. "I realized how crazy I was not to believe you," he said. "Forgive me--"

Sara interrupted him. There was no more he could tell her and it was painful to hear his self-deluded apologies.

"You must be exhausted," she said. "And I have some things to take care of." She stood, making clear that she wanted them to go.

"I'm sorry," Bert said. "I wasn't thinking." He got up from the sofa and pulled Wendy to her feet. "Maybe we'll have some dinner out and then pick up Mikey later. Would you like that?" he asked her.

Wendy nodded, her body limp with relief. Sara's interrogation was finally over and questions from Bert could be put off until the next day or, with any luck, forever.

Chapter 48

Sheila didn't want to go home. Not while the detectives were still there. She might have been needed to answer questions or make a fresh pot of coffee.

"She kept saying she didn't mind working late," Detective Spivak said. "If Maruri hadn't insisted, she'd still be here."

"She's a good-looking girl who likes cops or maybe I should say that she likes you." Roarke smiled as his partner's face turn pink. "Did you tell Maruri it was okay for him to go, that we'll lock up when we leave?"

Spivak, who had already noticed that Sheila was pretty, ignored the jibe and nodded. "I did, but he wants to stay."

Roarke looked at his watch. "He shouldn't have to wait much longer. Another half hour and we'll be out of here. Let's compare notes on what we've got so far and then get over to have a look around Hanson's apartment for ourselves."

"Everybody around here is ready to pin it on Bert Rudner," Spivak said. "Including the men on the warehouse side. They've got him tried and convicted. But it isn't going to be that easy, is it?"

"We'll know more after we question him," Roarke replied. "I want him and the girlfriend, the elusive Wendy Solomon, picked up first thing in the morning and brought to the station. I still think he's our man but what our guys found out from the men who work in the warehouse raises questions."

"And there's what the team who went to Hanson's apartment came back with," Spivak added, glancing at his notebook. "Like at the murder scene, there was marijuana and traces of cocaine. Plus cash. No doubt, he was dealing. There was also a little black book."

"Oh yes," Roarke said. "There's always a "little black book," isn't there."

Spivak laughed. "He must have had two of them because, unless there's some kind of code, this one doesn't seem to deal with the dope, just contacts with a bookie. Hanson appears to have been a go-between for bets on the track...ball games...you name it. Small-time stuff, but he took a cut and it added up to some tax-free income. Oliver Blakely shows up along with several of the men who work in the warehouse."

"Sheila Birney obviously didn't know what was going on. She was ready to swear on a stack of bibles that her Mr. Blakely would never do anything illegal, especially if it had anything to do with Rick Hanson."

" She nearly bit your head off when you asked her about it," Spivak recalled.

"We'll have to look into it. Hanson obviously had other sources of income. According to the lease agreement in his apartment, he was planning to move into one of those luxury places in the hills above the Strip. How could he afford to live up there on the salary he was getting here...even with his promotion? And that raises another question. How come this kid with very little experience, still wet behind the ears, had been made manager of the loading dock even though there were older, more experienced men ahead of him?"

"And be given the keys to every door in the building," Spivak added. He looked down at his notes. "According to Ed Walsh and Haru Maruri, Hanson was the only person other than themselves and Martin West who had full run of the place."

"Even so, the men he worked with didn't seem to resent him," Roarke said. "And I find that hard to believe."

He turned to the notes about the men who had worked with Hanson in the warehouse. Although Rick was friendly, he didn't socialize with them, other than the Monday bowling game, to which he hadn't shown up on the previous night. None of them had ever been to his apartment or even knew where he lived, except that it was in the neighborhood.

"And here's the part I find strangest of all," Roarke continued, "even though they'd all been at this company longer than he had, they didn't mind that he was promoted over them because 'he was a good worker.'"

"Yeah," Spivak said. "It's too good to be true except if he was dealing and they were buying and they're covering up.

Roarke nodded and turned to the next page in his notes. "And it's interesting that they didn't doubt his story about coming from a rich family but wanting to prove he could make it on his own."

"He must have been one hell of a good liar. Both Walsh and Maruri say they believed his story about being an orphan who was raised in foster homes where they starved and beat him until he ran away," Spivak said. "He told different stories to different people and everybody we talked to so far says they believed them, except the temp. She says she never believed he was the son of a movie producer and I think proves she knows more than she's telling. She must have known him better than she says."

"Or maybe she's a better judge of character. I'm beginning to believe she's been telling us the truth and her insights might be valuable. In any case, we'll have to find out where he really came from."

Roarke continued to go through the information they had gathered so far and make notations. "There's also the matchbook from Santa Barbara to look into. It could be an innocent coincidence," he said, "but it is interesting that Ken Ichiwara is in Santa Barbara and a matchbook from a hotel in Santa Barbara was found at the crime scene."

Both men closed their notebooks. "Let's get Hanson's apartment over with," Roarke said. Tomorrow is going to be a busy day."

CHAPTER 49

Sara reached for the peanut butter and jelly. Not particularly appetizing, but easy to prepare and preferable to leftovers from the pizza she'd shared with Wendy on the night before. She had too much on her mind to fuss with anything more complicated. Wendy and Bert had given her a lot to think about. And there was David.

In the two days since he'd left town she'd managed to become involved in a lover's triangle, a murder investigation and had been grilled by police as if she were a suspect. Not easy to explain.

Considering the matter carefully, she spread peanut butter on a slice of bread and carefully layered on the jelly. There was no reason for David to know anything about the murder until he got back to L.A. It would be simpler that way. By then she would be out of West Electronics and the murder, hopefully, will have been solved.

At the kitchen table, with a sandwich that, despite her precautions, oozed driblets of jelly, she had one of David's yellow legal pads in front of her along with two freshly sharpened #2 pencils. The notes she'd scrawled while listening to Wendy and Bert, along with the information she'd picked up on her own, needed to be put into some kind of order before the fragments slipped from her memory.

Pushing aside the inescapable questions as to why she was taking on this presumptuous and thankless exercise, or what David might think about it, she moved ahead, her focus on arranging the bits and pieces into a coherent sequence. A timeline for the day of the murder. Something she could use to get an idea of who might have committed the crime and who could be struck off the list of possibilities.

She was confident that she had enough information to pull it together. Unless, of course, it turned out that the murder had nothing to do with West Electronics. A possibility Sara had thought about before setting it aside. How would an outsider have gained access to Rick in the warehouse? It didn't fit with her assessment of him and the way he operated.

Although Rick was a braggart, he had also been discrete. Careful to keep the different parts of his life hidden and separate from each other. Secretive. With Wendy, for instance. She obviously had some knowledge of his sideline activities but wasn't allowed to have his address or phone number. His associates from outside activities, legal or illegal, probably knew even less about him. Almost certainly they wouldn't have known where he worked.

They would, however, have needed a way to reach him. A phone number. And that, Sara guessed, could have been managed by using an answering service. Like the ones she and most actors used so they wouldn't miss important phone calls. It would have been a way to control his life and keep various enterprises separate. He would have been safe from letting anyone get too close and safe from intrusion. Until he wasn't.

Interesting. And sad. To be so young and have had so much to hide. Still, until she could check it out, it was only a theory. Tomorrow she would ask Sheila about Rick's personal phone calls. If she was right, there would have been few, if any. If she was wrong, Sheila's information would still be of interest. She might remember something about the calls that had come in, who they were from and what kinds of messages had been left.

In the meantime, she moved forward on the assumption that the solution to Rick's murder would be found where she believed it to be. Among the people Rick had worked with, at West Electronics. She swallowed the last of her sandwich, wiped traces of jelly from her fingers and studied the newly created timeline.

<u>Before 5:00 o'clock:</u>
Ken Ichiwara leaves for Santa Barbara in the morning
Oliver Blakely leaves before noon and doesn't return
Martin West leaves at approx. 4:45
Bert Rudner arrives at approx. 4:50

<u>Between 5:10 and 6:05:</u>
Bert Rudner leaves office and sits in car
Sheila Birney leaves
Mark Cranston and Rick drive out together
Geraldine Fineman leaves
Ed Walsh leaves
Haru Maruri leaves
Cleaning Crew arrives at 6:00
Bert leaves minutes later

<u>Between 7:20 and 7:40:</u>
Bert returns approx. 7:20
Cleaning van leaves 7:30
Rick and Mark Cranston return shortly after
Mark Cranston drives out alone one or two minutes later
White convertible drives into garage at approx. 7:40
Bert leaves a few minutes later

Sara congratulated herself on being far ahead of the police. Without talking to Bert, they couldn't possibly know as much as she did about the movements of the people at West Electronics on the day of the murder.

She could also estimate when Rick was killed. If her timeline was correct, the murder must have taken place between seven-thirty, when Mark dropped Rick off at the warehouse, and nine-thirty, when Wendy got there.

There was only one flaw. The entire structure rested on her belief that Bert was telling the truth. What if he was lying? What if, instead of going home when he claimed, he waited until Rick was alone and went to confront him in the warehouse?

Rick, in his arrogance, would have invited Bert in, taken him back to show off his secret room, taunted him. Sara could picture Rick seizing the opportunity to further humiliate Bert, perhaps wanting him to be there when Wendy arrived, pushing him to the breaking point.

Sara shuddered and shook her head. It was possible, but she believed Bert. His reactions, along with the details he'd given her of what he'd seen from his car, had been convincing. It was Wendy's response that puzzled her. Why did she seem doubtful of Bert's innocence? Had there been some truth to her original claim that Bert could be violent? Or was it something else? Had she, perhaps, seen something incriminating when she was in the garage, something she didn't want Sara to know about?

Sara massaged the nape of her neck. There would be a lot more to find out about on the next day. In the meantime, her timeline would allow her to create a list of the people who could be eliminated from suspicion and those who remained suspects. With renewed energy, she turned to a fresh page in the legal pad.

ELIMINATE FROM SUSPICION

<u>Martin West.</u> Has keys to the building but left early. No evidence he returned to office. No discernable contact with Rick or hint of a motive

<u>Oliver Blakely</u>. No keys to warehouse. No evidence he returned to building that evening. Probably used Rick as go-between to place illegal bets--an unlikely motive for murder.

<u>Sheila Birney.</u> No keys to warehouse. No motive. Didn't like Rick but had little to do with him. Doubtful she could have inflicted the wounds on Rick's body, although it's possible. Leave that for police to figure out.
<u>Ask her about Rick's phone calls.</u>

<u>Gerry Fineman</u>. No keys to warehouse. Not much interaction with Rick. No discernable motive and probably not strong enough to inflict wounds.
<u>Ask about Mark's relationship with Rick, Rick's promotion, his relationship with Walsh and Maruri and problems with West Electronics insurance claims.</u>

<u>Wendy Solomon</u>. Impossible given the timing. It was less than an hour from when she left to meet Rick to when she called to be picked up. Not enough time to overpower and kill Rick (even if she was strong enough), clean up and walk to service station to call for pick up.
<u>Ask questions about Bert's supposed violent temper;</u>
<u>Ichiwara's 'business' with Rick; Mark's relationship with Rick.</u>

POSSIBLE SUSPECTS

<u>BERT RUDNER.</u> Could be lying about his movements after he walked out of West Electronics Motive: jealousy

<u>KEN ICHIWARA</u>. No keys to warehouse but presumably Rick let him in. May have been last person to see Rick alive. <u>Was Rick expecting him?</u> <u>Why had he come back from Santa Barbara?</u>

Motive: Unknown

<u>MARK CRANSTON</u>. No keys to warehouse but could have come back (by appointment?) and Rick would have let him in. <u>What was his relationship to Rick?</u>

Motive: Unknown

<u>ED WALSH</u>. Has keys to warehouse. <u>Why was Rick promoted over more experienced and qualified men in the warehouse? Was he aware of Rick's illegal activities? Was he involved in any of those activities?</u>

Motive: unknown

<u>HARU MARURI.</u> Has keys to warehouse. No apparent reason for direct contact with Rick. <u>Why crumpled note under asking Rick to see him in the morning? Did he have to sign off on decision to promote Rick? Could problems about insurance claims have something to do with Rick?</u>

Motive: unknown

Pleased with the result of her effort, Sara went over the lists one more time, making sure she had underlined all the information to look for on the next day. If there had been any lingering doubt about whether she'd be back at West Electronics, it was gone. She couldn't stop now, before it was over. Not until she knew who had gone with Rick into his secret place and ripped the flesh from his body.

CHAPTER 50

It was eight o'clock in the morning and Haru Maruri was already reaching for his third antacid tablet of the day. Anger and incredulity wrestled with each other in his gut.

"Tell me you haven't done anything yet," he said to Ed Walsh, who faced him across his desk. "Tell me you haven't tried to reach anybody? You haven't made any phone calls?"

"Of course not," Walsh replied. "I wanted to run it by you first. Don't I always?"

"I'm glad you had that much sense."

"You're the one not making sense," Walsh said. "The Long Beach warehouse has to be closed. We should get out of there now, before the cops get onto it."

"And where would you move the stuff to? Is there another warehouse lined up?"

"No," Walsh said. "But I'll work something out."

"Forget about the warehouse and think about protecting yourself. Rick was the link between you and the truckers for almost two years. If you contact them to move the merchandise, you'll remind them that you were the one who set it all up."

"The link between *us* and the truckers," Walsh said. "You'd better remember that. We're in this together. And who are you trying to kid?" he went on, his resentment reaching the boiling point. "You were damned careful to keep your name out of all the stateside arrangements. Don't you think I noticed?"

Maruri couldn't deny that he'd made sure there was nothing on this side of the Pacific to connect him with their venture. It had been no more than a sensible precaution. Part of their original agreement. Nothing to feel guilty about.

When the Japanese manufacturers had reached out to him, the scheme had seemed foolproof and Ed had agreed with him. It was a simple and profitable proposition. They wanted to get their products into the United States without going through government hassles on either side of the ocean and West Electronics would provide a perfect cover.

"You thought it was a great idea," Maruri said. "Too good an opportunity to pass up. You thanked me for it."

"And you set me up to take the blame if anything went wrong."

"That isn't fair," Maruri said. "I was obviously the one to handle the Japan side and you were a perfect fit for the stateside part of the operation. You never complained about what you were doing."

It was true that Walsh had never objected to doing his part, arranging for false shipping documents and handling logistics for separating merchandise brought in without permits from legitimate shipments to West Electronics. It was fine with him that Maruri handled liaison with the Japanese companies and their customers.

To Maruri, it had seemed harmless enough, helping those companies find a way around petty, troublesome regulations. They had rented a warehouse in Long Beach and he had convinced himself that, as long as no harm was done to West Electronics, he was not being disloyal to Martin West.

The complication was their need for a third person. Somebody to oversee the movement of the fraudulently documented merchandise from the docks to the warehouse and then to handle the shipment of orders to customers in the United States. Somebody they could trust. That was where Ed Walsh had made his big mistake.

He could have played it safe and found an old Army buddy, as Maruri had suggested. Instead he brought in Rick Hanson. Someone he saw as a younger version of himself who he could mentor and mold, who would fill the place of the son he'd never had and never would have.

And everything had gone exactly as planned until Rick got greedy. Until he went into business for himself, diverting West Electronics products and selling them for his personal profit. Until his thieving raised alarms with the insurance company and the suspicions of Martin West. Until he was dead and the entire enterprise was unraveling along with their lives.

"You're right," Maruri said. "You are more vulnerable than I am. It would take a long time for the police to figure out my involvement. But I didn't plan it that way."

"It doesn't matter what you planned," Walsh said. "I'm the one they'll come after."

"Is your passport up to date?" Maruri asked.

Walsh stared. "Are you saying I should run away? Leave the United States?"

"It's an option. I can't believe you haven't thought about it."

"Have you?"

"Of course," Maruri said, wearily. I'm putting my wife and the children on a plane this afternoon. And, if necessary, it would take me less than a day to pull it together and follow them."

"Why? Sending them away will make the police suspicious and you said yourself that they'll probably never come after you."

"But Martin will figure it out," Maruri said. "He won't make my involvement public. That would damage his reputation. But he won't want either of us working for him anymore and that's okay. I won't have trouble finding employment in Japan. It is my home and I've always planned on going back."

"Still? Even after all this time?" Walsh reached for his handkerchief and dabbed at the dampness on his forehead and upper lip. He looked confused and more than a little frightened, unable to imagine how anyone could prefer living someplace other than the U.S.A.. "I don't know where I'd go."

"Think about it. You wouldn't have to stay away for long. Just until the police are satisfied they have the killer or they give up looking. They aren't going to waste time going after either of us, especially if we're out of the way, and Martin won't push them."

"It could work," Walsh said. "I could go on a cruise. Around the world. Take it easy for a while. Money's no problem."

Maruri nodded. "Exactly. But try to be patient. If the police continue to concentrate on Wendy's boyfriend all this worry will have been for nothing. It could be they've arrested him by now. In the meantime, give some thought to planning that cruise. Maybe call the travel agency."

"First I need some aspirin," Walsh said, almost colliding with Sara as he stepped out of Maruri's office.

"What are you doing here?" he demanded.

"I'm just going to put up a pot of coffee," Sara said as she hurried past him.

"Bitch," Walsh growled and turned back to Maruri. "It's only eight-thirty," he said. "Why the hell is she sneaking around here so early?"

CHAPTER 51

Sara wasn't any happier to see Ed Walsh than he was to see her. He was the person she'd most wanted to avoid when she'd struggled out of bed at the first screech of the alarm clock. He was the reason she had pushed herself to hurry, leaving home without breakfast. Getting to work ahead of him was the point and her effort had been useless.

She was irritated, frustrated and hungry, with a craving, not for her usual slice of buttered toast, but a chocolate doughnut. It was a guilty pleasure which, had it been available, would have washed down beautifully with the steaming cup of fresh coffee she carried back to her desk. Instead she had a stale oatmeal cookie to nibble on. From a packet somebody had left in the coffee room.

At least the office was quiet now. Ed Walsh had disappeared. Returned, she supposed, to the little corner of the warehouse that the police were allowing him to use. And Haru Maruri, whose door was closed against intrusion, would assume she was dutifully attending to Mr. West's dictation. Let him assume. She reached into her handbag for the yellow sheets of lined paper that were covered with her handwriting and traces of jelly from the sandwich of the night before. The day wasn't going according to plan but she still had some minutes of privacy left before the others would arrive. There was no point to wasting them.

Sara, who had been a Luddite when it came to moving from manual to electric typewriters, was now a convert, grateful for the speed the sleek new IBM Selectric allowed her. Her fingers flew over the responsive keys, stopping only to raise her cup for an occasional taste of coffee. When Gerry Fineman came through the front door, the timeline had been reduced to one page of neatly aligned columns and she had started on the list of eliminated suspects.

"You're here early," Gerry said, her head tilted, like a timid little wren unsure of how to respond to an unexpected presence.

Sara smiled and nodded as she covered the yellow worksheets with a file folder.

Mark Cranston, who trailed closely behind Gerry, echoed her surprise.

Did they coordinate their comings and goings, Sara wondered? They certainly never seemed to be too far apart.

"It's only a quarter to nine," he said and looked at his watch as if needing to verify his perception.

"Thought I'd make up for being so late yesterday," Sara said brightly.

She was in the office uncharacteristically early on this Wednesday morning, but hadn't expected anybody to take notice.

It would make more sense if they asked questions when she was late. Nobody ever seemed to care about that. It was a curious reversal of priorities and totally irrelevant, since she had no intention of telling them or anyone else her real reason for getting to work early.

What she had wanted, when she'd forced herself out of bed that morning, was to get into the warehouse again. This time to have a calm look around. She had a feeling there was something she had overlooked, something she might remember if she had a chance to explore a bit on her own. And, if she got to work early enough, she had quite reasonably presumed that nobody would be there to question what she was doing.

She had expected that only Mr. Maruri would be in the building. Of the people who had keys, he was the one who arrived by eight o'clock to open the office for anyone who wanted to get a head start on the work day. She had hoped that he would have followed his normal routine and that the connecting door to the warehouse would also be open. As for Ed Walsh, everybody knew he hardly ever got to work before nine o'clock.

Sara had worked it all out. The police would not be there before nine o'clock or even later. The warehouse people had been asked not to return until the forensics team was finished. If Ed Walsh wasn't there, she would have a clear field. That was why, when she drove into the garage and saw the blue Oldsmobile parked next to Mr. Maruri's modest Datsun, it had come as a shock. She believed it was Mr. Walsh's car and it didn't take long to discover that he had indeed arrived ahead of her. Her well laid plan to look around the warehouse had to be postponed.

On the bright side, now that Mark and Gerry were here, there were other lines of inquiry to pursue. She tucked her notes into a desk drawer and trailed after them into the accounting office.

"There's fresh coffee," she announced, as cheerfully as she felt appropriate under the circumstances. "I hope you don't mind," she said to Gerry. "I know you usually put up the first pot in the morning."

"Of course not," Gerry said. "Thank you. Saves me the trouble."

Mark said nothing. He looked haggard, as if he hadn't slept at all the night before and Sara wondered again if there had been more to his relationship with Rick than one would have expected.

"I'm sorry for yesterday…for the way we treated you," Gerry said. "It wasn't on purpose. But it was all so awful. Finding the police here…and then trying to figure out what happened. I still can't believe it."

"Of course," Sara said. "I understand. And the police weren't making it any easier. I don't see them around this morning. They'll be back later, I suppose."

"Of course they'll be back," Mark said. "They'll search around and ask more questions and turn things upside down before they finally do what they should have done in the first place…find Wendy's boyfriend and arrest him."

"I guess it does look like he's the one who did it," Sara said, as this was obviously not the moment to declare herself on the side of Bert's innocence.

"Can't we talk about something else?" Gerry pleaded.

"Gladly," Sara said. "And maybe we can have lunch. I won't feel like going out by myself."

"That would be nice," Gerry exclaimed. She was surprised and pleased by the suggestion, ready to forego the sandwich she'd brought with her. "Mark can come too. And maybe Wendy… or Sheila."

"Of course," Sara said, although having Wendy or Sheila join them was the last thing she wanted. She needed Mark and Gerry alone if she was going to get any useful information.

"I don't think we'll see Wendy again," Mark said. "If I was her, I would be ashamed to show my face around here."

"You shouldn't talk like that," Gerry said. "We don't know that she did anything wrong. We don't, do we?" she said, turning to Sara. "And you believe she'll be coming back here, don't you? She wouldn't just disappear."

Sara was unsettled by the possibility Mark had raised. Like Gerry, she had assumed Wendy would be returning to West Electronics. What would become of her list of questions if Wendy pulled a disappearing act? She needed Wendy to show up again and she wanted her to show up today.

"Yes," Sara said, although she was no longer certain. "I think she'll be here later. After the police are finished questioning her."

"The police are questioning her?" Gerry said.

"I don't know for sure, but I would imagine she and Bert are at the police station now. I don't think the police were able to connect with them yesterday."

"So I guess we'll have to wait and see what happens," Gerry said, forlornly. "But we'll still have lunch, right?"

"Of course," Sara said. She looked over at Mark, hoping for a positive response. He said nothing.

CHAPTER 52

"**A**ren't you the early bird," Sheila said. "It isn't even nine o'clock yet."

Sara forced a smile. Even if she hadn't had questions for Sheila she would have wanted to get back on a more amicable footing. And she did have questions.

"I woke up early," she said. "Sleep was impossible. I kept thinking about everything that happened yesterday and I wanted to apologize."

Sheila, her jaw in a forward position, turned a suspicious eye on Sara. "What did you want to apologize for?"

"I know you were angry with me...when you all came back from lunch...and I don't blame you. But it wasn't my fault. I was waiting here to talk to you. I wanted to tell you what had happened. But the police wouldn't let me. You saw how they acted. How they made me sit here all by myself. It was--"

Sheila interrupted, unwilling to hear even a hint of criticism of the police. "I'm sure they had their reasons for doing it that way," she said. "But...if you really want to make up for it--" She rolled her chair over to Sara and lowered her voice. "There are some strange things going on around here and you're the one who can tell me what it's all about."

"Okay," Sara said, somewhat taken aback. This wasn't the reaction she had expected. "What do you want to know?"

Sheila inched her chair closer. "For one thing, how come you got so tight with Wendy? Last Friday the little princess didn't even have your phone number and next thing she was acting like your best friend and spending the night at your place. What's that all about? And how come you were the one to find Rick's body? What were you doing back in the warehouse? You have to admit that's weird."

Sara bit her lower lip and wondered how come she was being grilled by Sheila instead of the other way around. She would have liked to declare, loudly and clearly, that she was not the one who had discovered Rick's body. But that would open up questions about how and where she had found the body, the last thing she wanted to get into, especially with Sheila.

"I wish I could tell you more," she said, dropping her voice to a whisper. "But I'm not supposed to talk about it yet. All I'm allowed to say is that I was doing Wendy a favor." She gave Sheila a meaningful look. "You do understand?"

Sheila looked doubtful, but she had to agree. Since she assumed, as she was meant to, that the instruction to keep quiet had come from the detectives, there was no choice. e

"Okay," she said. "I get it. But after they arrest Bert you'll tell me all about it...right?"

Somebody else who had already tried and convicted Bert Rudner. Sara offered no objection. "I promise," she said. "As soon as they arrest Bert, you'll know everything. And I agree that he does seem to be the most obvious suspect. But Rick could have had other enemies. I mean, he didn't seem like a very nice person to me."

"He was a jerk."

Sara nodded. "When I was being questioned, the detective mentioned he was involved with gambling. That he placed bets for people around here. They asked if I knew anything about it."

"I don't know where that story came from." Sheila glared at Sara, her eyes blazing with suspicion. "They asked me about it too. They asked me if I knew anything about Mr. Blakely placing bets with Rick and I told them it was impossible. Mr. Blakely wouldn't have anything to do with Rick. But I'd like to know who told them that story."

"Don't look at me," Sara said. "Where would I have gotten it from? Maybe it came from one of the guys out back."

"Maybe," Sheila conceded, "but you're the one who is always sticking your nose into other people's business. Being where you shouldn't be."

"I don't know anything about Rick's gambling connections but there is something I've been wondering about," Sara said. "Something only you or Wendy would know about and you're the only one I can ask because I know Wendy wouldn't give me an honest answer."

Sheila made an inarticulate sound of approbation. "That's true enough," she said. "You can't believe anything Wendy says. What do you want to know about?"

"I was curious about Rick's phone calls. Did he get many personal phone calls and if he did, what kind of messages did people leave for him?"

"That's funny," Sheila said. Her forehead creased in concentration. "It never hit me before but I don't remember ever having any personal phone calls come through for him. Most of the other guys back there get calls. You know, from wives or girlfriends. But nothing for Rick."

Sara nodded. This was what she'd expected. He must have used an answering service that the police would be onto by now, getting information about who his associates were and what illegal activities he was into.

"I suppose it is strange," Sheila said. "I mean...you could say it's suspicious. Not getting any phone calls."

"You could," Sara replied, noting that Sheila's attitude had undergone a major alteration. She was positively glowing and Sara didn't think that the postman, who had just delivered the mail, was the cause.

"Do you think the police would be interested?" Sheila asked. "In finding out about Rick's phone calls?"

"Definitely," Sara said. "But I wouldn't want to be the one to tell them."

"Don't worry," Sheila assured her. "I'll take care of it."

"Do you have any idea when the detectives will here?" Sara asked.

"I don't know," Sheila said. "But they will have to come back. Even if they arrest Bert, they'll have to look for more evidence. They'll have to come back here, no matter what. Won't they?"

CHAPTER 53

A t eleven o'clock there was still no sign of the detectives and the funereal pall that had descended over West Electronics was thickening. That they would return was the consensus. But, when? Today or tomorrow? When they did show up, for how long they would they stay? Hours or days? When would life go back to normal and leave them free to forget that Rick Hanson had ever existed.

Sheila was, of course, the exception. Rick Hanson had already receded from her consciousness. It was the detectives she thought about and there was no way they could overstay their welcome. Especially a certain one of them who she was sure would ask her out on a date if he was given enough time to fully appreciate her attractions. Only then, would she would be able to accept the end of the investigation without too much regret.

For Haru Maruri and Ed Walsh, there was no expectation that life would go back to normal. But they could hope that an arrest had already been made, that the police would return to tie up loose ends and be gone without raising questions about Rick's salary increases, his precipitous promotions, or problems with insurance company claims. As they sat in their respective offices, each making contingency plans for the worst, their fervent hopes were for a swift end to the investigation.

Mark Cranston would agree. He was consumed with fear that the detectives would find out there was more to his relationship with Rick than a few drinks on the night of the murder. In his world, safety meant keeping the door closed on his private life. Staying in the closet. But the police seemed to have a way of catching on. For them, the closet often had a glass door. If they even suspected he was gay, he believed it would be enough to make them come after him.

Gerry, from across the space that separated their desks, could feel his anxiety. She felt frightened for him. Had he told her everything about the night of the murder? She couldn't help wondering. She would try to reassure him, but she knew he would not be safe until the police finished up their investigation at West Electronics and took their investigation elsewhere.

It was different down the the corridor, where Oliver Blakely sat in the privacy of his office. He wasn't worried about what the police might find out about him. He had already decided to tell the detectives about the bets he'd placed through Rick's bookie connections and wanted to get it over with. His wife was right. It was better for them to find out from him than from possible gossip around the office. He would also tell them about Rick's clumsy attempt at blackmail. The information might be valuable, especially if Rick had tried the same stunt on others. He lit a cigarette, inhaled deeply and opened the folder of orders that had come in so far that week. What he really wanted was a drink. Although it was still early in the day, he could definitely use a drink.

In the office next to Blakely's, it was anger that fueled Martin West's impatience. He didn't give a damn about the police or their investigation, he just wanted them gone. Work was at a standstill and would undoubtedly remain that way until they were off the premises. He was also personally offended at the cavalier way he had been treated and had intended to make his position clear that morning. Instead he had succeeded in making himself look foolish, if not in anybody else's eyes, in his own.

He had assumed that the detectives, realizing they had made a mistake on the previous day, would want to meet with him first thing in the morning. He was, after all, the head of the company. His thought was to turn the tables. To keep them waiting. It didn't occur to him, when he arrived after ten o'clock, that they wouldn't be there.

"What do you mean, they're not here? When are they expected?"

"I don't know," Sheila said. "We haven't heard anything yet. But the forensic people are back in the warehouse. Do you want me to--"

"To hell with the forensic people. Are we expected to sit around here like sheep waiting for those detectives to show up? How can I run a business when I don't know what's going on?"

He had lost control over his anger, made worse when he realized that the temporary secretary, the one he'd wanted to get rid of, was watching him as if he was a specimen in a test tube. Fortunately, the episode was over with quickly.

"Sorry for losing my temper," he said. "Didn't mean to take it out on you. The situation is difficult for all of us." He favored Sheila with a smile and ignored Sara. "Would you bring me a cup of coffee?"

Although he'd recouped his dignity, he knew that his behavior had been petty and unreasonable. Under ordinary circumstances, the police and the girls in the front office were people he would barely notice. Instead, he had allowed them to get under his skin.

Not one for introspection, he wasn't looking at the underlying reasons for his unease. He wasn't ready to face that there would be more unpleasantness waiting for him, even after the police were gone. Or that the problems at his company had festered because he'd allowed them to go unchecked for too long.

⋏

Sara had been surprised by Martin West's flash of anger. It was out of character, unless this was the way he reacted to situations he couldn't control. Had he been expecting the detectives to be sitting on the edge of their seats, waiting to question him? Possibly. Given his ego, it wouldn't have occurred to him that he was too removed from the people who worked for him to be of much use in the investigation. The detectives were probably not all that interested in what he had to say.

If they were anxious to question anybody, she thought, as she watched Sheila leave to bring Mr. West his coffee, it would be

Ken Ichiwara. By now they will have questioned Bert and they'll know about Ichiwara's return to West Electronics on the night of the murder. They must want to talk to him.

Sara wouldn't mind talking to Ken Ichiwara herself, but she barely knew him and couldn't think of a way to start up a conversation. Still, she wanted to know what had happened on Monday night. Did he get in to see Rick or had the warehouse door remained closed, as it had with Wendy? What was important enough to bring him back from Santa Barbara?

She doubted he would tell her the truth but it would be interesting to hear his lie, a preview of what he intended to tell the police.

⋏

When Ken Ichiwara had arrived promptly at nine o'clock that morning it was a pleasant surprise to find that the detectives weren't there yet. He dreaded seeing them. Although he didn't think they could know about his having returned to West Electronics on Monday night, Rick might have kept a record of their transactions. There could be unpredictable questions that he wouldn't be prepared to answer.

Still, rather than wanting to get the interview over with quickly, he was grateful for the respite. Delay worked for him. He had discovered, while still a teenager, if he could put off facing difficulties for long enough, they usually got resolved without too much inconvenience to himself. The longer the delay the better. Maybe the later the detectives got here, the less need they'd have to question him.

As the morning wore on he felt more confident. He resented being forced to sit at a spare desk in the accounting department where he couldn't be private or find a way to ignore Oliver Blakely's suggestion that he catch up with his sales projections, but Sheila had whispered to him that Wendy's boyfriend had probably already been arrested. If she was right, he might be back on the road by tomorrow morning.

Wrapped up in his expectations, Ichiwara barely noticed when Sara came into the room or that she had stopped just a few feet away from him, in front of Gerry Fineman's desk.

"Do you think we can go out to lunch before the detectives get here?" Sara asked.

"I don't see why not," Gerry said.

"I hate to leave because I know Bert has some really important information for them. But I didn't eat any breakfast this morning and I'm hungry."

Gerry looked doubtful. "You know what Bert is going to tell the police?"

Sara nodded. "I'm really curious to find out how the police will react."

"How could you know what Bert will tell them?"

"Wendy showed up at my apartment yesterday and he came to pick her up. He's really very nice and he told me all about it."

"All about what?"

"What happened when he walked out of here on Monday, after the argument with Rick," Sara said, enjoying the knowledge that the detectives who had grilled her on the day before would be furious if they knew what she was doing.

"I don't understand." Gerry said.

"He didn't go home," Sara explained. "He sat in his car, mostly on the other side of the street, and kept on eye on the people who went in and out. He was there for quite a long time."

"Did he see anything important," Mark asked. He was now standing by Gerry's desk.

"I think so. He watched as the building emptied out and then he saw the cleaning crew arrive. He saw them leave at around the same time you came back to the building with Rick. He told me that you drove into the garage and came right out again, by yourself."

"Then Bert must be admitting he's guilty," Gerry said. "Everybody was gone and he was the only one around here when Rick was killed."

"Not quite," Sara said. "There was somebody else. Before Bert drove away, there was another--" She stopped in mid-sentence. "I don't know what got into me. I've probably said too much."

Sara turned away from Gerry, aware but unrepentant. The detectives were undoubtedly planning to surprise Ichiwara with Bert's information and she had ruined it for them. If so, the damage was done. Too late to worry about it now.

"I'm going to make a fresh pot of coffee," she announced and noted that her quarry had gotten up from his desk and was following her into the coffee room.

"I could use a fresh cup," he said.

"It'll just be a few minutes."

"I was wondering why you think the police would take seriously anything Wendy's boyfriend tells them," Ichiwara said. "Sheila told me the police had probably arrested him by now."

"Sheila doesn't know that Bert saw an unidentified car. A white convertible. It drove into the garage around eight o'clock on Monday night."

"So what," Ichiwara said. "Who would believe him after the fight he had with Rick. And even if there was a white convertible, he could have waited and killed Rick after the convertible left."

"How did you know about the fight between Bert and Rick? You weren't there. You were in Santa Barbara."

"Sheila," he said, after a moment's hesitation. "Sheila told me."

"I don't know when she had a chance to do that. But I'm sure the detectives will check it out."

Ichiwara turned away. He had slipped badly. It was Rick who told him about the scene with Wendy's boyfriend. They had laughed about it. Now he needed back to his desk to prepare a plausible reason for whey he'd come back from Santa Barbara. He certainly couldn't tell them about the cocaine or that Rick had hinted at a sexual treat that would involve a third person.

Sara's voice, low and seductive, intruded on him.

"I'm sure, even if you did come back to see Rick on Monday night, you wouldn't have done anything to hurt him. It's obvious that you're not the sort of man who would do something like that."

"Of course not," he said, and turned to face her. She was closer than he had realized, almost touching.

"But if you were back there with him, in the warehouse," she said. "You might have heard or seen something that would help the police and they would be appreciative, I'm sure."

"There was something," he said and immediately drew back. Angry. As if she had drawn the words out of him against his will. "What are you getting at? This isn't any of your business."

Sara kept her voice intimate. "You're right. But think about what I'm saying. If you saw anything it could be important. It could put you in good with the police. And what harm would there be in telling me about it first? Trying it out? I won't tell anybody else. I promise."

"I didn't see anything." He hesitated. "But there were sounds. In the warehouse. As if somebody might be moving around. Rick went out and looked but he said everything was alright. By then, I was ready to leave so he walked with me to the garage door. I could hear him lock it behind me. He was alive when I left."

"Of course," Sara said. "And yours was the only car there... in the garage?"

"My car and Rick's Harley. That was it."

"You'd better come up with a good reason for why you came back to see Rick," Sara advised. "The police will want to know but I won't ask what you're going to tell them...unless you want to run it by me."

"What's going on?" Sheila said. She stood in the doorway, her eyes narrowed with suspicion. "I've been looking for both of you. The police let Bert go. Who knows why. And the princess has showed up." She turned to Ken Ichiwara. "The detectives are on their way. They called to make sure that you and Mr. West wait for them to get here."

"That's great," Ichiwara said, with a bravado Sara couldn't help but admire. She started to go after him.

"Not so fast," Sheila said, blocking her way. "You really had me fooled this morning with all that 'I want to apologize' business. You couldn't tell me anything because the police asked you to keep your mouth shut. Now you're going around telling everybody but me some story about what Bert saw on Monday night."

"I was going to tell you," Sara said. "As soon as I put up the coffee."

"The coffee is up. So tell me now. What was Bert going to tell the police...as if anybody would believe him."

"I believe him," Sara said. And while the aroma of fresh coffee filled the small room, she repeated what she had told the others just minutes earlier.

Sheila's jaw jutted forward. "I don't think the detectives are going to be pleased with you. I think they're going to be very angry at the way you won't stop sticking your nose into other people's business. And...just in case you're wondering...I intend to tell them what you've been up to as soon as they get here."

Sara sighed. "I wouldn't expect you to do anything else," she said to Sheila's retreating back. She followed her out and stopped once again at Gerry's desk.

"Let's go to lunch," she said.

Gerry nodded. "And Mark's going to come with us."

CHAPTER 54

"**A**nybody want to come to lunch with us?" Gerry asked.

Sara held her breath. She anticipated a negative response from both Sheila and Wendy but wasn't sure it would be forthcoming. Neither one disappointed her.

"I might be needed here," Sheila said. "But you can bring me a ham and cheese on white bread."

"Okay," Gerry said, and turned to Wendy. "But you can come. There's nothing much happening around here."

"I'll have an egg salad on rye," Wendy said, ignoring the invitation. "Bert wouldn't stop for lunch."

Sara, who wanted to be gone before the detectives showed up, was already out the door. "Where are we going?" she asked when they were settled in Mark's car.

"The Tick Tock. It'll be my treat." He was like a different person from the man who'd arrived at the office that morning. Gerry was also transformed, more relaxed and cheerful.

"I knew the police wouldn't find anything when they searched my car," Mark said, once they were seated in the restaurant and had placed their orders. "But I still believed I was the last person to see Rick alive, so naturally I worried that they would be suspicious. Now, thanks to you, I know there's proof that somebody was there after me."

Sara nodded. It would be unkind to remind him that he was still in jeopardy. He had a witness to his story about leaving Rick in the garage, but there was nobody to say that he hadn't returned later, either by appointment or on impulse.

"I am curious," she said. "When you dropped Rick off did you notice anything that would have some bearing? Did you see or hear anything suspicious in the warehouse?"

"I never went into the warehouse," Mark said. "Like Bert told you. I dropped Rick off and drove right out again."

"Before you dropped him off, did he say anything about his plans for later that evening...where he was going or who he might be waiting for?"

"No. But now that I think about it, there was a note on his bike. I'd forgotten about it. He read what was on the piece of paper, crumpled it and threw it away."

Sara's eyes brightened. This might be the note she'd found on Mr. Maruri's carpet. "You have no idea what was in it," she asked.

"How could I? I wasn't close enough."

"And that was it? Are you sure? There's nothing else that you remember?"

"Of course not. What more could there be?"

They were both holding something back. Mark looked apprehensive and Gerry, who had lowered her eyes, was nervously pulling at the napkin in her lap. Something more had taken place in the garage, but Sara didn't think either one was ready to let her in on it. Maybe if she took her questions in another direction.

"Did you know about anything illegal that Rick might have been involved with" she asked.

"Why are you asking so many questions?" Mark said.

"It's the police," Sara replied, glad that she'd readied an explanation should the question arise. "You know I barely knew Rick, but yesterday they were insisting I had a relationship with him. That something illegal was going on and I was in on it. I need information so I can protect myself."

"Of course," Gerry said. She looked at Mark, as if asking permission. "I did hear that he might be selling Marijuana. He was--"

"Gerry doesn't know what she's talking about," Mark said. "I never heard anything like that...and don't go around repeating it. Especially since Rick's dead and can't defend himself."

"I understand. This must be very difficult for you. Since you and Rick were such good friends."

"What makes you say that? What makes you think we were good friends?"

"I'm sorry," she said. "I just assumed...because you'd gone out for drinks together."

"That was unusual," Gerry said. "It was only the second time, wasn't it Mark? Because you didn't have anything better to do."

Sara was startled by how quickly he had reverted to the defensive, frightened man of earlier in the day. "It doesn't matter. What's important is that you didn't see anything suspicious and had no idea of what Rick was planning after you left him. That's all the police are interested in, I'm sure."

Sara hoped that her words were reassuring and turned, instead, to Gerry. She still wanted to know about Rick's relationships within the company.

"From what little I saw of Rick, he seemed young to be supervising older and more experienced men," she said. "I'll bet that made for some hard feelings."

"It would have bothered them a lot more if they knew how much money he was making."

"They don't know and that information is confidential," Mark warned.

"I'm not going to say how much he was being paid. Just that he'd had three raises in the two years since he'd been with the company. And they were big. He was making more money than either of us."

"It does seem odd," Sara said.

"Not to me. He was good at his job," Mark insisted.

"The other guys in the warehouse didn't think so," Gerry said.

"He must have had some good qualities," Sara said. "Or he wouldn't have been promoted."

"According to Mr. Walsh, he could do no wrong," Gerry said. "I never did understand why they were so tight together."

"What about the insurance company holding back on paying off claims? What was that about?"

Gerry leaned forward. "Lost merchandise. That's what they call it. I call it stealing. Cartons of tape recorders that were shipped from Japan but never made it to our warehouse. It started about six months ago."

"Could Rick have been behind it together with Mr. Walsh?"

"Of course not," Mark said.

Gerry disagreed. "It's possible," she said. "But the promotions and raises started almost immediately after Rick was hired. More than two years ago, long before merchandise started to go missing. I think there was something else going on that had nothing to do with stolen tape recorders and that Rick might have been in on it with Mr. Walsh."

"This is all in your imagination," Mark said.

"You know you agreed with me, way back in the beginning, that it looked like something funny was going on, even though we couldn't figure out what it was."

"And Mr. Maruri," Sara asked. "Do you think he was involved? He didn't seem to have much to do with Rick."

"No, but he would have had to sign off on Rick's raises. That's why I think they were all in it together. Or maybe Rick found out about something illegal involving Mr. Walsh and Mr. Maruri and was blackmailing them."

"That's ridiculous," Mark said.

"Maybe not," Sara said. "It might explain the note that you saw Rick read in the garage. The one he crumpled and threw away. I think it was from Mr. Maruri and in it he was asking to meet with Rick the next morning."

"How could you know that?" Mark said.

Sara paused, unsure of why Mark was glaring at her with so much distrust. "It was something the detectives hinted at...but maybe I got it wrong."

"You must have," Mark said. "Because the police don't know about the note. When they were asking me about what happened in the garage I forgot to tell them. I don't know where you got that story from unless you're making it up."

He looked around and motioned to the waitress for the check.

"You both should stop making things up and guessing about things you don't know about," he said. "And you'd better not start spreading those kinds of stories around."

"Of course not. You don't have to worry about me," Sara said. "I'm just a temp. And whatever we talked about here, I won't tell anybody else about it. I promise. After Friday, I won't be here anymore."

"I'll miss you," Gerry said, impulsively.

"Thank you," Sara replied. She glanced over at Mark who didn't look like he was about to echo the sentiment. "You're probably the only one who will."

CHAPTER 55

Sara trailed behind Mark and Gerry on their return from lunch. The police had arrived and, once again, she felt like the good girl about to be scolded for breaking the rules. Except this time, she couldn't claim innocence. The infraction had been deliberate.

"Detective Roarke wants to see you," was Sheila's greeting.

Sara squared her shoulders. "I'll go right in," she said.

"Hold it. They're not ready for you yet. Mr. West is still in with them."

"Mr. West?" Sara's eyebrows rose. "What about Mr. Ichiwara? They couldn't have finished questioning him already."

"Well they have. Not that it's any of your business."

Sara looked into the accounting department office and saw Ken Ichiwara sitting at his temporary location. The detectives hadn't spent nearly as much time with him as they had with her although he was a viable suspect.

"They didn't have him in there for very long, did they?"

There was no response. Sheila was unwrapping one of the sandwiches Gerry had delivered while Wendy rummaged through her handbag, searching for cash to pay for the egg salad on rye.

"Forget it," Gerry said. "My treat." She didn't wait for a 'thank you' which was just as well as none was forthcoming.

"The police are examining Mr. Ichiwara's car," Sara offered. "We saw them when we drove into the garage."

Again, no reaction. Sara shrugged and turned away. On her desk was a disc Martin West had left for her to transcribe. Why, she wondered, were the detectives wasting time with him? He was so removed from the day to day operation of the company, he couldn't have information that would take more than a few minutes to divulge. She picked up the disc and put it down again. No point in starting on it now. A summons from the detectives would be coming before she could make much progress.

Sara was no longer apprehensive about meeting with them. They would be angry with her for having made public what Bert Rudner had seen on the night of the murder, but she didn't mind. She could handle whatever lecture they had in store for her, and in return, she would give them information they might not be aware of. She took her notes from her handbag. Instead of Mr. West's dictation, she would use the time to get her thoughts in order and fill in what she had learned since that morning.

When Martin West emerged from his interrogation to announce that he was leaving for the day, Sara was prepared. The detectives, however, were not as anxious to speak to her as she had assumed. It was Oliver Blakely they called for next. Once again she was left with Sheila, who continued to ignore her, and Wendy, who, although she had no reason to be holding a grudge, was also giving her the silent treatment.

Sara supposed she should be grateful for that small mercy except she still had questions for Wendy. She pretended to concentrate on Mr. West's dictation while waiting for an opportunity to catch her alone. It came while Oliver Blakely was still in with the detectives. Wendy was off to the ladies' room.

"If Bert calls tell him I'll call right back," she told Sheila.

Sara allowed Wendy a head start and averted her eyes when Ken Ichiwara came into the front office. He too was leaving for the day.

"Will you be here tomorrow," Sheila asked. "Or are you going back on the road?"

"I'll be here," Sara heard him say before she moved to catch up with Wendy who she found washing her hands and studying her image in the mirror.

"I don't want to talk to you," Wendy said when Sara's reflection appeared over her shoulder.

"That's tough because I have questions for you."

"I don't have to answer your questions."

"True. You can do whatever you like. And so can I. I could decide to tell Bert the truth about you and Rick."

"Bert knows the truth." She stared at Sara, defiantly.

"Really?"

Wendy flushed and looked away. "Tell him what you want. He wouldn't believe you."

"Maybe and maybe not. Do you want to take that chance?"

Sara doubted she would ever carry through on such a threat, but she had enjoyed making it, like a character in a grade B movie. And, it worked. Or maybe Wendy just wanted to talk.

"What do you want to know?"

Sara rested her hip against the second sink. "Let's start with how come Mark and Rick got to be so buddy-buddy. Going out drinking together. How often did that happen? How close were they?"

Wendy laughed. "They weren't close. Rick thought Mark was pathetic. A jerk."

Sara winced at the casual cruelty. "If that's the way Rick felt why did he go out with him?"

"It wasn't for fun. Maybe they went for a drink a few times but Rick would have had a reason...like maybe he needed a favor...some information or something from the accounting department."

"Did they ever have arguments?"

"I don't know. Maybe. What do you care?"

"Forget it," Sara said. "Tell me about Rick and Ken Ichiwara."

"That was different. I guess you could say Mr. Ichiwara was like a customer. Rick used to get grass for him." She paused before adding, with a smile, "And maybe, sometimes, cocaine."

"Cocaine!" Sara exclaimed. Grass had become relatively common in the Hollywood scene but, as far as she knew, cocaine was still rare.

"Yes," Wendy said, gratified by Sara's reaction and prepared to scandalize her even further. "And Rick used to tell him that he was going to set up a threesome. You know like Mr. Ichiwara and

Rick and me." Once again, there was laughter. Wendy pointed a finger at Sara. "Don't look so shocked. He didn't really mean it."

"Are you sure?"

"Of course I'm sure. He used to tease me and say what fun it would be but I knew it was just to keep Mr. Ichiwara on a string."

"Did you know he was expecting to see Mr. Ichiwara on Monday night?"

Wendy shook her head. She wasn't laughing anymore. There was nothing funny about Monday night.

"I suppose Mr. Ichiwara could have come back from Santa Barbara for cocaine," Sara suggested. "Would that be reason enough? Or maybe it was a set-up. To have the three of you there. The long promised threesome?"

"You're horrible," Wendy cried. "Rick is dead and you want to find bad things to say about him. All I know about Monday night is that Rick was expecting me to be there at nine o'clock. And if I had been on time maybe he wouldn't be dead. And it was all your fault."

CHAPTER 56

Detective Spivak, the one who brought a sparkle to Sheila's eyes, was waiting for Sara when she got back to her desk.

"At last," Sara said. I thought you'd forgotten about me."

He didn't respond which, had Sara been paying attention, would have been a hint of what was to come. Instead, still confident the detectives would be interested in what she had to tell them, she grabbed her notes and followed. It wasn't until she was seated in Ken Ichiwara's pre-empted office that her certainty wavered. The two men ignored her. They seemed, instead, to be making preparations to leave.

"You look like you're clearing out," Sara said.

"We'll be with you in a few minutes," Roarke said.

"Don't worry about me. As a temp, I get paid by the hour."

Roarke looked up, clearly irritated. A man faced with a meal for which he had no appetite.

Sara couldn't resist smiling. "Please," she said. "Don't let me interrupt. I'm not in any hurry."

"If there's humor in the situation, I don't see it," Roarke said. "We take our jobs seriously and you came close to damaging our investigation. But, I'm not going to waste time. I won't ask why you took it upon yourself to question Mr. Rudner and I assume you're smart enough to know that making public what he told you made our job more difficult. I will, however, warn you that trying to subvert a police investigation is serious and could have unpleasant consequences."

His Sara condescension was insufferable. "That's not fair," Sara said. "I was not subverting your investigation. I was protecting myself."

Roarke was incredulous. "From what," he asked.

"From the insinuation that I had a secret relationship with Rick Hanson. That there was something I wasn't telling you about. Admit it. You didn't believe a word of what I told you yesterday. You even hinted I might have had something to do with Rick's murder. So how can you blame me for trying to find out what really happened? And I've made progress."

"By putting our investigation at risk?"

"You should be thanking me. If I hadn't let Mr. Ichiwara know about Bert seeing his drive into the garage on Monday night, he might never have remembered hearing noises in the warehouse. If he's telling the truth, a third person could have been hiding while he was there. I'm assuming he told you about that?"

"What he told us is none of your business and what happened in the warehouse has nothing to do with you," Roarke said.

"Does that mean you now accept that I had nothing to do with Rick or his murder?"

Roarke hesitated. "From what we have learned since questioning you yesterday," he said, "it would seem that your version
of events has been corroborated."

"I'll take that as a 'yes,'" she said.

"Take it however you like, as long as you remember that we
expect you to leave the investigation to us."

"Of course," Sara said, as she unfolded her notes. "But I have
gathered some other information. I think you'll find it useful."

"Obviously, I didn't make myself clear," Roarke said. And,
although he was surprised to find himself curious as to what this
woman had come up with, he gestured for Spivak to open the
door.

"You can go now. But remember, we expect you to stay out
of this investigation."

Sara remained seated. She could accept being treated like
an obligatory bit of business to be disposed of at their conve-
nience, but she had worked hard on developing her notes and
knew they contained information the detectives couldn't possibly
know about.

"In that case, you won't be interested in finding out that Mr.
Maruri left a note for Rick on his motorcycle the night of the
murder," she said. "And the next morning it was crumpled up
on the floor of his office."

The two men exchanged a look and Spivak closed the door.
He suspected that Sara was doing nothing more than making a
bid for attention. Roarke was less skeptical. So far, everything
Sara had told them checked out. Despite the irritating way she

kept cropping up in the investigation, he'd come to respect the way her mind worked.

"I don't know what bearing this note will have on our investigation," he said. "But, if you would fill us in--"

"Of course," Sara said. "And I'll begin by making it clear that the warehouse is Mr. Walsh's domain. He's the one supervises the men who work back there. Mr. Maruri has practically nothing to do with any of them, including Rick.

"This may surprise you, but we'd already figured that one out," Roarke said.

"Then you'll agree. It would be unusual for Mr. Maruri to write a note telling Rick 'I want to put an end to your nonsense' and that he wanted to see him 'first thing in the morning'."

Roarke leaned forward. Even Spivak was giving her his full attention. "How do you know about this note? Have you seen it?"

"I found it," Sara said and blushed as she explained how she came to see the crumpled piece of paper on the carpet of Mr. Maruri's office, next to the waste paper basket. "It seemed out of character for him to have anything out of place in his office. Especially something he was discarding. So...naturally...I picked it up and happened to see what it said."

"Naturally," Roarke said. "You went snooping around Mr. Maruri's office and found a note. You read it, but didn't bother to mention it when we were questioning you yesterday."

"I wasn't snooping and I didn't say anything because I'd forgotten about it. Remember...all this happened before anybody knew Rick was dead. At that point, it was just a crumpled piece of paper. A note that wasn't addressed to anyone specific.

"Wait a minute," Roarke said. "What makes you think it was meant for Rick Hanson?"

"Exactly," Sara said, as if he'd correctly answered a difficult question instead of asking one. "It wasn't until this afternoon, when I was having lunch with Gerry and Mark that I knew for sure how Rick fit into the picture."

"Lunch with Gerry and Mark?" Sara's story was taking a circuitous route and, while Spivak continued to scowl, Roarke was enjoying it. "For a temp, you certainly get around. Is there anyone at West Electronics who hasn't been subjected to your interrogation," he asked.

Sara regarded him with renewed interest. He seemed to be more amused than angry. An attractive man when he wasn't being self-righteous.

"All I did," she explained, "was ask Mark if he'd seen anything suspicious in the garage. He hadn't, but he remembered how Rick found a note on his bike, glanced at it, then crumpled it and threw it away. I didn't tell Mark or Gerry about what I'd found on the floor in Mr. Maruri's office."

"We appreciate your discretion. Do you still have this note?"

"Of course not," Sara said. "I dropped it where it belonged, into Mr. Maruri's wastepaper basket. I still don't know how it got from the garage into his office. I can't even be sure that the note I saw was the same one Rick found."

"I'm surprised there's anything you haven't figured out yet," Roarke said. "But I have to congratulate you on your interrogation technique. Mr. Cranston did not mention the note when we questioned him."

"It didn't seem important so, like me, he forgot about it. But when we were talking, and after we went over the scene in the garage several times, it came back to him. Memory works that way sometimes."

"What about your memory? Are you sure about what the note said?"

"Definitely. The part about putting an end to nonsense made an impression." Sara's face lit up with fresh enthusiasm. "It might still be there. The note. In Mr. Maruri's wastepaper basket. The cleaning crew hasn't been back in the building since Rick's body was found."

Roarke glanced over at his partner. "We'll look into it," he said. "In the meantime, you've done enough investigating. From here on in, you stay out of it."

"Of course," Sara said. "But I do have some notes about relationships within the company that you might not be aware of--"

Detective Spivak was on his feet, once again holding the door open for Sara. "We're already behind schedule," he said.

"And, I worked out a timeline for the night of the murder."

"We don't have time to get into it right now," Roarke said.

"It does look like you're preparing to abandon Mr. Ichiwara's office," she said. "Maybe taking the investigation in another direction--"

CHAPTER 57

It was no use. The detectives had practically shoved her out the door without giving away the slightest bit of information. However, what Sara saw in the front office, confirmed that the situation had changed. Both Wendy and Sheila were on the phone, calling the men who worked in the warehouse, instructing them to be back on the job in the morning. The forensics team was gone.

It would be nice if there was somebody she could talk to, somebody who more about what the police were planning. Mr. Maruri was the only possibility, but Ed Walsh had just gone past her desk and into his office, closing the door behind him. He'd probably be in there for a while. They would have a lot to discuss, especially if they were both involved in some shady enterprise that had included Rick Hanson. She didn't want to think of Mr. Maruri that way, but the suspicion was inescapable.

A few moments later the detectives also came through the front office and, without saying a word to anybody, left the building. Were they going to ignore the note that might still be in Mr.

Maruri's office? Sara hurried to the window from where she saw them get into an unmarked car.

"What are they doing out there," Sheila asked.

"They drove off but they'll have to come back," Sara said. "They've got a lot of stuff left in Mr. Ichiwara's office."

She stayed by the window. A new possibility had occurred to her. With Ed Walsh out of the way, this would be a perfect time to have a look around the warehouse. The building was practically deserted and the few people who were left weren't paying attention to her. It might be her last chance. She looked around and, holding her breath, moved slowly toward the door next to Wendy's desk.

Neither Wendy nor Sheila looked up as she opened it and walked into the dimly lit shadows. The only bright space was Mr. Walsh's glass enclosed office, looking like a department store window at night. Drawn to it, Sara took a couple of steps inside. Multi-colored travel brochures spread out on his desk brought her further into the room. She took a closer look at the array of tempting photos then moved away. Mr. Walsh's travel plans were not what she was here for. Her interest was in the different ways to get in and out of the building.

Sara was familiar with the heavy door next to Mr. Walsh's office. The one leading to the garage. She remembered Rick holding it open with his body on the morning of the day he died, a young man with a lifetime of possibilities ahead of him. She was surprised to find it unlocked. The police team must have left it that way but it was odd that Mr. Walsh had neglected to lock up after them, leaving the building and everyone in it vulnerable to some stranger coming in without being observed.

She stepped out to examine the landing. There wasn't much to see other than the large red buzzer Wendy would have pressed to let Rick know she had arrived and a few cars scattered around the garage. The Harley Davidson was gone from its usual place. Would there be anybody to claim it? Would there be anybody to claim the wounded body? To plan a funeral? To mourn him?

Sadness for the wasted life came over her as she went back inside and surveyed the length of the warehouse. Not far from where she'd found him, on the far end, was the drop-down gate to the loading dock that opened onto an alley behind the building. Next to it was yet another door, one more way to get in and out of the warehouse, one that had barely registered on her consciousness on the day before.

On the night he was killed, Rick could have let his killer in by that back door. Somebody he would have expected, who could have parked in the dark and deserted alley behind the building where neither Bert nor anybody else would have seen him. Or, without Rick being aware, one of the men who had legitimate access to every part of the building could have let himself in. Ed Walsh, Haru Maruri or Martin West.

Sara peered into the shadows, paying more attention than she had on the day before, when her only thought had been to disprove what she'd believed were Wendy's wild imaginings. Today, she looked around carefully, her senses alert, her focus on her surroundings.

CHAPTER 58

$\mathbf{S}$ ara was half way to the loading dock when Ed Walsh came into the warehouse. There was no sound to give him away. He slipped into a dark spot behind the men's lockers and watched, then followed. He moved slowly, sheltering between the pallets, the same as when he'd watched Rick on Monday night. Only then, he'd started out at the other end of the warehouse, the direction Sara was moving towards right now.

Sweat broke out on his forehead. On his upper lip. Like it was when he'd been hiding and waiting, having no idea what he expected to happen when Ken Ichiwara showed up.

It was only on impulse that he'd decided to be here. Only by chance that he'd heard them setting it up, Ichiwara and Rick, standing a few yards away from his office, on the landing outside the garage door.

"Be back here tonight. At eight o'clock," Rick said. It hadn't made sense and the words still swirled around in his brain.

"Eight o'clock...don't be late...I'll be here...waiting for you...here...bring the cash...there'll be a special surprise...don't be late...eight o'clock...bring the cash...bring the cash...bring the cash..."

If only he'd never heard them, hadn't felt impelled to find out what Rick was up to. Hadn't come back to the warehouse and gone scurrying around, coming in the back way and hiding, as if he hadn't the right to be there. As if this had become Rick's territory instead of his.

He kept his eyes on Sara. What did she want? There was no reason for her to be back here. Nothing for her to find. No way for her or anyone else to discover that he'd been here on Monday night. He'd been careful, parking in the alley where no one could have seen him. The sweat broke out again we he remembered the sound of his car scraping against the wall outside. But that was nothing to worry about. Those scratches could have happened anytime.

He was being careful now, as he moved forward on his rubber soled shoes. Not the ones he'd worn on Monday. He'd gotten rid of those along with the protective mats in the car. And, instead of using the toilet on this side of the building, he'd been smart and washed up on the other side, although it would have been better if he'd dumped the crowbar someplace away from the building. That damned crowbar. He'd just wanted to be rid of it. Maybe none of this would have happened if it had been where it belonged. If one of his men hadn't left it where he could trip over it.

He hadn't been looking for a weapon. He hadn't come back here to hurt Rick. He'd only wanted to find out what Rick was up to and help him back to their original good understanding. That's what he'd been waiting for, sheltered in the shadows. That's what he'd been hoping for when he heard the doorbell echo through the warehouse. Saw Rick walk slowly, in that graceful way of his, toward the door to let Ichiwara in. Watched them disappear into the aisle between pallets of packing cases.

It was when he'd crept closer, trying to figure out where they'd gone to, that his foot had come down on the crowbar. He'd picked it up and held onto it as he slipped back into hiding, frightened he would be discovered that way, crouching in the shadows like a thief.

He'd heard Rick came out to satisfy himself that the sound was no threat and go back to reassure Ichiwara they were alone. He'd inched forward again, toward the voices, waiting for what seemed like a very long time until, finally, both men came out from between the pallets and walked toward the front of the warehouse, arguing. Ichiwara was angry. He hadn't received all that he'd paid for. The special surprise he'd been promised wasn't there. Just a demand for more money and Rick was shouting at him to calm down.

"You have the coke," Rick told him. "And the extra money is going to a good cause. A sick friend."

Then Rick had laughed, as if he'd told the punch line to a joke. Remembering brought back the rage. The pain of the betrayal was almost unbearable. How many other people was Rick blackmailing and laughing about it? For how long had Rick been dealing cocaine out of his warehouse? What else could this have been about?

He had stayed motionless, hardly breathing, while Rick locked the door and returned to the passageway from where he and Ichiwara had emerged. Then, he'd followed, stalking Rick, like the animal he was. Silently, he'd squeezed his bulk past the cartons of West Electronics tape recorders until he came to the hidey hole Rick had fixed up for himself. Rick's back was turned away from him and he got close. So close he imagined Rick must feel him being there.

Without stopping to think, he'd brought the crowbar down on the back of Rick's head, moving quickly so there would be no time to counter the blow, but hoping there was a moment when Rick knew what was happening to him, knew he was getting paid back for his treachery. He'd brought the crowbar down over and over again slashing at Rick until there was nothing but raw flesh. Until the rage cooled. Until he looked down and saw what he had done. The mangled body. Torn apart as if a wild animal had attacked.

The money Rick had been holding was scattered and splattered with blood. He didn't touch it. But he wanted the key to the Long Beach warehouse and pulled at Rick's key ring until it came apart. Only there wasn't enough light. The keys went in all different directions and he was confused, gasping for breath, exhausted and, at the same time, exhilarated. The hell with the keys. He had won. This was his territory again.

His attention went back to Sara. Once again his space had been invaded. What right did this woman have to come sneaking around in his warehouse? What was she looking for?

"What are you doing back here?" he shouted.

The voice echoed and Sara stifled a scream as she whirled around to discover it was Ed Walsh who had come up behind her. She could see his fury as she backed away, desperately trying to come up with an answer for him, some acceptable reason for her being back here. A reason she should have prepared before venturing so far into his warehouse.

"I'm sorry," was all she could think of to say. "Really...I'm sorry." And she stumbled on the words as she repeated them several times. Not that it mattered. He was too angry to listen, perhaps because he knew as well as she did that there was no plausible reason for her to be here.

"Get out," he said. He grabbed hold of her arms and held tight, as if he hadn't the power to let go. "Nothing back here is any of your business. Get out and don't come back."

He still had hold of her when the door next to the loading dock opened and, in the sudden flash of sunlight, his grip loosened. There was no longer any doubt. This had to be the man who had killed Rick Hanson. Sara had suspected the truth earlier, as she'd made her way through the warehouse. She should have realized when she was reviewing her notes, preparing for the detectives. Ed Walsh was the only one who made sense.

It was Detective Roarke who had hold of her now and she was too grateful to mind.

"What are you doing here?"

"She has no business in the warehouse," Walsh said. "I told her. She's always sneaking around where she shouldn't be." He turned and walked away.

"We need to speak to you," Detective Spivak said, going after him and reaching for his arm.

Walsh shook him off. "I'll be in my office."

He exuded defeat, Sara thought. Maybe he knew it as all over. Had the detectives figured it out?

Roarke released her. "I told you to stay out of this. It isn't a game."

"I wanted to look around before the men come back to work tomorrow and it seemed like a perfect opportunity," she said. "While Mr. Walsh was in with Mr. Maruri. I thought I'd have more time."

"I can't believe you don't understand how dangerous this is," Roarke said. "Playing detective. Nosing around where you don't belong. Now get back to your desk and--"

"I know," Sara said. She spoke softly, responding to the concern in his voice. "I should mind my own business."

It was then they heard the shot. Like an explosion in the cavernous warehouse.

Spivak, who had been following Walsh, allowing several yards between them, was running.

"Don't move," Roarke said to Sara. And he too was running.

Sara saw Spivak reach Walsh's office then turn to Roarke. She heard him call out. "He's gone."

Slowly, Sara made her way to the front office, averting her eyes from what must be a terrible sight.

The detectives were now behind her. They herded her, together with Sheila and Wendy into the accounting office. "Stay here," Spivak directed. "You'll be able to leave soon. In the meantime, stay here."

Chapter 59

The forensics team had returned to the warehouse, but they wouldn't be staying for long. This time there was no mystery about what had happened. Ed Walsh had ended his own life. Before he could be taken in for questioning about the murder of Rick Hanson, he had put a bullet through his brain, adding yet another layer of color to the travel brochures on his desk.

On the other side of the building, the late afternoon light, gray and heavy with the possibility of rain, shrouded the almost empty offices. Haru Maruri, speechless with shock, had taken sanctuary behind a closed door. Sheila, still hoping for a sign of interest from Detective Spivak, was determined to stay at her desk until he and the temp, who had once again managed to be where she shouldn't have been, were gone for the day.

The object of her resentment was in Ken Ichiwara's office with the detectives, surprised and gratified that Roarke thought she might be able to fill in pieces of information the police investigation had not yet uncovered. It was at his request that she'd brought her notes with her.

"I eliminated the women immediately," she explained. "There were no motives...except maybe for Wendy. And she wouldn't have had the physical strength."

Detective Spivak, who believed they had more than enough information to close this case, wasn't interested in digging for more, especially if it came from Sara Fisher.

"I'm going to check on the forensic guys in the warehouse," he said. "See how long before we're out of here."

"Sounds good," Roarke said and turned back to Sara. "Go on. After you eliminated the women--?"

"I looked at Bert Rudner. Jealousy is a strong motive but he wasn't familiar with the building. He wouldn't have known how to find his way to the ladies' room...or the men's room for that matter. Add to that, he didn't have a key to the door between the front offices and the warehouse...he wouldn't have known to look for it... and he wouldn't have recognized it even if it had been visible in the blood and gore around Rick's body."

Roarke had come around and was looking over her shoulder. "Is that Mark Cranston's name? Next on your list?"

Sara was acutely aware of the man standing so close behind her and unsure of how she felt about it. "He also seemed unlikely," she said. "Even if he'd returned after Bert saw him drive away, I don't think Rick would have let him in. He was expecting Ichiwara and Wendy. And again, it was a question of the keys. Mark didn't have a key to let himself in."

The detective pulled a chair over to sit next to Sara. "What about Ichiwara?"

"He was more of a possibility. That he drove all the way back from Santa Barbara did look suspicious."

"His story is that Hanson needed emergency money for a sick friend. Ichiwara came back to help out."

Sara dismissed the sick friend with a wave of her hand. "I suspect drugs. Marijuana? Or maybe cocaine? Wendy did mention that Rick might be dealing cocaine?" She looked at Roarke for an answer, having decided not to mention the threesome Rick had been hinting at which might have been another reason for Ichiwara to show up.

"There were traces of both drugs at Rick's apartment and in the warehouse," Roarke admitted. "But that's between us. We have no proof about what Ichiwara was after."

"Whatever brought him back, I couldn't come up with a motive for murder."

"Blackmail?" Roarke said.

"Possible. But, once again, Ichiwara had no way of getting into the offices on the other side to wash up. If he had, he wouldn't have made the mistake of going into the ladies' room. The killer needed to have keys to every door."

"Which narrowed it down to Martin West, Haru Maruri or Ed Walsh."

Sara smiled. "Can you picture Martin West striking out with a crowbar and winding up all bloody, washing up in the ladies' room? No. If Martin West wanted to get rid of somebody, he'd hire a hitman.

"Leaving you with Maruri and Walsh."

Sara nodded. "The way they tolerated Rick's arrogance. The raises and promotions over more experienced people. If anybody was a candidate for blackmail it was one or both of them."

Roarke agreed. "But, how did you zero in on Ed Walsh as the killer."

Sara's hand went to the bruise on her upper arm.

"You were crazy to go back there alone," Roarke said.

"I suppose," Sara said, remembering the warmth of his hands on her arms. "But I didn't put it all together until I was in the warehouse. Until then, I was assuming the killer came in from the garage. Only when I focused on the back door did I realize the full importance of the keys. The killer had to have access to all the doors and, just as important, be somebody who acted on impulse. On raw emotion. I saw the body and couldn't believe the killer slashed out like that in cold blood.

"It came down, then, to Ed Walsh."

"It had to be. If, as I believed, Martin West was not a credible suspect and Mr. Maruri, even if he'd had the strength to overcome Rick and inflict those injuries, didn't have the temperament to act out so impulsively."

"He also happened to be at home with his wife," Roarke said. "And West was at a dinner party in Brentwood. We eliminated the others pretty much the way you did. Which also left us with Ed Walsh. And I agree that killing Rick was, most likely, not premeditated. There are too many other ways he could have done it that would have been easier to cover up."

"What's frustrating," Sara said. "Is that we can't know when Walsh showed up at the warehouse. Was it before or after Ichiwara arrived? Did he even know, for sure, that Hanson would be here? If he did, how did he know?"

"Frustration is part of the job," Roarke said. We rarely have all the information we'd like. In this case, all we can assume is that he came back to the building and parked in the alley. There are fresh scratches on his car and traces of matching paint on the wall outside."

"Whatever reason he came back for, I don't think...from talking to Wendy... that he knew about the secret place and the dope dealing before he got there on Monday night. It would have come as a terrible shock if, in the warehouse, he found out what was going on. Added to the probability that he and Maruri were being blackmailed, it would have pushed him over the edge."

"It could have happened that way," Roarke said. "If Walsh was hiding and overheard the conversation between Rick and Ichiwara."

"Ken Ichiwara did say they heard a noise," Sara said. As if somebody else was there, moving around in the warehouse. It must have been Walsh."

Roarke agreed. "And, there's no guess work about what happened after Ichiwara was gone. We know that Walsh followed Rick back to that secret space and killed him. Attacked him from behind. Rick probably never knew what hit him."

"It's horrible," Sara said.

"It would have been a lot worse if he had struck out at you in the warehouse."

Sara looked down at her notes. It seemed unmistakable that the detective was coming on to her and she fought the urge to respond.

"I do have one more question," she said.

"Just one?"

The way he was looking at her left no doubt. He was coming on.

"I was wondering if you're going to go after Haru Maruri," she asked, as she refolded her notes.

Roarke shook his head. "We don't believe he had anything to do with the murder. And we're not sure what he and Ed Walsh were up to, except that it involved a warehouse in Long Beach where they may have been receiving illegally imported merchandise from other manufacturers using West Electronics as a cover. That makes it Martin West's problem. But I'll be surprised if he wants to pursue an investigation targeting his second in command. In any event, if there's a crime to follow up on, a different division will handle it."

"I shouldn't say this, but I'm glad that Mr. Maruri will be out of it. I like him," Sara said.

"I'm not saying that he wasn't involved in some criminal activity," Roarke cautioned. "And I expect that you won't discuss this with anyone else."

"I understand and I want to thank you for being willing to talk about all of this with me. Even though I could see that your partner doesn't approve."

"I'm sorry to see it end," Roarke said. "I thought maybe we could continue, catch up with each other later this evening. Or some other time."

They were both standing, closer than they should have been. But Sara had David to consider and, not to be overlooked, there was the gold band on the ring finger of Detective Roarke's left hand.

"I appreciate the invitation but it wouldn't be a good idea," she said.

CHAPTER 60

Once again, it was curiosity that propelled Sara back to West Electronics on Thursday morning. How could she not be there? She wanted to find out how she would she be treated--how the people there would be treating each other--what it would be like in the aftermath of such terrible events. As it turned out, whatever she might have imagined was nothing like what she found.

All was peace and harmony when she came through the door at quarter past nine. As if nothing out of the ordinary had happened. No murder. No investigation. No suicide. Sheila was as pleased to see her as she'd been on the Monday before the murder. Wendy smiled, as if their old relationship was still in place. In the accounting office, Gerry was her warm and friendly self, while Mark was polite but reserved.

Sara would have been equally startled had she known how easily Rick Hanson and Ed Walsh had slipped from the consciousness of the men in their private offices. Although Ken

Ichiwara would be without the supply of drugs he preferred to travel with, he exuded good cheer as he prepared to go back on the road. He even found a moment to sidle up to Sara's desk and murmur how much he looked forward to taking her to dinner at some unspecified future date.

Oliver Blakely, whose equanimity had never left him, gave a routine reminder to Ichiwara about overdue sales projections before getting back on the phone to his regional sales managers, yawning discreetly while they discussed sales figures and checking his watch frequently as he anticipated his first scotch of the day.

Martin West, who saw no reason why his new-found commitment to oversight of the company should interfere with a morning visit to his mistress, arrived at eleven o'clock and, after allowing Sara to bring his coffee, graciously announced his wish that she stay until Elinor's return, which he now knew would be in two weeks. Equally gracious, Sara surprised him by advising that, although she was appreciated the request, a previous commitment made it impossible to comply.

Haru Maruri, who did not have the luxury of forgetting the deceased, nor the time to mourn, had already made several calls to find replacements for Ed Walsh and himself. As much as he wanted to walk away, he couldn't leave the company before finding people to fill those positions. It would amount to an admission of guilt, something he couldn't allow. Instead he must behave with scrupulous propriety until he was safely on the plane to Japan.

Having put the wheels for his departure into motion, he turned to his letter of resignation. Without implicating himself, he would name the criminal activity that had taken place under his watch and give it as his reason for leaving, refusing to claim ignorance as an excuse. He would state that it had been his responsibility to know what was going on and that the company had been harmed because of his dereliction. He had dishonored himself, which left resignation as the only option. It would be effective as soon as the necessary replacements could be found, and no later than the end of the following month.

The decision was irrevocable. Not that he believed Martin would raise objections. He was already suspicious and must be using his own connections in Japan to investigate. But that would take time. Maruri intended to be long gone before Martin could discover how completely he had been betrayed. He looked once more at the carefully composed letter, to be submitted in his own handwriting. When Sara opened the door, a preferable alternative presented itself.

"I'd like you to type this up for me," he said, pointing to the paper on his desk. "It is, however, highly confidential."

"Of course," Sara assured him. "But before that, I do want you to know that tomorrow will be my last day."

"I'll be sorry to lose you," he said. "As will Mr. West. He has expressly requested that you remain."

"He told me. But I do have other commitments and the Meacham Agency can have an excellent person here for him on Monday morning. Shall I ask Sheila to make the call?"

"Please."

Back at her desk Sara read his letter and wished she could discuss it with Detective Roarke. It seemed to confirm the suspicion that Haru Maruri had been involved in activities that were at best unethical and, at worst, criminal. Why else would he be leaving Martin West so abruptly and with so short a time in which to fill two key positions in his company?

"West Electronics is going to be a very different place when you're not here," she said, when she brought back the letter.

"Perhaps it will be better."

"Perhaps. But I don't think so."

⚓

Wen Sara left his office, she decided to postpone Mr. West's dictation for a few more minutes. She wanted to finish a shopping list for David's dinner the next night. It was just as well he hadn't been around while she was mixed up in the extraordinary events of this week but she missed him now. He would disapprove of how she had involved herself, but too much had happened for her to keep it from him.

"I'll leave work early and pick you up at the airport," she'd insisted when he'd called on the previous evening. "I'll cook dinner. Pasta and salad and a nice bottle of Chianti."

"I can't wait to see you with or without the pasta."

"You can have it all," Sara said, laughing. She thought about how close she had come to making a mistake; how close she had come to being carried away by the appeal of something new and slightly dangerous. But she had always avoided married men and she certainly didn't want to risk her relationship with David for what would have, of necessity, been a brief interlude.

Content, she finished her list with only the slightest twinge of regret for the detective. David would be with her tomorrow night. She had the warmth of his arms to look forward to. And there'd been a call from her agent. She had an interview at Four Star next week.

ABOUT THE AUTHOR

Originally from the bustling city of New York, author Irene Mattei feels at home in America's metropolises. She currently lives in San Francisco but previously resided in Los Angeles. Her professional life is just as diverse as her residential map. Once an actress, Mattei moved on to become a market researcher, an advertising account manager, and even a vice president of sales and marketing at a sleek electronics company. As Oscar Wilde might have put it, hers has been "a life crowded with incident."

Thanks to her breadth of experience, Mattei has been given a wealth of material with which to create gripping stories. Drawing upon characters and situations she's come upon throughout her colorful life, Mattei develops authentic fictional elements that perfectly complement her natural storytelling ability. As a lover of golden-age mysteries, she is inspired by classic authors like Christie and Sayers.

Made in the USA
Charleston, SC
13 January 2017